ENTER THE SAMURAI

WADE PETERSON

THE STORY SO FAR

In the beginning, Ryan the Creator cried out and begat the Badlands with all its people, and it was good. When the people broke, the Creator abandoned the Badlands and created other cities as he saw fit. As decay spread through the lands, a madness grew within him and manifested the avatars. He summoned his twin sister, Jasmine the Redeemer, to help him heal the world, but she too was broken and flawed. In her wisdom, she expelled herself and Ryan from the world to wreak havoc no more. The people were left behind, living in their echoes.

The fallen avatar Kikuchiyo, the Blood Weeper, was given a holy command to purge his brethren from the land so the people might live for themselves. And it came to pass after many years, that the Blood Weeper faced the last and mightiest avatar in the dreaming sands between worlds.

— —THE BOOK OF THE PEOPLE, UNKNOWN

1

The new meat arrived as the sun dipped behind the Wall's anvil-headed cloud tops and turned the sand blood red. Gatehouse guards rose and unslung their rifles as a rooster tail of dust appeared over the rise. Minutes later, one of the camp's runabouts, a small wheeled sand buggy, sped through the gate with a bound man on its cargo rack. Four guards dragged the man through the camp, past the fences topped with concertina wire, and stopped at the cell next to Skye's. Skye pressed against the viewing grate built into the blue-black metal door, wincing at its sun-soaked mesh scorching his face. The new guy muttered in a strange language and his long black hair had partially fallen free from a topknot. They had beaten him nearly unconscious, which surprised Skye not at all, though this guy's arms and legs were thick with the corded muscle of a fighter, which made him wonder if it had been a difficult capture. They threw him into the cell without bothering to take off the manacles and double-wrapped a heavy chain through the door's D-bolts.

The two guards may have had proper names, but Skye christened them Horse Laugh and Stink Eye. Stink Eye, on account of the surly expression he wore at all times, and his partner, Horse Laugh, who reckoned the entire world was funny. Stink Eye's notions especially tickled

Horse Laugh, usually hollered abuses followed by a beating from the long bamboo cane he carried inside the wire.

"Welcome to your new home, meat," Stink Eye said.

Horse Laugh guffawed. "Yes, welcome to Outpost 242. Balmy weather and spectacular views of the Wall, the sandstorm that never comes. We do apologize for its constant headaches. Would you like to leave a wakeup call?"

Stink Eye shoved him in the back. "Enough of that."

"Jeez," Horse Laugh said. Stink Eye didn't relax until the padlock clicked shut. He caught Skye looking and snapped his cane against the grill, driving Skye back. Stink Eye came right up to Skye's door and glowered.

"Don't worry, your secret is safe with me," Skye said with a wink. "Have you ever thought about getting a bigger stick?"

Horse Laugh snorted, but got it under control as Stink Eye turned his glare on him.

"Tomorrow, Skye," Stink Eye said, turning back around, "you just wait until tomorrow."

"Tomorrow... tomorrow," Horse Laugh sang before braying.

The guards walked away and Skye went back to the cell door once they cleared the inner wire.

"Hey, you hear me?" he whispered.

His chains clattered and scraped against metal, but the newcomer did not speak.

"You got a name?"

No response, only thrashing.

"Hey, save your energy. They run you into the ground while starving you besides. Tomorrow, they'll make you learn this funny dance and beat you if you don't do it right. You hear?"

Silence. The winds off the Wall picked up, whistled through the camp, and Skye felt another headache coming on.

"Have it your own way, then." Skye pushed away from the door and lay down. Minutes later something bounced off his roof, followed by another and another until a steady cascade drummed against his hot box. The light outside dimmed as more sand, metal fragments, and other detritus rained down on the camp from the Wall.

The woman next door began singing, and his headache eased. Her name was Cora, a former fleet necro. He envied her, only having to walk simple circles in the exercise yard and never touched, by cane or otherwise. He wondered if he might have seen her perform in one of the Paradise City clubs, would like to think he would have remembered a beauty with a voice like that. Then again, he had been preoccupied with other matters back then.

Fortunately, nobody here recognized him from those days or he might have ended up against the wall and shot rather than swept up with the other dregs and shipped out here as a "candidate." He had always been lucky that way.

The singing stopped, and moments later Cora lightly tapped a message on her wall.

U OK? Cora asked.

Skye checked outside to make sure the guards were well away before he rapped a staccato reply.

Y. 3 SLVRS. U?

OK. NRLY RDY. U REST.

He considered a moment, then sent: BUTY SLEP?

Her faint laugh made him smile and she signed off with a quick double tap. He closed his eyes and wished he could let her sing him to sleep. Instead, he started picking the metal splinters from his hands, knees, and feet, courtesy of the day's dancing lesson in the exercise yard. He examined each sliver and separated them into piles.

2

———————

An overhead scream woke her. Cora peeled herself from the metal floor, rubbing her bare arms to regain some sensation. The ornithopter swung around and landed in the exercise yard. The guards in the towers straightened, appearing competent for the first time in weeks. A man hopped from the thopter, dressed in heavy black leather with silver thread glinting in the morning sun. Guards streamed from the blockhouse, pulling at their uniforms and falling into a ragged formation. The camp's commandant, a potbellied man without a hint of tan, shoved his way to the front, calling to the newcomer who waved as he headed for the inner wire gate and the camp's hotboxes. The commandant bawled at those nearest him, and they rushed to catch up with the man in black.

The VIP's inspection started at the back row, and as soon as the group was out of sight, the other guards fell out of formation. One of them picked up a stone and threw it side-arm at a black-and-white dog sleeping in a runabout's shadow nearby. Idiots. Cora didn't know if it was the guards' poor marksmanship or pure luck keeping the cur alive, but somehow no matter how often the guards yelled, threw rocks, or on one drunken occasion, fired shots at it, the dog stuck around. Her family's enclave always kept a dog around because the animals didn't like deaders. Some could even sense those already changing and help the 'clave sort the starving from the cursed. The side-armed rock went wide and the dog's mismatched eyes stared down the guard a few seconds before trotting over to a stack of petrol barrels and resuming his nap in its shadow.

The inspection party reached her row and she got a good look at the VIP, eating an apple and peering into a cell. Her stomach twisted and she swore out loud. Doctor Ian Astbury had the same shoulder-length blond hair and blue eyes she remembered, but a sandy beard now camouflaged his baby face and he somehow wore a colonel's insignia on his collar. His black cavalry Stetson with custom necrotic glyphs around the band complemented the standard Imperial-issue duster billowing behind him as he walked. Murmuring to the commandant, he peered into Cora's cell and the imitation of a smile spread across his face.

"And how are we today?" he asked as he took a bite from his apple. Cora said nothing, hoping he wouldn't recognize her. His expression seemed free of all malice and guile, but she knew better. At her silence, Astbury squinted and his jaw slowed. He glanced at the apple and rolled his head back to the sky.

"Oh, how gauche am I? You wouldn't believe how busy I am, hardly any time to spare for a proper bite. Have you eaten? No, never mind, don't answer that. I'm sure the commandant and has rigorously adhered to the diet I prescribed for one such as yourself. And the exercise program, yes?" He turned and regarded the commandant whose jowls flapped as he nodded. "Yes, we'd be careful with you... Clara, is it? Katherine... Coral..."

"Cora Pierson," said the commandant.

Astbury tapped his chin. "Did we go to the Academy together? That is, you seem familiar."

"I was a few years behind you," she said.

Astbury snapped his fingers. "The 'claver girl!"

The epithet hit her in the chest. She couldn't escape her upbringing, even in this forsaken place.

Astbury took a last bite of his apple and looked around for a place to discard it. The commandant offered an open hand and with a shrug Astbury placed it in the man's palm.

"One question," she said.

"Yes?"

"Who sold me out?"

Astbury blinked and looked at the commandant, who hastily shook his head. "I haven't the foggiest, Miss Cora, but then again I don't concern myself with logistics. I imagine this is a disappointment for you after all your training and what I assume was a modest career, given where you are now, but cheer up, you can still serve the Prime. I expect the next time we meet you'll be coming back with me. Isn't that exciting? I believe you will be the commandant's guest for perhaps another..." He pursed his lips and hummed a tune popular in Paradise City's heyday. The hairs on Cora's arms rose, and something stirred in her brain. She took an involuntary step forward before stopping herself. Astbury nodded. "Yes. Almost ready, a week at the outside. Just in time, really."

Had Astbury controlled her? Summoned her like a deader?

It couldn't be true. She might be dying — her hunger pangs had disappeared long ago — but she was a necro and however terrible she'd been at it, her ability to influence deaders gave her immunity to the Badlands curse, even if she was Badlands born. Necros died, period. So no, Astbury was just playing games with her head. Simple malnutrition and sleep deprivation had made her open to suggestion. Regardless, she didn't intend on dying just to prove Astbury wrong.

Astbury had already moved on. Cora watched him take a quick look into Skye's cell, cluck his tongue, and murmur to the commandant, who nodded at every utterance, then flipped the apple core away when Astbury wasn't looking.

At the newest prisoner's cell, Astbury slapped the cell door and laughed out loud. "A fine catch, commandant, and a wonder you didn't lose anyone in the process," he said and rattled the cell's chains. "He'll make a fine addition, assuming we can find the correct regimen. Until then, it would do you well to use a heavier chain on his cell." He flicked a finger at the padlock. "And perhaps a second one of those. Show me his personal effects, if you would."

Astbury turned back to the blockhouse, with the commandant struggling to keep up. Cora dragged herself to the cell's coolest corner, farthest from the sun, where a small hole served for all of one's waste needs, not that she'd had a reason to use it in a while. She was too thin. She should be sweating and hungry. When Cora had first arrived guards would linger and ogle, dropping unsubtle hints about special treatment for certain favors, but their gazes and illicit offers stopped weeks ago. Her skin stretched tight across her cheekbones and sagged in the hollows; her knuckles looked swollen compared to her fingers. No, this wasn't good at all. She leaned her head back against the wall, sitting over the toilet she'd had no use for and stared at the metal roof, wondering when things would start turning for the worse, and figured it would be soon.

Cora tapped out a quick message on the wall.

TONIGHT.

Skye double-tapped an acknowledgment and Cora crawled to the door and began singing, disregarding her growing fatigue. Skye hummed along next door. His tone was off and he rushed the tempo, but not bad for an amateur. She could work with it. She concentrated and began tracing her finger around her cell door.

3

At full dark the Wall began churning, building for the night's storm, and the camp's arc lights lit with a sharp snap. Not long after, guards emerged from their blockhouse in strange stone-like armor and entered the inner wire. Skye watched a pair haul a limp body from the cells and set it into the cargo space of the dead-eyed VIP's ornithopter. Other pairs followed, and he watched sixteen bodies packed and arranged. Skye had only reckoned four casualties since he arrived and wondered why his captors bothered hauling the poor bastards out rather than just burying them or tossing them in the burn pits at the camp's edge where the Wall's constant winds carried ashes away to become someone else's problem.

A guard tripped and let out a muffled curse as he came to a knee and fumbled at a loose strap. The armor wasn't designed for mobility, with its stone-like vambraces, chest plate, and greaves strapped over a quilted body suit. The full helmet with its integrated goggles and gas mask looked hot as hell too, and Skye would have felt sorry for the man under normal circumstances. Battle armor always made him feel like a waddling beetle. As he watched another pair hauling a body, the guard holding the feet tripped and the corpse's leg tore free at the hip. His partner stiffened, and a moment later the corpse began thrashing around.

It cried out in a dry hiss soon taken up by the mass in the thopter's cargo bay, which also began undulating and squirming.

The VIP strode from the blockhouse in his black duster and two long swords sticking from his belt, which sent the new guy next door ranting and rattling his chains. The necro took in the scene and began chanting and stomping his feet. His voice carried throughout the camp with syllables that teased at the edges of Skye's understanding. The words were like thick syrup in his ears, set to the rhythm of the man's feet. The chanting stopped, and Skye blinked, shaking his head and realizing time had passed he couldn't account for. The camp was still again, quiet apart from the wallstorm's howl and dark muttering from cell next door. The guards carried the body to the thopter and placed it with the others — also quiet.

"Trooper," the man in the black duster said.

The clumsy guard trotted over and saluted.

"Were you not given specific instructions on proper cargo handling?"

"Yes, sir."

"And yet, this." He pointed to the dismembered leg still kicking on the ground.

"Sorry, sir, this armor is so—"

"Perfectly designed for the task!" the man in black shouted.

"Oh, come on, sir! Whoever designed this kit should be shot."

"That's enough, Rogers!" the commandant barked. He turned to the man in black. "Colonel Astbury, sir, I apologize for Trooper Rogers' insubordination. Be assured I will make an example out of him."

Astbury stepped forward and tapped Rogers' helmet. "Your lid, trooper."

Rogers hesitated, then took off his helmet. It was Horse Laugh. His eyes were wide and skin extra pale under the arc lights.

"Trooper Rogers, you damaged a valuable piece of the Empire's property and vital part of my research program."

"It was an accident," Horse Laugh stammered, but Astbury held up a hand.

"I could forgive that, but then you blamed your incompetence on your equipment. Equipment that none of the others had problems utilizing.

Equipment I assure you has been rigorously designed and tested. Can you guess by whom?"

Skye would have stared ahead and remained silent had he been Horse Laugh.

Horse Laugh's mouth twisted as he fought against his natural impulse and lost. "Someone who's never had to wear it," he blurted.

Astbury shifted his weight, and a chill settled in Skye's guts.

"The armor is for your protection, Trooper Rogers, in case this happens." Skye had seen faster draws, but not many. The gun appeared in Astbury's hand like magic, and Horse Laugh had only enough time to blink at the gun's barrel before it barked. His body collapsed, missing the top half of its skull.

Astbury holstered his sidearm, strode past the stunned guards, and scooped up the twitching leg. He tossed it into the cargo bay and slapped the ornithopter's fuselage. The engines pitched up, sending dust everywhere, and Astbury's thopter was airborne before the commandant came to his senses and shouted at his men.

Skye's stomach rumbled, and he hoped his luck would kick in before it came time for a trip with Astbury.

WHEN THE WELD POPPED, Cora startled. She had been working on it for so long she wasn't sure what to do next. She pushed the cell door, finding it only held in place by residual corrosion and the chains wrapped around the handle and latch. Whoever had welded the door hinge to the cell had done a terrible job. Rushed, uneven, bubbling seams that not even a first-year apprentice would have turned in. Breaking them had taken only a few necrosonic talents and time.

She went to the cell's far corner where the wall met the floor and felt along the seam for her pin stash, made from metal slivers stuck in her boots from the exercise yard, secreted and refined over the past weeks when not working on the door. Delicate work, that, requiring precise voice control to draw out the metal and harden it for the next task. Her raw throat burned and she doubted it would ever be the same again.

The camp guards had been on edge with Astbury's leaving, but after a few hours of darkness and the howling wallstorm sandblasting anyone not under cover, they had reverted to their half-assed selves, ditching their fancy armor for desert uniforms with goggles and scarves, going through the motions of running a secret prison camp and research facility but in reality a shit detail with nothing to do but pace the perimeter and let the subjects waste away. The inner wire patrol passed, and would not come again for at least another two minutes and fifteen seconds. The tower guards, barely visible in the wallstorm's haze, were undoubtedly sneaking drinks from flasks or perfecting the art of sleeping while standing up. She wound her fingers through the cell door's grating and pushed with her shoulder. The door broke loose with a groan, and she froze, listening for an alarm. After thirty pounding heartbeats, she lowered the door to the sand, careful not to rattle the chains or let its upper edge clang as she propped it against its frame. She wiped her sand-scoured face with fingers numb and swollen from the strain and then shimmied through the gap and into the shadows of Skye's cell.

RDY? she tapped.

Double tap.

She waited for the guard to pass, not allowing herself to look directly, lest he get the feeling of being watched. *Just a shadow, nothing to see here.*

The guard passed.

She let out a breath, and with a last glance up at the guard towers, crouched before Skye's door. She stuck her makeshift picks in the padlock and pictured the mechanism as she worked, nudging each locking pin as Skye whispered a countdown. She bit off a curse as shaky hands bent her pick and she had to start over. She could do this, she told herself. It was an ugly lock, a stupid lock compared to others she had known before and opened with ease.

Yeah, with proper picks and someone watching your back.

"Thirty," Skye whispered.

The last pin stuck for a moment, then gave as she teased it past the sticking point.

Damn sloppy operation. Would it kill them to oil these things?

She twisted the cylinder and winced as another needle bent. Damn the dust!

"Twenty."

Ping!

The upper needle snapped in half and flew away, the other half now jammed in the lock with only a nub protruding.

"Problem," she said.

"Fifteen— Hide!"

She caught the nub under her fingernail and twisted. Blood flowed. The cylinder turned and caught.

"Ten."

Cora jimmied the lock's hasp and gave the cylinder one last push. The other needle snapped, but not before the cylinder completed its turn. She crawled into the shadows and waited as the guard stopped and turned her way.

Her heart galloped loud in her ears. She tried averting her eyes, but they betrayed her, drifting back and waiting for the guard's next move. She gripped a handful of sand, ready to throw it in his eyes. She would have to rush under his cane, get him to the ground, bite through his neck—

Metal screeched and chains rattled from a cell down the row — the new prisoner's cell. The guard's head snapped around and brought up his cane. Cora crept around, following the guard's tentative approach. He peeked into the cell and shouted, banging his cane twice against the door. The rattling ceased, and the guard backed up with eyes locked on the fresh meat's door before turning and hurrying away. Cora waited ten seconds before leaving the shadows.

"Hurry," Skye said.

Cora opened the lock and removed the chain. Skye slipped out and hid in the shadows while she replaced the chain and padlock. It wouldn't pass close inspection but might buy them a few extra minutes.

"What'd you manage?" she asked.

Skye opened his hand, revealing six finger-length metal shards.

"Those must have hurt," she said.

"The beatings kept me distracted. Come on, let's go."

Skye and Cora darted from cell to cell, keeping to the shadows and marking the patrol. They came to the back row, near the camp's reeking garbage pit which still smoldered from the afternoon burn and had accumulated a fresh pile for tomorrow's daily offering. The camp dog circled the pile, sniffing and pawing through the mess. Skye ran up to the wire while Cora kept watch. He set the thickest shard into the wire's gaps and started twisting. His arms shook as the wire stretched, then broke with a metallic snap like a gunshot. Cora's head swiveled, sure that someone would have heard, but to her relief, only the dog noticed.

"Hurry up," she whispered.

Skye's shoulders bunched as he went to work on the next wire. In thirty seconds, they broke through the inner curtain fence and crossed to the outer. Skye passed her a metal shard, and they went to work on separate wires. Skye's wire went quickly, hers wouldn't budge after the first twist.

"Just hold it there, and I'll get it after this," Skye said through clenched teeth.

The dog abandoned the garbage pile and trotted over to them.

"Git!" Skye said. Two ears, one white, one black, perked up and the dog wagged its tail. Skye's wire snapped, and he took over Cora's.

"Shoo!" Cora said, waving the dog away. The dog's nose sniffed at her outstretched hand and darted back a step. His ears flattened and he let out a low growl.

"Back up, Cora," Skye said, straining with the last wire.

She held up her hands. "Nice dog, you're okay, we're okay..."

The dog's hackles rose as he crouched and bared his teeth.

"No-no-no!" She waved her hands and the dog lunged, barking. Moments later, a rifle cracked and its bullet struck at her feet.

"Go!" Cora shouted.

Another bullet ricocheted between the wire breach and the dog.

"We're blown," she said.

"Plan B," Skye said, and pulled her back from the wire.

"What Plan B?" she asked.

"Spring that other guy out — diversion," he said.

"No way. We don't know him."

"He's chained in a metal box and they're still afraid of him. While they're busy with him, we'll slip away."

A siren blew. Spotlights snapped on and began sweeping the ground. They darted back to their cells and Cora jerked her head back around a corner as a tower guard took aim.

"I can't pick a lock with a rifle scope on my back," she said.

"Got you covered." Skye scrambled to Cora's loose door and shouldered it open. A shot rang out from the northwest tower and it pinged off the door. "This guy can't get you from his angle."

"What about the other guy?" But as she looked, the inner gate's posts blocked the northeast guard tower's view.

Skye nodded to the blockhouse, where four guards in full armor rushed out, two with canes, two with full-length riot shields. "You have until that crash team gets here."

"This is a rotten plan," she shouted as she crawled to the cell door.

A bullet ricocheted off Skye's improvised cover, sending the door ringing. "Rotten plans are all I've ever had," he said.

She pulled two pins and went to work on the lock, which seemed in better shape than the one on Skye's metal box. Footsteps approached and when she glanced up, she froze. Red smeared down the prisoner's face from eyes to jawline. His stare bored through her and her bowels turned to water. A name floated into her head. A name her gran always struggled speaking aloud when she read Cora her scripture.

Blood Weeper!

Skye shouted her name, but she was petrified, certain death gazing back at her. He broke the stare and focused on the oncoming crash team.

"Open it, Badlands child, and you will live," said the Blood Weeper in a ragged voice.

This was the worst possible plan, she said to herself but her fingers worked, probing the lock until the third locking pin cleared and the hasp opened with an easy twist.

She cleared the chains from the handle and scooted back. The Blood Weeper stepped free and took in a deep breath. Blood dripped from beneath manacles at each wrist, down short lengths of broken chains and onto the sand.

"Twins save us," Cora whispered.

The Blood Weeper began swinging his chains. He spared a glance at Cora and Skye and nodded once before sprinting down the row at the oncoming crash team. The guards locked shields and drove them into the ground, bracing to meet the charge. The Blood Weeper let out a guttural yell, jumping to the side, rebounding off a nearby cell and landing behind the guards. One chain swung around and wrapped around a cane, the other caught under a helmet and snapped the guard's head back. The Blood Weeper twisted and fell to the ground, sweeping a leg that sent the stunned guards tumbling. The remaining pair turned and tried bringing their shields to bear, but the Weeper reached out and twisted one guard's helmet around with a sickening crunch and sent the other flying back with a heel kick. He followed up with another strike to the fallen guard's throat. The Blood Weeper became a whirlwind of elbows, fists, and kicks sending all four guards to the ground, unmoving. The Weeper picked up a body and held it before him as he headed for the front gate.

"Let's go, Cora," Skye said and pulled her to wobbly feet.

They fled the cells and made for a runabout parked near the blockhouse. The Weeper made for the nearest tower, and if his human shield was still alive, his fellow guards did not care, firing round after round as the Blood Weeper disappeared in the wallstorm's haze.

Cora and Skye ran across the compound, bullets whizzing past their ears. They slid behind a runabout and Cora crawled into the driver's seat and fumbled for the starter. "No keys!"

Skye ducked as another bullet whizzed past. "Can't you hotwire it or something?"

"In the dark, in a firefight?" She lowered herself to the floorboards. "I got nothing better to do, go find me some tools."

Skye crawled into the back of the runabout and began looking through the cargo bins when gunfire sent them diving to the ground. Cora made herself small behind the runabout's wheels as the commandant and his chief, the one Skye called Stink Eye, fired at them from the blockhouse. Bullets hit the sand before her, and Cora backed away, trying to keep the runabout between her and the commandant. Skye crawled back to the bins and started tossing things onto the ground, swearing with every quick burst the commandant sent their way.

A screwdriver hit the sand, and Cora snatched it up and scampered into the runabout. She exposed the ignition's guts, then ducked as a burst hit the windscreen and glass pebbles showered her.

"Up top!" Stink Eye shouted.

The Blood Weeper appeared on the blockhouse roof wielding a cane.

Stink Eye leaned out, took careful aim, and Cora didn't think; the screwdriver flew from her hand, tumbling end-over-end. She had never been much of an athlete: clumsy, winded easily, always the last one picked. She prayed for Jasmine's hand to guide her missile true, but it was not to be. The screwdriver sailed wide of Stink Eye and clattered against the blockhouse wall. The submachine gun's muzzle flashed, though it wavered as Cora's failed throw made Stink Eye flinch.

The Blood Weeper leapt down and swept his cane in an arc as he twisted in midair. The cane's tip fractured as a bullet hit it. The Weeper cried out on landing, dodging another wild burst. Stink Eye cursed and slapped at his gun, ejecting a magazine and fumbling for another.

In one motion, the Blood Weeper rolled to his feet and plunged the cane's shattered tip through Stink Eye's chest. The commandant popped around the doorway and triggered a long burst into both men. The gun went dry, and the Weeper dropped Stink Eye and swung his arm around in a flat arc, palm striking right over the commandant's heart. The gun fell from the commandant's dead fingers and the rest of him soon followed.

Cora shook herself, conscious that she was in the open, staring, an easy target. Then she realized that apart from the wind, the camp was silent. The Blood Weeper raised his arms and roared, turning his gaze to the runabout.

"Oh shit," Cora said.

The Blood Weeper took one step and his brows knotted. He brought two fingers to a red stain on his chest and came away rubbing blood between them. He... faded. For a fraction of a second, the commandant's body and blockhouse's open doorway showed through him as if he were mist. The Blood Weeper grunted and began hyperventilating. His ghostly form darkened over the next several seconds as he became substantial once again. The Blood Weeper then took one more step towards her before collapsing.

4

Skye stood over the man's body, gathering the courage to check for a pulse. Blood flowed from at least three bullet wounds. Cora pointed a submachine gun at the man with her lips pressed in a tight line, and Skye wondered if she was going to finish him.

"I know what I saw," she said.

"He looks solid enough to me." Adrenaline did strange things to people. Toss in a few weeks of solitary and malnutrition and who knew what cocktail was pickling her brain? He was surprised he wasn't seeing things too.

"At least he bleeds," she said, and lowered her gun.

That snapped Skye from his own post-adrenaline fog. He knelt and found the man's pulse, still going but weak. "I'm surprised he took so few hits."

"It was said bullets couldn't touch him, he'd swat them out of the air no matter how many."

"Who?"

"Him. That's the Blood Weeper, Kikuchiyo."

"Hell he is. He's just a man." Skye opened a med kit.

"You sure you want to do that?" Cora asked.

Skye dressed the worst wound where a bullet had passed through the upper chest. "Of course. I think he's earned it."

"You said we were only using him as a distraction."

"Worked out better than I thought." He smiled. "Just lucky, I guess."

Cora's grip on the gun tightened. "If you had grown up in the Badlands, you'd know better."

Yeah, and he might have eaten the long pig and worshiped the Twins too. Fortunately he had been born outside all that bullshit, though arguing with a woman death-gripping her weapon seemed like a bad idea. Skye started wrapping the bandage across the man's chest. "Are you going to help me or not?"

Cora stood for a moment longer before putting the gun's safety back on and kneeling. "This is a mistake, you know." She helped him with the bandage. "Jasmine guide us."

"I don't believe in myths."

"Neither do I," Cora said.

Skye checked the cells after they had finished, finding them empty save for one containing a corpse rotten with beetles and blowflies. Scratches lined the walls as if the man tried clawing his way out at the end. Why the guards had left the poor bugger in there when he had witnessed several bodies hauled to the burning pits, he couldn't understand. Not everyone here turned deader, and he wondered if they were the lucky ones. That's what he hated about this place, all the time alone with nothing but questions for company. He left the guards where they fell, not looking too closely at how they died. It would just be asking another question.

By dawn they had scoured the camp and came away with a few weapons, fewer bullets, food, water, and keys to the runabout. As they loaded up, their patient shouted. Skye turned to find the dog sitting a few feet away from the man, regarding him through mismatched eyes and ignoring the verbal assault.

"Hey, cut it out," Skye said, walking up to the man. "You'll rip something open."

"Get it away," the man said.

Skye crouched and spared a glance to the dog, who thumped its tail against the ground.

"You're still on my shit list, Dog," Skye said. Dog let out a long yawn.

"Filthy animal," the man said, and struggled to rise. Skye put a hand on the man's chest and pressed gently.

"Look, mister, you got a name?"

The man fell back with a groan.

"Cora over there thinks you're the Blood Weeper, but I reckon she's been locked up in the hot box too long. You don't look like the Devil to me. Which one of us is right?"

"There is no Devil in this place."

"Uh-huh. So what's your handle?"

"Kikuchiyo."

"Mercenary?"

"Samurai."

Skye wondered if the man had taken a few too many blows to the head, or was just a mercenary cashing in on the myth for extra notoriety. He was a phenomenal fighter, sure, but he didn't kill with a glance or bat bullets from the air. Anyone who could take out airships by himself would never get captured by the idiots running this operation.

What does that say about you, buddy?

Hey, that's different; I was drunk.

"What do you reckon, Dog?" Skye asked.

Dog barked once.

Skye snorted and shook his head. Fine. He'd play along until he figured out the guy's angle. "If you say so, Mister Kikuchiyo. But for now just lay back and rest, okay?" Skye shooed the animal away, and Kikuchiyo lay down, scowling at Dog. "We'll be back in town soon and get you somewhere you can hole up and rest."

Who knew, it might even be true.

Cora cobbled a stretcher together and they put Kikuchiyo on the back of the runabout. The samurai's eyes drifted to the hilt of a long knife Skye had found in the commandant's office. Kikuchiyo held out a hand to them.

"They took my swords," he said.

"Forget it," Cora said, and brought her weapon up.

"It can't hurt," Skye said.

"I'm sure you won't feel a thing when your head rolls free."

"Kikuchiyo here wouldn't do that. We saved his life, didn't we?" He turned to the wounded man, raised eyebrows asking the silent question.

Kikuchiyo sat up with a grunt and gave a shallow bow. "I will not use my weapons against you, Cora Pierson, or you, John Skye."

How had Kikuchiyo known his name? He didn't recall the guards saying anything.

"Swear on your swords," Cora said.

"His swords?" Skye asked. "The ones Astbury took?"

"They hold his soul."

"Bullshit."

"It's scripture," she said. Evidently, for all her necro schooling, she hadn't outgrown Badlands mysticism.

Just when I was beginning to like her.

Kikuchiyo winced and pressed against his bandages. "They no longer hold my soul; a vow on them holds no meaning. I will swear on my honor."

Skye snorted. "That's not much," he said. "Thin coin of the desperate."

"It is all I have left," Kikuchiyo said.

Cora shifted in her seat. "Like you're one to talk, Skye. It's all any of us have in the end. Give him the knife."

Kikuchiyo stuck the knife in his sash and gave them both an awkward bow, though it seemed to Skye that Cora received a deeper one.

"Did you find my bag?" Kikuchiyo asked. "Or a small box filled with blood vials?"

"No," Cora said.

Kikuchiyo grunted. "He took those, too."

"What of it?" Skye asked.

"It is of no matter," Kikuchiyo replied, but something in his voice made Skye wonder.

Cora started the runabout up and they left the camp, but not before Kikuchiyo made them stop and help him to the gatepost where he carved kanji symbols into the wood.

"So they remember," was Kikuchiyo's only explanation.

～

Cora drove the runabout over the well-worn tracks between the dunes, the Wall on her right. She welcomed the darkness and not worrying about the great dust plume behind them attracting a thopter and riddling them with high-caliber rounds.

"When we get to Motorhead, we should split up," Skye said, scratching at his beard. "I reckon that gives us the best chance, the Imperials having to split up and all. With luck, our trails will be too cold to follow."

Maybe Skye was right. If she could take the runabout, she could be hundreds of miles away before the Empire checked on Outpost 242. She could lose herself in the Badlands, maybe not with her mother's clan, but some other. Even a middling necro like her would be useful against wild deaders.

No. She was done with 'claves. She'd have to come up with an alternative plan. Cora checked on the Blood Weeper in the rearview mirror, who seemed to take every bump and jostle without complaint, though he had to hurt. She'd have to get clear of him too, promise or not. She caught up to something Skye had just said.

"... so at least they won't know where to start."

"Wait, what?"

"The fuel dump."

"What about it?"

Skye grinned, a sly thing that doubtlessly worked wonders on most girls. It filled her with dread. "The fire. Probably spread across the whole camp by now."

She slammed on the brakes and held her breath as the dust cloud passed. Skye coughed and swore at her while the Blood Weeper just covered his mouth and nose and lay there with his eyes closed. As the dust cleared, she made out a black smudge in the sky behind them.

"Idiot!"

"What?" Skye said. "It's not as if there's anyone around to see; looks like a campfire from here."

"That's no campfire," said the Blood Weeper. "That is a beacon."

"Who asked you?" Skye snapped.

"They will come," said the Blood Weeper.

Cora stomped on the accelerator and wrestled the runabout as it fish-tailed down the road.

"Hey now, settle down," Skye said. "Ain't nobody going to chase us. There's jack-squat for miles."

"You just bet all our lives on that," Cora said and tightened her grip on the wheel. "That guy Astbury? He's the top Imperial necro, the Prime's right-hand sociopath. He's not going to let this go."

"I know all about *Colonel* Astbury. So he lost a deader farm, big deal," Skye said. "He's probably got a dozen more. I bet he's too busy fussing over which general to humiliate at some dinner party to even notice. Speaking of which..."

Skye pulled ration bars out from a bag and offered one to Cora.

He may as well offered her a turd. "No thanks," she said.

Skye shrugged and tossed the bar over his shoulder to the Blood Weeper, who caught it without looking.

"It'll be fine, really," he said and ripped into the bar. "For all anyone knows, we could be survivors rushing to send word."

"Or when they count the bodies, they'll find all the dead guards but no prisoners," Cora said. "Math."

Skye's chewing slowed, but he resumed with a wave of his hand. "*If* someone happens to notice the secret hidden base is on fire, and *if* they decide to investigate, and *if* they're smart enough to figure out what happened, *we'll* be long gone." He paused. "In separate directions. Those are good odds."

"And him?" Cora jerked her head at the Blood Weeper. "He can't walk."

"We all know the legends of the Blood Weeper, I'm sure he'll be up and around before we hit town." He turned in his seat and grinned. "Isn't that right, friend?"

The Blood Weeper said nothing.

Cora concentrated on the road ahead. Too late to change Skye's bone-headed move now, the best chance they had was reaching town quick and quiet. After that, she'd have to see. Skye tried catching her gaze, she didn't meet it.

"They are good odds, really," Skye said. He twisted around to the

Blood Weeper for support, but the samurai's eyes were closed. "I've been staying one step ahead of the Empire for years."

She sniffed. "Right."

"Hey, that was bad luck. And they weren't actually looking for me, right? Wrong place, wrong time. What's your excuse?"

"I trusted people."

"Yeah, funny how that happens." Skye sat back with a smug look on his face and Cora wondered if a quick brake check would help wipe it off.

The rattle of 10,000 nails on a tin roof came from the engine just before the wheels seized. The runabout became a 60mph brick heading into a dune. The steering wheel bucked and tore at her grip while the back end broke loose and began swinging around. Time slowed. The dune loomed. She prayed to the Twins for a soft impact.

5

———

It wasn't unheard of to find a powder patch, a kind of sand the consistency of talcum powder that could bog or even swallow small vehicles whole. Fortunately, the powder was only deep enough to mire the roundabout's front wheels. Fortunate even that it kept them from hitting the dune at full speed and further damaging the frame. Skye dug at the sand while the Blood Weeper, recovering faster than Cora thought possible, hobbled back along their path searching for lost parts.

The bad news? The power plant was fried.

"You can fix it, right?" Skye said, taking a break and tearing into another ration bar. She glared at him.

"Oh, you hungry now?" he asked, offering her the bar with a bite missing. The earthy-sweet scent of chocolate and peanut butter hit her and turned her stomach. Leave it to the Imperials to twist her favorite flavor into something horrid when there were corners to cut and pennies to pinch.

"I'm fine." She turned away and breathed out through her nose to clear the smell. "No, the problem is this thing's powered by a four-phase squirrel-cage motor."

"Why's that bad?"

"One of the squirrels is dead." She pointed to the mini-dynamo wired to four forearm-sized cylinders. Three each held a film-eyed squirrel in arrested decay spinning on a rotisserie. Cora pointed to the fourth, which held a charred lump.

"Okay," Skye said. "No spare, I take it."

"Nope, and I don't see any suitable substitutes around here, and even if we did, we don't have the tools to properly balance the load anyway."

"So that means what?"

She puffed her cheeks as she considered the job. "Thirty minutes to rewire the dynamo, another thirty to disengage one set of wheels from the powertrain, and we limp into town at one-quarter speed after however long we take digging ourselves from the sand. If we're lucky, we'll make Motorhead by tomorrow night. Does that change your brilliant plan any?"

Skye leaned in and whispered, "Maybe. We should get rid of the dead weight."

The Blood Weeper gingerly bent down and picked up something from the sand. "I thought he was your new best friend, seeing as how he killed all the guards for us," she said.

"We broke him loose and bandaged him up afterward. Sounds even to me."

"What if we run into more trouble?"

"I don't trust him."

"I don't trust you."

"Of course you can trust me. I could have abandoned you back there but I didn't."

"Because you still need me."

He flashed that irritating smile. "Isn't that why anyone sticks around?"

"We're responsible for him."

"When did this happen? You said helping him was a mistake."

"I did, but then you talked me into it."

"What is this, some kind of honor thing?"

She turned back to the engine. "Something like that."

He put a hand on hers. "Don't be an idiot."

She was an idiot? She jerked her hand away. "If you're so smart, why don't we switch jobs?" She offered her wrench to him and raised a brow.

Skye mumbled something about clearing more sand and left her to it, which was fine by her. Busy hands kept her mind off the problem of how Astbury had briefly turned her into a puppet. She needed food she could hold down, not that disgusting crap Skye was eating. She promised herself to eat something once they were back on the road.

An hour later, she was nearly done. The Blood Weeper slept on the stretcher while Skye lounged in the driver's seat with another ration bar and canteen.

"What were you in for?" Skye asked.

Cora cranked on the wrench, moving the fitting all of a sixteenth before locking up again. What were those monkeys doing all day that they couldn't have bothered maintaining the engine?

"Does it matter?" she said.

"Just making conversation," Skye said. He pulled a face and put the ration bar away.

"Hit a bad one?" Cora asked. Serve him right if he did.

"No, just lost the taste for it. I'm hungry, just not for this."

"That's not good," she said.

"Whattya mean?"

"Well, you were at the farm for a long time; the change might be coming on you." There! The cable came free with a groan.

"Bullshit. I'm not turning deader," he said.

Cora reached out and placed her grease-stained fingers on his forehead and tapped a quick rhythm. "Hmmm. There's something there."

"And?" For the first time, his self-assured smile disappeared.

"You need to be careful."

"Your professional opinion?"

Cora shrugged.

"You were in that camp longer than me, necro lady. And you're not eating either."

She shook her head. "I would know if it were happening to me, wouldn't I? It's different for necros."

"Then why ship you to a deader farm?"

"Made the wrong friends."

He laughed and took a swig from the canteen. "I hear that," he said.

It would be too embarrassing to admit she walked right into custody, taking her orders at face value. What an idiot! Who she had pissed off, she didn't know. She even knew something was wrong with the situation. She knew! But she had walked into that transport anyway, like some pre-programmed robot.

"That's why we can't split up," Cora said. "You'll need me to keep you from transforming."

"You think I'm stupid? No, I move faster alone. Plus, if I turn deader you would all be in danger."

"Nah, you'd be a pushover. In fact, it could help us. Harness you to this runabout, I bet you could power it all the way across the desert." She slid under the chassis and attacked the linkages on the rear wheels, knocking rust from a coupling and setting to work. "If you're set on leaving, best of luck. Keep eating real food because if you start getting stomach cramps, you'll have to make the tough choice on your next meal."

"What choice is that?"

"Whether you're going to eat human flesh or a bullet."

Skye blanched, and she wondered if she had gone too far teasing him, though she was only half-joking. City-born never worried about such things, privileged with ignorance until they found themselves in the Badlands. She was debating on whether to soften the message when the Blood Weeper sat up.

"We need to go," he said.

"You hear something?" Skye asked.

"We have been here too long. We must keep moving."

Cora reefed on the last bolt and the coupling came loose. "Okay, we have power to the front wheels and the rear pair are decoupled. Let's get this knobber on the road."

She winced as she turned the key and breathed out a sigh when the engine caught and stayed smoke-free. She gently applied power after the boys shoved sand ladders under the wheels and began pushing against the front bumper. The Blood Weeper worked without complaint, though he struggled. After much cursing, the runabout lurched and they were free. She took a drink from a canteen and it hit her stomach like turpentine. She decided on waiting a little longer before trying solid food.

Bloody high-top sneakers littered the highway. Something gurgled and wheezed in the ditch's tall grass. He wanted to run, but his legs were concrete and approaching the thing in the weeds step by step on their own. He had to get away. He couldn't face it again. Where were his swords? Naked, he took another step.

Kikuchiyo woke up to the sound of cursing. The runabout ground to a halt and the others got out while he lay on the stretcher, weak and useless. He let the memory of the bloody highway fade, and focused on a nearby building: weather-beaten clapboard, corroded tin lanterns flanking batwing doors, a twisted plank boardwalk. The runabout's headlights rested on a hand-painted sign nailed over a rough-hewn awning: THE KILMEISTER.

They had reached Motorhead, then. A town of lowlifes with delusions of civility.

Something was off. In a place where even on a quiet night dozens might stroll the boardwalk, gather in the street, or hop between saloons, the place was deserted. He reached for the reassuring solidness of his katana but found only the knife.

"We should turn around," Cora said.

"And go where, exactly?" Skye replied.

The honorless one, Skye, was right. Motorhead was the only settlement for hundreds of miles. The Empire had left it alone mostly, preferring to let others risk themselves combing the desert after each night's wallstorm for artifacts: metal scraps, loose book pages, or tattered clothing. Lucky prospectors returned with hand tools, antique pistols, machine parts, or gore-splattered swords. The rarer and more lucrative finds were nearer the Wall: functional mini computers, drugs, and vehicle wrecks, though the closer one got, the more dangerous it became. Evidence of monstrous creatures crisscrossed the sand, and it became practical and later fashionable to use their remains in everyday life. Beetle husks with wing cases hard as titanium were sewn into bulletproof vests. Hollowed out cockroaches the size of runabouts were regularly reclaimed and used as such. Prospectors came back with tales of tracks created by thousand-legged creatures and single bus-sized footprints with undisturbed sand for hundreds of feet in every direction.

Kikuchiyo didn't believe them. Prospectors drank a lot, usually alone.

"We'll scout around, you keep an eye on the runabout. Okay?" Skye said to him with a smile. Cora strode off without making eye contact. Kikuchiyo sat up, stifling a groan. It wasn't difficult, the pain. He and pain were old companions. It had been his ally, fueling his body with unbeatable strength and an invincible defense. Now it victimized him, leaving him weak, vulnerable, and mortal.

Cora and Skye peered into buildings, wary and whispering. They wasted time with cowardly stealth when surprise and momentum would serve them better, but he hadn't the strength to argue. He wondered if they would abandon him here, as Skye suggested. His body might be broken, but his ears worked perfectly. He slid from the stretcher and leaned against the runabout while he adjusted the knife in his sash. At least his headache had abated. Motorhead's drunken founders established their town at the very edge of the Wall's influence, a balancing act between greed and basic mental function.

Movement.

Kikuchiyo put a hand to his knife and crouched, shunting the pain aside. A shadow flickered behind a stack of bins; dust from a careless step drifted through the air. He centered himself and measured the distance he would need to cover and added seven steps for a feint and a dodge. His body wouldn't take a leap or a roll, but no matter, it was but one opponent. And if he was wrong, he would adapt or die.

I keep my promises.

Mismatched eyes behind a black-and-white muzzle emerged, and shame washed through him. A dog. That same accursed mongrel from the camp. Its tongue rolled out as it recognized him and it took a tentative step with white tail wagging. Kikuchiyo bent for a stone at his feet and whipped it, hissing as wounds reopened. The rock sailed wide and clattered against the building. Kikuchiyo couldn't believe it, to miss a throw at a mere fifty yards was impossible! The dog emerged from the bins, padding towards Kikuchiyo.

Sweat prickled at his brow as he stooped and found another stone.

"Away," he said to the animal. "Go!" He faked the throw, and the dog flinched and turned as if to go back. Weakness flooded through him and he flailed at the runabout's fender for support, but his hand faded from reality and passed through the steel.

Blood of the Redeemer, not like this!

He fell face-first. His world narrowed to a bright pinprick as blackness closed in from all sides. As consciousness left, voices shouted and a dog's panting grew louder.

6

Skye crept through the empty mechanical shop, wary of an ambush. The last time he had been through town, runabouts being rebuilt or scrapped for parts filled the shop's triple bay with at least four more jobs waiting out back. The back lot was empty now. The air stank of rust, copper, and hydraulic fluid, but its scrap bins and grease-stained tool benches were empty, the shelves held only dusty outlines, and the overhead hoists were missing their gears and chains. He poked at greasy rags piled on the floor, and several iridescent bugs scurried away into the shop's darker corners. Motorhead was home to nearly a thousand people, but no more. Maybe he would find a clue to what had happened, but his gut told him not to bother. Whatever happened to Motorhead had been fast and thorough.

Outside, someone shouted.

Skye rushed out from the shop to find Kikuchiyo sprawled on the ground and Dog sitting on his haunches nearby. Through some trick of the light he seemed to see through the man, but as he approached the effect faded. Ozone stung his nostrils. A lightning strike? Someone with an electro gun? He scanned the area, but could find evidence of neither. Skye reached out for the man's shoulder and steadied him as he pushed to his knees.

"You all right?" he asked.

"I am fine," Kikuchiyo said. Dog let out a single bark, then took off running as Kikuchiyo flung a rock at him.

"That mutt ain't worth the trouble," Skye said, and helped Kikuchiyo to his feet. "You bleeding anywhere?"

Kikuchiyo shook off Skye's hand. "Leave me."

"Hey, I'm not the one that shouted and fell the fuck down."

The knife pressed at his ear before he could react. Kikuchiyo's dirty face leaned closer. "I said, leave me."

"Put it down," Cora said.

Kikuchiyo turned enough for Skye to see Cora standing ten feet away with her submachine gun trained on the samurai's head, the muzzle steady. The blade didn't waver.

"My stroke will fall before you pull the trigger. You would feel my blade's kiss before the third round leaves the chamber, if you felt it at all."

Cora's eyes went hard. "Maybe. That still gives me two shots to put you down. It only takes one to get the job done."

Skye didn't like either option, seeing as it would either be his jugular or stray bullet to the head.

"Hey," Skye said. "Remember that time we all escaped from the prison camp where they were farming deaders? Remember when we cooperated and didn't kill each other? Those were good times, right?"

For a few moments, Skye figured it could have gone either way, then Kikuchiyo lowered his knife and walked away, ignoring the gun Cora still aimed at his back.

"You've got a light step," Skye said to her.

Cora lowered the gun but kept watching Kikuchiyo as he walked into the town's trading post. She let out a ragged breath. "I thought you were leaving," she said.

Skye gave her one of his best smiles. "Looks like you can handle that merc just fine, but wouldn't you rather have someone watching your back?"

"I'd never turn my back on the Blood Weeper."

"Then who's gonna keep you safe while you sleep?"

The corner of her mouth twitched. "That line work for you often?"

He spread his hands. "More often than you'd think. Anyway, there's nothing here to work with unless you found another runabout or thopter."

She shook her head. "They've stripped the stores bare, or nearly so."

"Nothing left in the shop but the bones."

"Think they evacuated?" she asked.

"Maybe. Most people came here because it was their only chance to scratch out a living. I'm sure some might bug out if some big nasty appeared, but there's always a few who would stay even if..." He smiled and glanced back at Kikuchiyo. "Even if the Blood Weeper himself came for a visit."

Cora watched Dog trot across the street and enter the trading post.

"I can't believe he followed us here," Skye said.

"You burned down his home," Cora said. "What did you expect he'd do?"

"Ah, he'll be fine."

Dog shot out of the trading post, a rock clacking at the floorboards behind him. A scowling Kikuchiyo followed moments later with knife in hand. Dog disappeared around the corner and Kikuchiyo nodded once, then began carving kanji on the door.

AN HOUR LATER, Skye gave up. The buildings had been stripped of anything useful, but more troubling were the things left behind. Family photos, wooden knick-knacks, redstone trinkets, Paradise City china and coffee mugs — all left in place. The sentimental things people rushed into burning buildings to save, just abandoned? And not a fork, coin, teapot, or scrap of metal left in the entire town. These people hadn't gone away on their own, they had been moved, probably at gunpoint, and their homes professionally looted.

He found Cora sitting on the runabout's bumper, watching Kikuchiyo carving up another wooden post.

"What's he doing?"

"Dunno, but it keeps him happy." She pointed to three identical symbols carved along the boardwalk.

"Looks just like the one he left at the camp," he said.

"Yeah. So, find anything?" she said.

He shook his head. "We should leave. Head for the Badlands."

"And eat what?" she said. "It's two weeks and we're already in the hole."

"It's one of the few places free from Imperial control."

"Why go there when we can make it work here? We wouldn't have to worry about shelter."

"I thought you were worried about pursuit," he said.

"I thought you wanted to split up and hide. Why not hide here?"

"You mean starve in some stranger's house?"

"It's our best bet," she said.

"It's a sucker's bet," he said. For a 'claver, she sure was sour on the Badlands.

"A caravan's bound to come. If we don't exert ourselves…"

Kikuchiyo interrupted them with a shout. He took a few steps into the street, cocked his head and closed his eyes.

Skye cocked an ear. Wind. Creaking doors. Cora's wheezing. He hadn't noticed that before; how sick was she?

"Incoming," Kikuchiyo said and pointed east. "Ornithopter."

Skye opened his mouth to argue, then the telltale drone reached his ears. "Right. Move the runabout inside the garage. We'll hide there until it leaves."

Cora slid in behind the steering wheel and tried starting the runabout. The dynamo caught, then made a spine-cringing squeal and seized.

"Fucking squirrel!"

Skye nodded. "Bugger. Okay, let's push it."

He threw his shoulder behind the runabout as Cora pushed with one arm and steered with the other. Kikuchiyo, of no help at all, limped behind.

"There is not enough time," Kikuchiyo called after him. "They will see you."

"I've always been lucky," Skye said, and clung to the thought as he lurched from side to side, digging into the packed earth. He was lucky. His legs would be strong enough to hold the sprint to the garage. He wasn't tired.

34

The runabout bumped along at a slow jog, the drone of the ornithopter growing louder in his ears. He willed his legs to go faster. Something fell from the runabout's cargo rack. He glanced back and found Kikuchiyo bending to pick it up.

"Hurry, Blood Weeper, or you'll get left behind," he called and sprinted for a few more seconds. The runabout pulled away and he stumbled, but Kikuchiyo's powerful grip latched on his shoulder and kept him upright. The ornithopter sounded almost on top of them, and he hoped to Twins there was a building between them and the pilot. The runabout had enough momentum to carry it the last dozen yards and Cora hopped in behind the wheel and guided it into the garage, stopping at the far wall as Skye and Kikuchiyo made it inside. Skye put his hands on his knees and checked over his shoulder.

No sign of the thopter, though it was close by.

"Close the door," Kikuchiyo said.

Skye shook his head. "They'll see," he managed.

Kikuchiyo cocked his head and pointed at the wall. "Passing north and coming around." His fingertip tracked the thopter's movement. "Be quick, or they will see the vehicle."

Skye groaned but went to the sliding door. Miraculously, its rails hadn't been stripped for scrap. He leaned into its wide handle and forced his screaming legs to push once more. With a squeal, the door began moving.

"Hurry," Kikuchiyo said.

Really? Thanks for the help.

He gave it another shove, switched his grip, and started pulling. The door chattered and bucked, promising a grinding halt if he let up. The thopter's wail grew louder as it turned back towards town. With one last heave, the door rolled past him and slammed shut.

Just above the rooftops, a needle-bodied thopter with an oversized turbine on its ass-end screamed down the street. The pilot sat in an open cockpit, but rather than desert robes and goggles, standard since the days of the Caliphate, the pilot wore the same stone-like helmet that had gotten Horse Laugh in so much trouble. Good. That meant the pilot couldn't see shit. The thopter pulled a tight turn over Motorhead and the three of them backed further into the garage's shadows.

"Single seater," Cora said. "We can take the pilot if he's stupid enough to land."

"He won't. Just a quick peek and report back. If he sees nothing, they won't be in any hurry to get here."

"If we're lucky," she grumbled.

He winked. "I've always been lucky, Cora."

She sniffed.

The thopter's shadow passed, followed moments later by a miniature sandstorm that rattled the window frames. "Dumbass won't be able to scout shit if he keeps that up," Cora said.

Skye clucked his tongue. "Like I said, lucky."

The thopter's banshee wail pitched higher as it came around for a second pass.

Nothing interesting here. Go home, flyboy.

"Just hold tight here. He won't see us."

"And what then?" Cora said.

"Then we bug out," he said.

"And get caught on the open sand?"

He waved her off. "We can move at night."

The thopter's scream echoed as it circled the town.

Cora folded her arms. "What about the wallstorm?"

"This far out, we can chance it."

"I don't like it," Cora said.

He turned to Kikuchiyo. "What about you?"

Kikuchiyo didn't answer, fingertip tracing that same kanji symbol on the grimy window. Then his attention focused on something outside and moments later, Dog began howling outside the door. Kikuchiyo muttered as he left and picked a rifle from the runabout.

Skye hissed as he tried and failed standing on wobbly legs. "Get back here!"

"The pilot will see the animal, and report it," Kikuchiyo said over his shoulder. "This cannot happen."

Cora raised her submachine gun, but Skye pushed it aside and shook his head. He didn't like it either, but Kikuchiyo was right. "Make it quick."

Kikuchiyo slid the door open a fraction and poked the barrel out. Dog's ears perked up and he stopped barking. Kikuchiyo brought the rifle to his shoulder and stared down the barrel for several seconds. The thopter's scream grew louder.

"What are you waiting for?" Skye said. "They'll see the muzzle flash!"

The rifle rose and Kikuchiyo squeezed off three quick shots. The thopter broke off and banked hard. Kikuchiyo braced rock-still against the doorjamb before firing two more shots. The thopter's engine whine turned into a buzz saw's rattle as it fled to the east. Kikuchiyo cast the rifle away and turned back into the garage. Thin smoke trailed behind the thopter and it began corkscrewing.

Skye blew out a ragged breath and his rifle rattled in his hands. "I should do you right here! What were you thinking?"

"I was shooting the ornithopter down."

Skye pointed at the disappearing thopter. "Does that thopter look like it's down to you?"

Kikuchiyo shrugged. "Ran out of ammo."

"You idiot!" Skye said. "Now they know we're here for sure!"

Kikuchiyo met his gaze but remained annoyingly calm. "They will be wary and cautious in their approach, which gives us the advantage."

"I agree," Cora said. "Give me thirty minutes to fix the problem squirrel and we can bug out."

"Oh, really?" She shrugged at his glare. "It's hours until dark. If they send out another scout, they'll catch us in the open. You were pretty clear earlier about it being a bad thing."

She lifted her chin and came a half-step closer. "If they catch us here, we're pinned down with no way out. You were all for leaving a minute ago."

"In the *dark*. In *secret*. It was a splendid plan before this dumb bunny started shooting Imperials in broad daylight!"

"There." Kikuchiyo pointed west. "That is the path."

Cora blinked. "To the Wall?"

Skye poked his tongue into his cheek as he stared them both down. "Suicide is it, then?"

Cora shrugged. "They won't find us in there."

"For good reason. The closer we get, the more it'll fuck with our minds. You thought the headaches were bad now, the nightmares? Just wait until you start hallucinating while the sand grinds your face off. One hell of a way to get lost."

Cora counted on her fingers. "We can stay and wait for an Imperial patrol looking for the idiots who burned down their deader farm and winged their thopter, take a Mickey-Moused runabout into the desert with no cover and no supplies for a hundred miles, or head west and chance the Wall," Cora said. She kicked the roundabout's tire. "It's the least terrible option."

The thopter disappeared over the horizon, struggling yet airborne. It would have radioed ahead by now, and another flight could already be on its way. Poor odds all around, and only one choice kept him out of Imperial hands.

"Come on, Skye, where's that luck you're always talking about?" Cora said.

"Fine. Let's hope you two don't use it up."

7

They broke down halfway between Motorhead and the Wall, one a barely visible smudge behind them and the other billowing and rippling ahead, filling the western sky. Cora re-tightened the scarf around her face and blinked sand from her eyes. Skye, her self-volunteered assistant, brushed a hip against hers as he leaned over the engine compartment. Deliberate? Now? Here? She wondered if biting his nose off would make him lose interest.

"How much longer?" he asked.

She said, "The more asinine questions you ask, the longer this takes." Skye winced and held his hands up. "Nearly there. Why don't you take five and I'll let you know."

"Okay," he said. He gave a tight smile and flopped down onto the runabout's stretcher with an arm over his eyes. Right. The headaches. Skye's head must be pounding. If the Blood Weeper suffered, he bore it better, sitting on the sand with hands in lap, breathing deeply. The sand curtains eddied and curled, teasing half-remembered shapes from her childhood. She wanted to get closer, sure everything would come into focus if they went a bit farther.

She hummed a tune and tapped a beat on the flukey squirrel's canister, trying to coax out a few more watts. The damn thing was sputtering and when it went for good, she doubted the remaining pair could make the runabout do more than lurch. The engine needed more attention than she could give it, even under the best conditions. Truth was, she had always been a middling necro and had to work her ass off to accomplish the most mediocre result, but at least it got her out of the enclaves and into the city. Then again, staying in the 'clave would have spared her this.

A flash in the corner of her eye made her look up. She scanned the desert and it flashed again, beyond Motorhead's smudge. Then another, and another. She grabbed a pair of binoculars and tried making sense of what she saw. The blobs on the horizon resolved into a dozen anvil-shaped vehicles of red-brown metal, each the size of a modest building. Dots swarmed around them like gnats — thopters and runabouts. As the dozen crested the dune, the flat tops of another dozen appeared.

Cora pushed the binoculars into Skye's hand. "Imperials."

"How many?"

"All of them, I think. Great idea, setting the camp on fire."

She had the dynamo firing a few minutes later and was composing a blistering rant she'd deliver to the engineer who thought routing an air intake over the necrotic transfer case was a good idea when a shadow fell over her workspace.

"Five minutes, Skye," she said. "If you want to be useful, hand me that socket."

The hand delivering the tool was not Skye's. Scripture popped into her head.

Blood Weeper! His touch means death!

She might have yelped. She definitely bashed the back of her head. Her gun lay at her feet.

"Sorry," she said. "I thought... Sorry."

"The Imperials approach," he said. Cold eyes met hers, and she glanced away.

"I know. I saw the metal things."

"Sandcrawlers," said the Blood Weeper.

"You know them?"

He was silent for a few moments. "From another life."

More awkward silence.

"They're huge," she said and instantly regretted it. The Blood Weeper grunted and kept staring at her. She shifted from foot to foot. Was he angry with her? Another dumb question. Scripture clearly said he was always angry. "I'm almost done."

"I require a tool," he said.

"Yes? A tool?" Twins, she sounded stupid!

"Something that scratches metal."

She bent over the toolbox, glad to have an excuse not to look at him, and rifled through the contents though she knew them all already. "I don't have a scriber or awl... how about a screwdriver?" She held it up.

He snatched it from her hand in an eye blink. "It will do." He turned and left. After she collected herself, she went back to assembling the dynamo and didn't ask about the new vibrations running through the runabout's frame or the metal-on-metal screeching. Where she needed a screwdriver, she improvised.

She slammed the hood shut, and when she strapped the toolbox back in place, she noticed the passenger-side door had a new kanji symbol on it. Skye caught her looking and leaned in.

"It's his name," he whispered.

She shot him a questioning look.

Skye shrugged. "What he says."

"And he's been leaving it everywhere we've gone. Do the Imperials know what it is?"

"I don't know if they can read it, but I bet they recognize it."

Idiots. You're both idiots.

A column of fire erupted within Motorhead. Seconds later, the explosion's sound reached them. More columns appeared and bits of the town tumbled through the air. Gun smoke puffed around the sandcrawlers as they came into range and pounded the town with salvo after salvo.

"Glad we didn't stay?" she asked Skye.

"I was about to ask you the same thing. You were for it before you were against it."

What was his problem? "They're called facts," she said. "When you get enough of them, you're allowed to change your mind."

"You can't play the result and call it a win."

The Blood Weeper rapped his knuckles against the door and pointed. An ornithopter squadron streaked over the town and dropped bombs onto the few buildings still standing. When the destruction ended, runabouts emerged from behind the sandcrawlers and charged ahead. The Blood Weeper turned away and pointed his chin at the Wall.

"Move."

Cora grimaced and started the engine. The dynamo hummed off-key, and the runabout lurched ahead.

"I liked him better when he was unconscious," Skye muttered.

"Hush. He's easily insulted."

Skye sniffed. "If he wants to kill me, he'll have to get in line."

As they reached the Wall's leading edge, Cora discovered it wasn't just one big storm but several smaller storms with dust devils dancing and twisting around each other. She aimed the runabout at a break between two cyclones, a dead zone a hundred feet wide. Skye pinched the bridge of his nose and hissed with the runabout's every bump and lurch. Even the Blood Weeper grunted from time to time but kept watching their backtrail. She hadn't experienced the headaches yet, though a pressure in her head ebbed and flowed. To her relief, the pressure had eased as the runabout climbed the final dune and entered the gap.

Did we get away with it?

Maybe the Imperials weren't interested in them. Maybe they wouldn't follow the runabout's tracks right away. Maybe the winds had erased the tracks. Maybe she'd live through the next few hours.

Too many maybes.

The ground leveled out and she opened the throttle. The runabout's headlights did little in the gloom, mostly illuminating sand grains tearing at the scarf wrapped around her face. Lightning erupted in deep purples and greens from the hearts of billowing thunderheads; actinic whites and blues from cloud-to-cloud strikes lit the path ahead with a hellish beauty. Several gaps appeared ahead and she cranked the wheel to the leftmost, following its twisted path. She could be getting them hopelessly lost, but it felt right somehow, and really, who was complaining at this point? At each fork in the path she let the pressure in her head guide her, until the runabout's lights went out and it coasted to a stop.

Skye peeked out through his hands and she shook her head. She popped the engine hatch open, unsurprised to find the problem squirrel reduced to ash. The remaining two weren't looking too well either, but she salvaged their cylinders anyway. Even damaged deaders had value. Skye tossed supplies into a bag and didn't protest when she added the power cells. He leaned in and shouted over the wind.

"We need to keep moving," he said.

"Can you? You look like shit," she said.

Strong teeth flashed in his quick smile. "Got no choice, this gap won't stay open forever."

Cora fished around the runabout's tool kit and held out a tow rope. "Tie it around your waist."

"Why?"

"If the winds shift and we get caught, you won't be able to see your hand in front of your face."

"Afraid I'll wander off?"

"Yes, along with all that gear you're carrying."

"What about Kikuchiyo?"

She regarded the Blood Weeper, already tying another length of rope around his waist and adjusting his knife.

"If you can convince him to carry anything, be my guest. I'll go first, then you, he can take the rear."

"Why?"

"Because I want you between us when he goes psycho."

"I'm touched."

"Let's hope not."

The Blood Weeper and Skye were soon grainy images behind her as the gaps between storms collapsed and the howling wind had become just a sound, something she tuned out until the Blood Weeper's line jerked and brought them all up short. The samurai's head tracked something unseen, and when his gaze found hers he seemed surprised and shook himself before continuing on. Likewise, Skye walked hunched over, constantly checking over his shoulder and swiping the air at some personal phantom.

For her own part, the wind and sand suggested shapes and sounds in the same way clouds or a half-heard song might, only more so. In the corners of her eyes, skeletons with glowing eyes reached for her while a blue whale floated in the air with an oil derrick caught in its tail. A tall figure dressed in robes and the long-nosed mask of a plague doctor stopped to watch as she passed before turning and disappearing into the darkness. Voices whispered in agitation, joy, anger, and sorrow. Feathery touches ran along her spine as insects crawled ever upwards on a quest to lay their eggs in her brain.

All false, of course. It wasn't hard to ignore it, as one would with a nearby conversation at a restaurant or static on the radio. For her, anyway.

The Blood Weeper trudged on ahead with a gait like he was trying to shoulder the Wall's winds aside with each step. He muttered curses under his breath, dark words she couldn't understand but made her shiver all the same. Skye kept up his own single-sided conversation with his imaginary tormentors in a furor that grated on her nerves.

"Would you kindly shut the hell up?" Cora said over her shoulder. "Some of us are trying to concentrate."

Skye shook his head as if to clear it and took quick steps to catch up to her. "This is a sucker's bet."

"One you made."

Skye's response was cut short as his foot came down on loose sand and he bobbled the recovery.

"Sorry, didn't catch that," she said.

He spat sand and grimaced. "In any room, someone has to be a sucker. If you can't figure out who it is, then it must be you."

"So who's the sucker here?"

He blinked. "Can't you figure it out?"

"But this was your idea!"

"Don't I know it."

Cora shook her head and trudged on, throwing an arm over her eyes as she crested the dune. The winds tugged at her clothing, sand probing at the seams and finding its way in. A droning wind surrounded them, punctuated with other buzzes and rattles, making her wonder what else whipped past her besides sand. Occasionally, she maneuvered around

44

twisted metal wrecks buried in the ground and she began glancing up from time to time, expecting one to come hurtling down on her head.

They came to the Wall's center, though how she knew she couldn't say. The rope at her waist jerked each time the men stumbled, and a dull ache settled in her lower back. At least the ornithopters wouldn't find them in here, even if the pilots were crazy enough to follow. The surrounding air darkened as the storm swelled: white to gray, gray to brown, and brown to red. The droning around her grew louder and thunder rumbled ahead. She couldn't make out anything beyond arm's reach and the rope behind her disappeared into the red dust. She leaned into the wind with each step, tugging at the rope each time it dug into her hips, wondering if the Blood Weeper would kill her later for such impudence as to suggest he moved too slow. She could simply cut the rope and leave him behind. Leave them both behind.

The rope went taut and vibrated like a guitar string, almost pulling her from her feet. As she swayed, it went slack and dropped to the ground. She resisted the impulse to pull at it and instead followed it back to its severed end. The pressure in her head increased. She was going the wrong way. She called out, a shout barely louder than the howling wind. To the left, something? She took a closer step and panic began gnawing within her. What if it was one of the Wall's hallucinations? What if she picked the wrong direction and got even more separated from the others and they all wandered in ever-widening circles away from each other, or worse, if the Blood Weeper came upon her and mistook her for an enemy?

She took another step, seeing nothing. The pressure in her skull turned into a headache, pulsing with every step. A black shape in the storm. She took two more steps and found the Blood Weeper, kneeling with knife in hand and swiping the air to either side, eyes unseeing, punctuating each slash with an explosive breath. The rope around his waist was missing entirely.

"Blood Weeper," she called.

He whirled to face her and leveled his blade.

Did he remember his promise? "It's Cora."

Nothing. He shuffle-stepped closer.

"What do you see?"

The Blood Weeper plunged the knife behind him like a man paddling a canoe and as quickly reversed the grip so the knife's tip pointed at her belly.

"There's nothing here, Blood Weeper. Look at me."

He shuffled to the side, angling his head, but he still looked through her, at a point over her shoulder. The wind's howl took on the flavor of Skye's shouting voice. She gathered herself to shout back and stifled it as the Blood Weeper lunged. She fell and scrambled backwards as the knife tip came ever closer with the Blood Weeper's quick thrusts.

"It's the Wall in your head. Push past it!" she cried.

She rolled and scrambled to her knees. The Blood Weeper struck at invisible enemies to his left and right before charging her again. Her arms and legs were heavy as concrete and wouldn't let her stand. She threw herself to the side again as the blade swept down, stopping short as the Blood Weeper grabbed her ponytail and placed the knife's edge to her throat.

"I'm not your enemy, Kikuchiyo," she said.

His eyes focused on her face for the first time. The knife quivered, then withdrew. He fell to his knees beside her and with effort, sheathed his weapon. Cora wanted to collapse but pushed to her feet and steadied trembling limbs.

"We need to find Skye. Are you under control?"

"*Hai.*"

She swallowed the lump in her throat and held a quivering hand out to him. The Blood Weeper took it and rose to his feet, coiling her rope's severed end around his hand and motioning she should lead on. Cora focused on Skye's shouting through the pounding headache at her temples, telling her she was heading the wrong way.

Gunshots popped nearby. She took off at a run, hoping a bullet meant for one of Skye's phantoms didn't hit her by mistake, or the Blood Weeper would slip into another episode and cut her down from behind. Would she even know, or would she turn off like a switch? Would it hurt? She pushed the thought away and squinted into the darkness.

Another gunshot buzzed past her ear.

"Skye!"

"They followed us in!" Skye was close.

"Who, Skye?"

"The Imperials!"

She had him now, a shadow ahead and to the right. "Look, we're coming in. Don't shoot us!"

"Roger that, laying covering fire."

Something knocked her to the ground as Skye's burst passed overhead.

"Hold," the Blood Weeper said into her ear. He left in a running crouch, zigzagging as Skye fired another burst.

"Don't kill him!" she called after the samurai. She crawled on elbows and knees, close enough to see muzzle flashes like a strobe light, then a darkened shape flew in and knocked the shooter down. When Cora arrived, Skye writhed on the ground holding his wrist. The Blood Weeper had disappeared.

"You're okay now, Skye," she said. "We've got you."

"The Imperials," he hissed.

"They're not real. It's the Wall messing with your head."

"Someone cut the rope and was coming for me."

"That was the Blood Weeper. He had an episode too, but he's better now, I hope."

Skye sat up and shook out his hand. "Is he? Where'd he go?"

"I don't know."

Gunfire erupted from the darkness. They flattened themselves to the ground and Skye pawed the sand. "He took my weapon."

Cora mentally slapped herself and unslung her submachine gun. Had the Blood Weeper been lucky, or had she? He might not have stayed his hand if she had been shooting at him. She looked for a target in the darkness, a muzzle flash, a shape, anything. Hopefully not a hallucination. She'd risk hitting the Blood Weeper. Another shot passed close by but no flash, nothing to home in on.

"He's moving with each shot," Skye said. "We should too."

They crawled. Gunfire erupted from their left and another burst answered it. Her weapon rattled in her hands. Skye looked back at her.

"I'm okay," she said.

"You won't be if you just sit there. Either take a shot or give it over."

Another bullet whizzed past her.

"Close, but not at us," Skye said. "He's just firing blind. You going to return fire?"

Shadows and sand blended together. "There's nothing to shoot at!"

"The Blood Weeper'll get lucky, eventually. Give over." He held out his hand.

"Nothing makes sense!"

"Welcome to the jungle, baby." He reached for her gun. She snatched it away and swung the muzzle to him. They stared at each other for several moments before a strangled cry broke out, fading to a gurgle.

Cora lowered her weapon. "That's the Blood Weeper. He doesn't need a gun."

Skye scowled at her. "You sure about that?"

Cora shrugged and rolled to her stomach, keeping one eye on Skye. "We'll see."

"Yeah, we'll see."

A shape appeared from the darkness, and she trained her gun on it with a finger on the trigger just in case. The Blood Weeper emerged, dragging a body behind him.

"Imperial pathfinder," he said.

"Told you I wasn't seeing things," Skye grumbled and approached the body wearing that same melted stone armor as the camp guards. Skye removed the blank-faced helmet and worked his jaw as he turned the trooper's head. "Just a kid. Dumbass guttersnipe conscript with wasted talent." He closed the trooper's eyes. "Better luck next time."

"How'd he find us?" Cora asked.

Skye turned the helmet in his hands. "Designed for the task? Isn't that what Astbury said?" He put the helmet on and swung his head from side to side for a few moments before removing it and wincing. "Some light amplification, air filtration, and noise damping. There's some kind of radio built in too, but I don't see the speakers. Most importantly, it seems to take the headache away."

Cora took the helmet from him and put it on her head. The pressure in her head eased, but rather than relief, she felt dizzy. The stone helmet buzzed at her ears, tickling them with questions from a distant voice. She ripped the helmet off and took several deep breaths before handing it back.

48

"The stone itself vibrates," she said. "I wonder how they do it."

"Not important," the Blood Weeper said. He rolled the body over and pulled a bundle of flags attached to telescoping poles. "Markers. His squad will follow them here. We must be elsewhere."

"Yeah." Skye removed the trooper's web belt and fastened it around his waist, then checked the holstered sidearm. "Nine-millimeter, no extra mags. I don't suppose you kept my submachine gun, or his main?"

The Blood Weeper leveled a stare. "No."

"Do you know where they are?"

"In the sand."

"Right. You wanna trade, Cora?"

Cora tightened her grip on the gun, but Skye waved her off. "Fine, but I'm keeping the helmet. Lead on."

They re-tied the rope and set off in the direction the pressure in her head insisted on, thoughts too busy to pay any more attention to the cavorting demons and skeletons at the edges of her vision. Would Astbury have sent Imperial pathfinders? For all that he seemed interested in them, it was a hell of an expenditure for a few escaped prisoners. Damned quick response, too, even with Skye's boneheaded pyromania and the Blood Weeper's graffiti trail. They must have already had a contingent of sandcrawlers outfitted for operations in the Wall nearby.

Several minutes later, it hit her. Imperial pathfinders didn't chase escaped prisoners, they scouted invasion routes. The soldier wasn't there for her; there was an army coming through the Wall.

Time had no meaning. After hours, days, weeks, or merely a series of eternal minutes, the blackness lifted without warning and they were free in clear air. Before them, sand grains danced across a cracked hardpan stretching out to distant mesas and hills under a sky filled with dark clouds. The pressure in Cora's head faded, less urgent yet still lurking. Skye pulled off the pathfinder's helmet and scrubbed though sweat-slick hair while Kikuchiyo knelt and shut his eyes.

Cora poured out the sand from her boots and watched the wind gather and fling it at the Wall. She had made the crossing with nothing worse than flaking skin and throbbing joints, the assaults from the Blood Weeper and Imperial pathfinder notwithstanding. Not bad for a little necro from the Badlands. The more she thought about it, the more she suspected her upbringing and training had toughened her mind against the Wall's mental assaults. It would also explain the pressure in her head, perhaps some potent necrotic power source or phenomenon amplified by the Wall that overloaded untrained minds. It would be worth researching, she thought, something at one time she may have proposed doing herself. But she wasn't a necro anymore, she was an escaped convict. Maybe if she were more accomplished, if she had studied harder, none of this would have happened.

No sense in dwelling on it.

She scanned the horizon and made out a rocky outcrop promising shelter from the winds. They would get there by nightfall if they made good time, hopefully ahead of any other Imperial troops.

"Come on, boys. We can't stop now."

The shelter turned out to be little more than a man-high rise on the plain, some optical trick making it look huge from a distance. They sat huddled together as the gloom turned to full darkness and temperature dropped. Skye tore the ration bar's wrapper open with his teeth while Cora fidgeted with hers.

"You need to eat," Skye said. "Even if you don't feel like it."

She set the food aside. "I'll get to it later."

He opened his mouth to say something, then thought better of it. His face twisted after taking a bite from the bar and he chewed mechanically, seeming to keep the stuff down through sheer force of will.

"Yours taste like dust too, Kikuchiyo?" Skye asked.

The samurai put down a stone he was scratching a kanji symbol on and tore a hunk from his jerky. He looked around the camp as he chewed, remarking finally, "It is adequate."

Skye nudged her with his elbow. "You were right, he isn't human."

She caught herself laughing and froze.

The Blood Weeper's eyes narrowed and his hand closed around the rock.

That idiot's mouth just killed us both — it wasn't my fault!

She swallowed as his gaze slid from her to something over her shoulder. She turned and crept a hand to her weapon only to find that mutt Dog at the edge of their camp watching them.

"How'd he find us?" Cora said.

"Smart dog," Skye said. "Lucky, too."

The Blood Weeper weighed the rock in his hand and sucked at a tooth. Dog tensed, ready to run. The samurai let out something between a laugh and a grunt and tossed his jerky to Dog, who snatched it in the air and trotted around the camp, stopping ten feet away from the men. Satisfied he was still out of arm's reach, he settled down and started gnawing.

Skye grinned. "Change of heart, Kikuchiyo?"

The samurai went back to etching his name on the rock.

"I had a dog once," Cora said. "She'd follow me around outside the 'clave."

Dog finished the jerky and looked to Skye. Skye laughed and rose slowly, holding out his ration bar. "It's nothing special, but you're welcome to it."

Dog crept forward, nose working. Skye stretched his arm and Dog sniffed the outstretched hand, then lunged for the food and ran back to his spot. Dog ate it in five quick bites.

Skye nodded. "Proves what I've always suspected. In any army, the generals and quartermasters eat the best. Everyone else takes their cut down the supply chain until there's nothing left for line troopers but dog food."

Dog thumped his tail against the ground.

Cora looked at her uneaten jerky stick. Dog finished Skye's offering and looked to her, ears forward.

"You haven't eaten," the Blood Weeper said without looking up.

Her face went warm. "You're not my mother. I'm not hungry, he is."

She crouched and slowly duck-walked to Dog, holding out the dried meat like Skye had. Dog went still and his ears flattened.

"It's okay," she cooed. "Just wanna give you a treat." She took another shuffle forward and Dog growled.

"Cora," Skye said.

"It's okay," Cora said. "Dogs like me."

"You sure?"

"Come on, boy." She wiggled the jerky at Dog, who stopped growling and glanced between her and the outstretched offering.

She took another step forward and Dog's nostrils flared.

"That's it. We're friends, right?" She took another step.

Dog snarled and lunged at her, barking. Startled, she scrambled back. Dog bared his teeth and growled.

"I don't think he likes you," Skye said.

Cora backed away towards her original spot. Dog advanced on her until the Blood Weeper uttered a command Cora didn't understand. Dog froze, still growling. He repeated the command and Dog backed off, returning to the fire's far side.

Cora sat and wrapped her arms about herself.

"Don't take it too hard, some dogs are just assholes," Skye said. "Maybe you smell funny." He picked up the discarded jerky stick and brushed it off. "Still okay. You want it back?"

"No thanks, I'm not hungry."

He leaned closer and rested a hand on her forearm. It was warm and firm, skin not so leathery and cracked as her own. She imagined she could feel his pulse, blood pumping through water-rich muscle. She imagined—

"You okay?" he asked.

She looked over his shoulder and flinched at the Blood Weeper's icy stare.

"I'm fine," she said and turned away.

8

Skye woke up to an eagle's scream. Long finger-like wingtips stretched and finessed currents high overhead as the bird circled their camp before moving on. He took it as a good omen.

He stood and stretched, working all the kinks out of his body from sleeping on the hard ground. Breakfast was another unappetizing ration bar, washed down with a couple swigs of water. Kikuchiyo was already up and around, pacing the perimeter and ignoring Dog, who lay with head on paws, brown and blue eyes watching the samurai's every move.

Skye shook his canteen. "We need to find some food and water, or this jailbreak is going to end real soon," he announced.

Cora mumbled something. When he asked her to speak up, she glared at him and turned away. Skye considered asking her what was going on, but changed his mind. If the woman wanted to talk, she would. He looked to the samurai, who set his carved rock down and stood back a moment before bending down and turning it imperceptibly.

Skye nodded. "You all make wonderful points. Motion carried, we go that way." He pointed.

"Why there?" Cora asked.

"See those sticks on the horizon?"

"No."

He rummaged in the pack and handed her the binoculars. "They look like masts to me. Masts mean boats, and boats mean water."

Kikuchiyo squinted and grunted. "Sharp eyes."

Skye shrugged. "Clean living."

The samurai said nothing, but Skye thought he almost smiled.

Cora lowered the binoculars and stood. "It's as good a destination as any, I guess."

"For someone who was dead sure about life yesterday, it seems to have left you now," Skye said.

Cora flipped him a middle finger and started walking away. Skye turned to Kikuchiyo. "What?"

Kikuchiyo looked at him for a moment. "Bad phrasing."

AT THE MOUTH of a bowl-like canyon they found the boats but no water. Downslope, a man o' war lay buried on its side, rusted cannons still jutting from its gun ports. The desert had preserved the ship so far, but it had a few decades left at most before becoming buried or succumbing to dry rot. Hundreds of feet away on another sandbar lay the rusting turtle-like domes of ironclads, riveted hulls with a single turret sprouting twin cannons. On the valley's far side sat larger steel vessels painted gray with turrets filled with cannons big as trees fore and aft. Galleons, triremes, longboats, and submarines littered the sands with gaping holes in their hulls while more wrecks were unidentifiable, just a gigantic wooden rib or part of a keel jutting from a dune. They lay scattered on the ground like children's toys, resting on their sides and spilling their innards across the sand, lifeless but for the fluttering of ragged top sails and faded pennants.

Skye's stomach soured as he stepped into the graveyard. He imagined the jealous dead in all those ships watching him stomp through their realm, just waiting for him to screw up. They reached the half-buried man o' war and though no longer seaworthy, it felt good to have something substantial between him and the other ships.

"Who has a navy?" Skye said. "I've only read about these things in stories."

"No one has that much water," Cora said. "The scriptures talk of the Eastern Sea and the Maelstrom, but I've never seen enough water to float a canoe."

"What's a canoe?" Skye asked. Cora shrugged.

Kikuchiyo placed a hand on the man o' war's hull. "This is not of Ryan, or Jasmine."

"And how would you know that?" Skye said.

Kikuchiyo tapped his breastbone. "The Blood Weeper shared Ryan's soul. Everything he created is as familiar to me as a man's house is to him."

"And Jasmine?" Cora said.

"She was a healer, not a builder," Kikuchiyo said.

Delusional, the both of them. But also dangerous, so no need to call anyone out on it.

"So what's this?" Skye asked.

Kikuchiyo shrugged. "It is of the Twins' world but not of them."

"There's another godling walking around?"

"I don't know."

Cora snorted. "Great."

"Should we bother trying to salvage any of this?" Skye said. "There might be water, food, weapons."

"Anything here is probably rotted or next to useless," Cora said.

"It can't hurt to try," Skye said. He looked to Kikuchiyo for support, but the man ignored them, already busy carving lines into the ship's hull. Skye turned to Dog and said, "What do you think?"

Dog thumped his tail against the ground.

"Good enough."

Skye found his way inside by hanging onto protruding cannons and kicking at the battle damage until he found a weak plank and made a hole large enough to fit through. Light filtered in through smaller holes perforating the hull, cutting the gloom and keeping him from knocking his head on the low ceiling. He felt his way across the pitched deck, stomping on the decking and tugging on frayed ropes before trusting them to hold his weight. The place smelled of rust and tar; disintegrating cloth heaps and splintered wood piled against a far wall. A few soot-stained lanterns clung from hooks but held no oil.

The footsteps scrabbled above him and he called out a warning about the rotten wood. He slung himself through another gangway to the lower gun deck and tripped over a boot sticking out from under a fallen beam. The floors and walls were painted a bright white, which helped him navigate the dark shapes of the cannons in various stages of reloading on their carriages. A shadow caught his eye.

"Anything?" Cora called down.

Skye held his breath and carefully inched around the carriage lest the tethered cannon break loose from its fraying ropes. A body in a striped shirt and soot-stained white pants lay draped with an arm over a gun barrel, leg crushed under the cannon carriage's wooden wheels.

"You'll want to see this," he called back.

She slid through the gangway with a simple grace that caught his attention.

"What?" she said.

Caught staring like a jackass. He smiled and said, "Nothing, watch your head."

When she came close, he held out a hand and pulled her up. Her palm was smooth, but cold.

"How long has he been dead, you think?" she asked.

Right, the body. He shook his head to clear it. "A better question is whether he was ever alive." He lifted the crewman's leg and removed the boot with a tug. Rather than a skeleton or mummified flesh, the leg was just stuffed canvas. A seam in black thread ran down the leg, gaping in places to reveal foam beads and cotton batting.

"A dummy?" she asked.

Skye stepped back. "Let's keep looking and not touch them."

They found more stations crewed by uniformed mannequins, some with smiling faces painted on their misshapen canvas heads, others left blank. Stuffing leaked from bullet holes and wooden shrapnel wounds, with the odd blackened or severed limb adding to his unease. When they reached the ship's kitchen, they discovered cupboards filled top-to-bottom with animal crackers. Cora frowned as she opened a sealed carton and found it empty.

Sky picked up another carton filled with nothing but air. "I don't think we'll find food and water on this boat," he said.

Cora sucked in a breath and pointed past him. Skye turned and stared at a mannequin nailed to the wall and skewered with arm-length splinters, its batting soaked through with blood. Cora nodded. "I think you're right. Let's try another."

Thick gray steel armored the next ship, which bristled with gun turrets.

"Destroyer, World War Two," Kikuchiyo said.

"You've seen these before?" Cora asked.

"World War what now?" Skye added.

Kikuchiyo tapped his head. "Ryan's world knew these things. I recognize this ship, and possess the memory of a great war. Colorless images on a screen, pictures in a book, old men suddenly mute in the middle of telling their war stories and leaving the room. If there is more, I cannot say; scholarship was not one of Ryan's focuses."

The destroyer, unlike the sailing ship, was mostly upright but split in the middle like it had been broken over a giant's knee. They explored the inside, and besides another stockpile of empty cookie boxes, found little salvage: another rope that might hold a man's weight, writing paper, and around the neck of a stuffed mannequin in a khaki uniform, binoculars with one working lens. The tanks held oil and diesel, armories filled with shells for the guns, but no water or food. Kikuchiyo emerged from a passageway with a machete at his waist.

"I don't think there's anything here for us," Cora said, gripping her gun tighter and looking away from the samurai as he wrote his name on the bulkhead with a grease pencil. "We'd be better off moving on."

"Moving on to where?" said Skye. "We should find another place to cross the Wall where the Imperials aren't looking. We can double back to Motorhead if they're gone or find some other settlement."

Cora turned to inspect a rusted spot on the hull. "You want to go through that madness again?"

Skye tapped the pathfinder's helmet. "We can take turns wearing this to hold off the hallucinations."

Cora picked free a hand-sized rusty flake and began pinching off little pieces. "I'm not certain I can take us back."

"We'll have to take that chance. I don't think wandering around hoping for water is a winning strategy."

Kikuchiyo motioned them towards another ship, long and oval like an airship's envelope but made from metal. "This way," he said.

"You're kidding me," Skye said. The yellow cigar-shaped hull had crossed revolvers intertwined with thorny rose vines painted across its bow. Several hatches on the upper deck lay open in double rows. Why would they need so many? It reminded Skye of an airship, but it would be too heavy to fly. No visible weapons, either. A troop transport, perhaps?

"Missile submarine, nuclear powered," Kikuchiyo said.

Submarine didn't mean anything to him, but nuclear did. Nukes made spiders and lizards grow fifty feet tall, leveled cities, or gave you a third arm while your hair fell out. He wasn't ready to go bald. "What makes you think it's any different in there? If it's crewed by mannequins, their galleys only stock phantom animal crackers."

"If the destroyer had oil, the submarine's reactor will have water," Kikuchiyo said over his shoulder. Dog finished a yawn with a clack of his teeth and trotted after the samurai at a respectful distance.

Cora shrugged at Skye's questioning look and picked at a paint flake. "Can't hurt, unless it's radiated."

Ray of light, that woman.

The submarine's hatches were out of reach and its smooth hull gave no convenient handholds, leaving one entry point: a gaping hole amidships that was likely the ship's deathblow. Skye leapt for the edge and pulled himself up, feet scrambling for purchase. He looked quite dignified, he was sure. He finally got a boost from Cora and clambered onto a jagged metal outcropping. The hole sat inconveniently between decks and he would need to either climb up or crawl under the twisted decking to go farther. He peered into the darkness and reached out to steady himself as he leaned inside.

Jagged metal bit his hand. "Damn it!"

"You okay?" Cora said.

He pulled his hand back and watched the blood well in his palm. "Yeah, shallow scrape. I'll survive."

"If it doesn't get infected."

"Aren't you just all sunshine and joy," he said. "It's fine, see?" He showed her his hand, and Cora stilled as her nostrils flared. She shook herself and turned around.

"Get that covered, now," she said and walked away with quick strides.

"Yes, Mother," Skye mumbled to himself. Then he took a second look at the scratch and mentally shrugged. It'd be fine.

Something scraped inside the submarine and Skye had a brief glimpse of glowing yellow eyes as an arm reached for him through the breach. Everything went white for a moment, and when it cleared he was looking up at the sky and the pain began radiating down his spine.

The arm withdrew from the hole above, and a howl echoed through the sub. Kikuchiyo appeared at his side, dragging him away onto a rise where Dog stood with hackles raised, barking. Running feet banged and echoed through the sub until a hatch on its topside tower screeched open.

Skye had seen deaders before, close enough to note their filmy eyes and catch their lungs' faint rattle, like leaves scraping across pavement. He had been stuck behind their chain gangs on boulevards where their sluggish pace and uncoordinated lurching made them Paradise City's number one traffic nuisance. They could be dangerous at arm's reach when uncontrolled, sure, but even in the Badlands wild deaders were only a problem when encountered unprepared, by surprise, or in large groups.

The deader leaping from the tower was a species that broke the rules. It loped with the easy predator's stride and instinctively dodged Cora's gunfire with glowing eyes locked on his, brown wrinkled lips pulled back from bleach-white teeth. Skye pulled his sidearm and took careful aim, ignoring the talons sprouting from the deader's fingers and few seconds remaining until they would reach his flesh. His rounds hit its torso, throwing it off balance but slowing it not at all. Skye shifted his aim down to the thing's kneecap and pulled the trigger.

Click.

"Out!" Skye shouted out of long habit and reached for a fresh magazine that wasn't there. The deader closed to ten feet.

"Your pardon," Kikuchiyo said, and stepped before Skye, machete extended. The creature roared and swiped at the samurai, who moved the machete a fraction. Steel parted flesh and the taloned hand sailed through the air, still wiggling.

Kikuchiyo pivoted and aimed a cut at the deader's neck, but the thing dropped to the ground and grabbed Kikuchiyo's ankle. He plunged the blade through the deader's torso and shouted in fury as the deader pulled the samurai to the ground.

Skye ran without thinking. He lowered his shoulder and bowled into the deader. His fingers found the creature's straw-like hair and pulled. Great clumps came loose, delaying the deader long enough for Kikuchiyo to roll free. The deader snarled and twisted, sending them tumbling back down the bank. When they stopped, Skye was pinned on the bottom with his hand on the deader's jaw, pushing and failing as its teeth sought his throat.

A shadow fell and someone shouted. The deader inexplicably looked up for a moment, and its head tumbled free as Kikuchiyo's blade passed.

Skye pushed the deader off him and crab-walked away. Kikuchiyo stood over the body, ready for another strike, then relaxed and sheathed his machete.

Cora ran up and pushed him back to the ground, turning his head from side to side as she searched.

"Any bites, cuts?"

"I don't think so."

She turned his injured palm over and paused before muttering, "You're fine," then suddenly stood and walked back to his weapon. "Here." She tossed it over.

"It's empty."

"Maybe you'll find more ammo."

"Yeah, maybe. Or maybe I'll find this boat's crewed by more of those things rather than stuffed mannequins."

Thirst won out over caution and they boarded the submarine, creeping along its passageways, ready to shoot or skewer anything leaping from the gloom. Shredded mannequins filled the compartments, the work of claws and teeth rather than bullets and explosions, but thankfully they encountered no glow-eyed deaders. As expected, there was no food in the galley, but they had better luck in the engineering compartment and the defunct reactor's stainless steel water tank. After consulting with what Kikuchiyo called a Geiger counter and outright praying on Cora's part, the two proclaimed it clean.

Skye swirled a beaker and sniffed at the water. "How do you know it's not poisoned from leached metals and such?"

Cora snatched the beaker from Skye's hand and gulped it down. "Tastes fine to me," she said. Her stomach gurgled ominously, but she held up a hand at his protests. "It's fine. You should be more worried about that cut on your hand."

She might have a point, he thought, but moot since there were no proper bandages or ointments to be found. He murmured an apology to a mannequin and tore a strip from its uniform for a hand wrap. He counted himself lucky finding a box of flares under the mannequin, and while still feeling lucky, chanced a drink. The water went down warm and bland, neither refreshing nor convulsion-inducing. They refilled their canteens and left the wreck to contemplate their next move.

"Our best bet is to go back over the Wall and skirt around the Imperials," he said.

Cora sniffed. "That's a horrible idea."

"What about you, Kikuchiyo?"

The samurai shook his head.

"Okay, nice knowing you." He stood up but Cora pulled him back down.

"You'll get killed doing that. Stay with us," she said.

"You think there's some kind of living out here? No supplies, no shelter, no future. Back home, I have a chance."

Cora looked at him like he was an idiot. "You go off alone, you'll get lost."

He tapped the pathfinder helmet. "I've got this."

"Which won't save you from the wrong end of a gun or a 'claver's barbecue."

"And you know a lot about 'clavers and eating your fellow man?"

Her eyes narrowed. "I know what people say about us, and what's true and what isn't."

"So what goes on at a 'claver's barbecue, then? Is there a special sauce?"

She punched him in the chest. "Don't get distracted. It's like this: leave us, you die. Stay with us, you might live."

"You're a sucker for hope."

She arched an eyebrow and looked past his ear. "Think so? Think you can survive on your own against one of those?" She pointed.

Two creatures the size of school busses emerged from behind a partially burned galleon. Tubular brown-and-black bodies undulated over the sand on a hundred tiny black legs as shovel-shaped heads tipped with shining mandibles swung from side to side. One creature's head plunged into the ground and came up with a wriggling, runabout-sized beetle. The other screeched and grabbed for its companion's meal. The two fought until the beetle's head tore free in the usurper's mandibles and both started devouring their prizes.

"I think we should move," Cora said.

"Good idea," he said.

They put the sub between themselves and the creatures and made for the canyon's edge. As they ran up the slope, Dog began yelping and running around in circles. Skye slowed up and veered toward the animal as the ground started trembling.

"Run!" Kikuchiyo shoved him forward.

Behind them, the sand shifted and billowed moments before another centipede-creature burst to the surface in a geyser of sand. The body was easily twice that of the others with dusky red skin and barbed mandibles longer than he was tall.

Kikuchiyo pulled his machete free and relaxed his shoulders. Skye glanced back at Cora, frozen in midstride and fumbling for her weapon. Kikuchiyo charged in, parrying the creature's slashing mandibles and getting tossed aside. It followed the samurai's roll and took another swipe, catching him in the ribs and hooking him through his kimono. The machete scraped across hard chitin.

Cora fired a burst that raised only dust clouds from the creature's armored flank. It turned to Cora for a moment before it remembered the samurai stuck on its mouthparts and whipped its head from side to side. Kikuchiyo fell and scrambled away from a spear-tipped foot. The beast advanced, body-plowing the sand before it, including the sand under Kikuchiyo's feet. The samurai floundered in the shifting sand, legs pumping as mandibles snapped behind him.

Skye fumbled at his belt for the flare. He twisted the cap open and struck it, igniting with a hiss and dripping red sparks.

"Give it another burst!" he shouted at Cora. Kikuchiyo ducked a slashing mandible and backpedaled awkwardly. Cora's gun barked and bullets raked the worm-thing's side. It turned, but stopped as soon as it saw the flare. Its ponderous bulk curled to face him.

"Come on, big ugly." He waved his arm and the beast's four tiny eyes tracked the magnesium flame.

"Get out of there, Kikuchiyo!"

The beast misinterpreted his shouting for a challenge, rearing up as tall as a building and bellowing, mandibles spread wide enough to catch an ornithopter. On an impulse, Skye heaved the flare right at the beast. Mouthparts snapped and the flare disappeared down its gullet.

He'd always been lucky that way.

The beast's roar hitched and a shudder ran down its length. Skye believed it might die on the spot but then it roared again, this time in a pitch that rattled his teeth and sent daggers through his eardrums. It coiled itself like a spring and launched with legs churning. Skye's legs couldn't move fast enough as it closed the distance. Mandibles scissored at his heels, anise and carrion breath blew hot on his neck.

Something struck him from the side and he tumbled down the slope. Cora. The beast passed close enough for him to reach out and touch a leg had he wanted. Cora untangled herself from him and pulled him to his feet.

"Back to the sub!" she shouted.

They couldn't make it, but what else could he do? He followed as several tons of angry worm-beast-thing tried to turn around.

"You too, Blood Weeper!" she shouted at the samurai, who staggered to his feet.

They ran, and Skye wondered if he would have the gumption to sacrifice himself for the others or if he would let one of them play the hero. He had a feeling it was all academic anyway, as the beast would likely smash them to jelly and hoover the remains afterwards.

A black dot streaked from the canyon rim into the beast, trailing a thin black line of exhaust. It slammed into the thing's head and burst in a bright pink cloud. The beast roared and emerged from the cloud like a runaway train. Skye pulled Cora to the side and the pink-spattered beast rumbled past them, barely missing Kikuchiyo and Dog as they jumped aside. Its undulating legs lost synchronicity and the creature plowed head-on into the yellow submarine with a crash that rang the sub's hull like a demonic gong. The beast shuddered and crumpled to the ground.

"You okay?" Cora said.

Skye nodded and followed the black contrail back to the canyon rim, where three figures stood in black desert robes and full-face respirators with long bird-like beaks. Two held rifles loosely in their arms and the other loaded another bulbous rocket into a launcher braced at his feet. One figure raised a hand and beckoned.

"What do you think?" Cora said.

Behind them, the beast let out a sound somewhere between a bellow and a groan. It shook itself and tried to regain its feet before collapsing.

"Can't stay here," he said. "If nothing else, they should be able to tell us how to find food and water."

"Unless we're the food," Cora muttered.

"They could have killed us already if that's their plan."

Cora brushed herself off and nodded. "Yeah, but it's easier when your livestock walks to the slaughterhouse rather than having to push, pull, and drag them yourself."

"Voice of experience?" he said with a grin. She didn't return it. Skye stifled a sigh and waved at Kikuchiyo, pointing at the figures in black. The samurai returned a *hai* and sheathed his blade. "One problem at a time. I like our odds better with them than with that." He jerked his head back to the sub.

"Hmm," Cora said, but followed.

9

———

The figures in black waited for them at the canyon rim. Their outer robes of rough homespun covered spindly bodies in close-fitting black vinyl undersuits. The dark goggles and beaked breathing masks were also integrated, leaving no part of their skin exposed. The three stared at them, eerily still and silent. Cora suspected they stared specifically at her.

"Thanks for saving us," Skye said, holding out his hand. The figures in black dipped their heads but did not reach out.

"The Bath Tub is a breeding ground for the sand furies and their grit-terpillar pups," said a muffled voice.

"Among other things," Cora muttered.

"Indeed. You are fortunate to have survived your folly. Now we leave. Follow."

The figures turned and walked with a slow deliberateness. Cora's body yielded to a silent compulsion and fell into lockstep behind them. Panic flooded through her and she willed herself to a stop. They paused and turned around as one. The one in the lead tilted his head and she felt the pull at each joint, the urge to move just *so* and surrender.

"Cora?" Skye put a hand on her arm, and the compulsion disappeared. The three in black resumed walking as if nothing had happened.

Relief and anger swirled within her and her fingers stroked the submachine gun's frame, reassuring her it was still there. She was still in control.

"I'm fine," she said.

Skye stepped closer and tightened his grip. "You're not."

She shook her arm loose. "I will be." Skye started to argue, but the Blood Weeper pushed past them.

"Move," he said.

Submitting to that compulsion was the last thing she wanted, but there was no other path she could see. Fine. She would play along, but on her own terms, and she promised herself she would stay a step ahead of it. Cora squared her shoulders and left Skye behind, fully in control of her body. He just stood there and she wondered if he really would abandon her. With a look back at the sand fury trying to coordinate dozens of wobbly legs, he sighed and jogged to catch up.

Even when the canyon rim had disappeared from sight, Skye kept looking back over his shoulder.

"Second thoughts?" Cora said.

"All the time. Right now, I'm more worried about yon beastie coming back to finish what it started."

The one with the rocket launcher waved his hand dismissively. "We will be outside its territory before it recovers."

"You have nothing to worry about," another said.

"So that place is a nursery?" Skye asked.

The one in the lead spoke up. "The Bath Tub. It is an old dream where a great battle took place on a great ocean."

The grenadier added, "Until its dreamer woke up, and the water drained away."

"The dreamer?" Cora asked. "You mean Ryan the Creator."

The figure made a strange figure with its fingers and a gesture. "Not that one. The Wall is the dreaming sand's response to his meddling, though it stretches the skin separating the dreamers and the dream thin indeed. You will find this place not as stable compared to what we knew in the Badlands."

The Blood Weeper snorted. Skye shot him a questioning look, but the other man shook his head and kept plugging forward. Dog trailed behind and, she noticed, upwind.

"So you're not from here originally," Skye said.

The grenadier touched its chest. "I am Mortensen. Hobbs, Ross," he added, pointing at the others. "We were Badlands cursed, but found our way here, as you did, by heeding the call."

"What call?" Skye said.

"You made it through the storms without succumbing to madness. No living mind can traverse quickly enough, without guidance," Mortensen said.

"Without the call," Ross said.

Hobbs's beaked mask turned to the Blood Weeper. "Reckon he'd make it, though." Ross looked to Mortensen, whose shoulders lifted a fraction.

Skye shook his head. "Bullshit. People scavenge around the Wall all the time. It's not pleasant, but with a bit of luck someone could make it across."

"They might make it close to the Wall, perhaps even a few hundred feet inside, if they are clever, cautious, or lucky, but none survive the horrors for long; they wander in circles and go insane before the storm claims them," Mortensen said.

"Unless they hear the call," said Ross.

"Not us," Skye said. "The Imperials on our tail forced our hand. Believe me, they won't stop because of a little sand and wind. We found them using this." He held up the helmet. "It keeps the headaches away."

Mortensen reached for the helmet and turned it in his hands. He tapped its smooth faceplate with a gloved finger before handing it back. "Perhaps, but the sands are always shifting; so too the safe path."

"Yes, only those guided by the call may pass." Ross said.

Skye ran a hand through his hair. "I keep telling you, I heard no call. Did you, Kikuchiyo? Cora?"

"No," she said.

"I find it unlikely," Mortensen said to her.

"Believe what you want," Cora said, staring ahead.

Mortensen cocked his head. "You recall the creature you faced in the submarine, the chap with glowing eyes?"

She nodded.

"They are feral Eddies, deaders who found their way to the dreaming desert but for one reason or another, chose not to follow their instinct and come with us. The dust, dream stuff all around here, they breathe it in, you see. It seeps into their skin and warps them."

"You become more of what you actually are, and less of what you wish to be," said Hobbs.

Hobbs dipped his head. "If you do not change with it, you remain feral and we can no longer help you."

"I don't understand," said Cora.

Skye said, "Sounds like Utopian claptrap to... wait, are we infected with this dream shit?" He unraveled the cloth from his hand and inspected the gash. It had turned gray at the edges and black veins traced under the skin. Cora's tongue ran over her lips and she had to look away. "Shit," Skye said, and re-wrapped his hand. "Is there a cure?"

Mortensen nodded. "Once we get to Twisted Bluff, we will take you to the queen and she will know what to do." Mortensen then raised his hand, bringing them to a halt. Ross drifted to the side and stomped his foot repeatedly on a flat rock. Then he dropped to his knees and put an ear to the stone.

Skye's whisper tickled her ear. "If I start turning into one of those things, you know what to do, right?"

"Silence, please," Mortensen said. Skye reached for her shoulder, and she pushed him away. Moments later Cora felt a pulse under her feet, then several more. Ross brushed sand from his robes as he rose and nodded.

"Our transportation is coming. Please restrain yourselves from any sudden movements or threatening gestures," Mortensen said, gazing at each of them through his dark goggles. "And mind the dog."

Dog growled, but stopped at the Blood Weeper's grunt. A rumbling approached and soon three enormous lizards appeared. Cora remembered a Badlands-salvaged poster she saw in the market once, bound for a collector in Paradise City. It featured a giant reptile with small eyes set into a gigantic head filled with teeth looming over a pretty lady wearing torn furs. At the time, her younger self was torn between gaping at the salivating monster and puzzling over the woman's impractical outfit, but she remembered the bold-faced words: "ACTION! ADVENTURE! DINOSAURS!" The lizards before her lacked the vicious fangs, but their pebbled skin, muscular frames, and hardened talons on three-toed feet gave them the same intimidating presence. They wore saddles and harnesses and each came up to a figure in black and nosed for treats or leaned into slaps to the neck.

"Dinosaur?" she said aloud.

"These are thumpers," Mortensen said and swung up on a saddle. "Perhaps inspired by dinosaurs, but a dreamer's creation. Fortunately for us, they also breed, and are docile enough to ride."

"Really?" Cora reached out to Mortensen's mount. The lizard hissed and snapped at her hand.

"Temperamental. Ornery. But ridable," Hobbs said.

"Stay away from their heads," Ross added.

"Right," Cora said.

The thumpers traveled swiftly, lurching from side to side at a pace faster than a man could run. Mortensen and the others rode easily, able to balance an extra rider in their saddles and keep their mounts under control while sparing the occasional glance at the horizon, wary for danger. To someone who grew up in the Badlands, their sealed under-suits and masks seemed unnecessary. Sure, it was nice to keep the sand and dust out, but they looked stifling. She grew up wearing layers of robes that not only kept the dust away but also insulated the air against her skin from the searing desert heat. Was this dream dust more harmful than they were letting on? Did the masks hide awful disfigurements?

The land here was not so much different from home — sand a little looser, odd half-buried objects she couldn't identify — but the air smelled the same. It would be tough living, but people could survive out here. Clearly Mortensen and his crew had figured it out, and she knew she could too if only her hunger and mounting headache would let her think!

There was one bright spot. Though still hungry, she no longer drooled over her companions.

THEY TRAVELED until they came upon a rusted-out pickup truck on an escarpment. Mortensen tilted his head back and gave a subtle salute to another figure in a hook-nosed bodysuit sitting behind the wheel with a scoped rifle, who nodded back. Minutes later, they crested a ridge overlooking a plain dotted with sandstone hoodoos, scrub trees, and mounted figures in black herding thumpers and thumper-sized gritterpillars between crudely fenced-in lots. All roads led to the valley's center and a cleft in a red and ochre sandstone mesa with a colossal helix of pearlescent stone rising from its center.

"Twisted Bluff," Hobbs said.

Mortensen nodded. "Home, shelter from the wind, and easily defended."

"Apart from that giant crack running down the middle," Skye said.

"Even the mightiest fortress needs a gate," Ross said.

"Gate? You could fly a thopter through that gap," Skye said.

Ross pointed to the low clouds, purple-black and roiling towards the Wall. "What fool would fly through that to get here? And the Wall? No ornithopter could survive the trip."

Skye snorted. "There's a whole treaty violation's worth of warships a few hours ride from here. Who's to say there isn't some air force out there waiting to be found?"

"We are not mindless imbeciles. We have many layers of defense, starting with the curtain wall itself—" Ross began.

"Skye, let it go," Cora said and gave him a look. To Mortensen: "Easily defended from what?"

"From those who would hunt us," said Mortensen.

"Complete and utter bullshit," Skye muttered.

The cliffs surrounding Twisted Bluff reached over a hundred feet high, but the gate protecting the cleft was a hodgepodge of metal salvaged from automobiles, road signs, metal roofing, water tanks, appliances, and armor scraps coaxed from wrecks in the Bath Tub. What it lacked in armor was made up in firepower with several machine gun and heavy weapon placements on towers and the cliffs above, manned by more figures in combinations of robes, coveralls, and mismatched uniforms worn over their sealed body suits. Cora noticed also some figures with limbs stretched twice normal length clambering up the sheer rock face with ease. At the gate's entrance, the guards were significantly bulkier and wider in the shoulders than Mortensen's crew and armed with broad-bladed pikes and cinder block-sized pistols. Their heads turned with goggles glowing from within.

Mortensen led their thumpers past the gate and up an incline through artificial switchbacks made from old Cadillacs buried nose-first into the ground. After clearing the last switchback, the armed militia gave way to civilians who walked around in the same masked body suits worn under dungarees and long-sleeved work shirts, or suit coats with watch chains dangling from waistcoats. Other figures with female curves wore long high-neck dresses, or opted for more feminine takes on the men's denim and long sleeves.

Various passersby nodded or tipped their Stetsons and bowlers in greeting as Mortensen and his crew traveled along the long dusty street. The masked figures strolled at ease, entering the wooden storefronts of shops carved into the walls, calling to each other from the boardwalks, and haggling along wooden corrals filled with gritterpillars and thumpers. The street ended at an archway leading into the twisted bluff itself. Cora felt its pull and shifted in the saddle. She wanted to leap from the thumper and run through the arch and also lash herself to the beast so she wouldn't.

"A damn straight shot through the middle of town," Skye muttered.

"By design," Ross said. "The quasi-dead are drawn here by instinct, compelled to enter the labyrinth and begin their rebirth. They are not to be impeded."

"It's not the deaders I was thinking about," Skye said. Ross's back stiffened in the saddle, but settled at Mortensen's gesture.

"Quasi-dead, if you please, Mister Skye. Our city's plan is as much for our safety as the quasi-dead's. This close to the labyrinth they can be… impulsive," Mortensen said. "But the labyrinth must wait. Our way lies up the spire."

"So what, you worship these quasi-dead?" Skye asked.

"No, but we have come to an accommodation with them. You will see."

The thumpers veered away from the archway and up a ramp

following the spire's natural twist. It seemed the same stone as the pathfinder's helmet and when Cora remarked on it, Mortensen nodded and called it pearlstone, a material difficult to work with but useful in its own way, though he wouldn't elaborate on it. Cora's hunger sharpened the higher she climbed. She distracted herself by picking out black algae stains against the curtain wall's red sandstone that reminded her of home. When she cleared the rim and looked out over the plains, the dark clouds overhead weighed heavy on her, though she knew it was only a trick of perspective. She shook her head and pulled her shoulders back. They came to a fortress at the spire's top, four stout walls and a gate constructed from the same pearlstone as the spire, and the pathfinder's helmet.

Where Twisted Bluff's front gate was all sloppy salvage, this gate looked as if carved by a master sculptor. The seams between blocks were so tight she doubted she could fit a fingernail into them. The gate swung open easily, though it had to weigh tons. Ross collected the thumper's leads and headed for a nearby stable, while Mortensen and Hobbs took them to a low building covering the entrance to a warren of tunnels descending into the spire's heart.

The tunnels were no wider than her shoulders. She struggled taking full breaths as the walls closed in, and tiny blue lights dotting the walls left her blinking away afterimages. Hobbs and Mortensen had no problem walking single file and avoiding the irregularities in the rock she and the others kept bumping into. She imagined any invading army would have nightmares, defenders able to hold off larger numbers almost indefinitely. Every intersection looked the same and she was soon lost, until Mortensen made a last turn and she found herself in a large room with more soldiers in hooknose bodysuits, some standing guard at doorways with automatic rifles, others moving from one hallway to another. One long-limbed figure hung spider-like from the ceiling. Mortensen stopped before two guards and jerked his head back to Cora and her group.

"I'll be needing an audience with the queen," he said.

The guard nodded and indicated a rack beside him. "Check the weapons."

Mortensen set down his rocket launcher and added the fighting knife from his belt. Cora did the same with her submachine gun. The Blood Weeper looked at the rack and crossed his arms.

"No."

"I'm sure you'll get them back when we're done," Cora said.

"Your weapons will not be disturbed," Mortensen said.

"No."

Guns swung their way and Cora didn't like anyone's chances in the enclosed space, herself least of all, if the Blood Weeper started taking exception.

Skye ejected the magazine from his sidearm and inspected the chamber before setting it in the rack. "Don't be such a bitch," he said. The Blood Weeper's hand went to the machete and the guards flinched. Cora stepped between the men and put a hand on the Blood Weeper's arm.

"Please," she said. "Mortensen saved us, saved you. He's an honorable man. If he says they will not be touched, then they will not be touched."

The Blood Weeper's arm flexed under her fingertips. Was he about to draw the weapon, or was he holding it in place? His jaw worked, and he shifted his grip, drawing the knife and machete from his sash. He placed them carefully in the rack and glared around the room, leaving no doubt what would happen if they were disturbed.

"This way," Mortensen said and they entered another long winding corridor.

"Stop taunting him," Cora whispered to Skye.

"He takes himself too seriously."

"You don't take him seriously enough."

"He's not really the Blood Weeper," he whispered.

"He's more than just Kikuchiyo."

Three turns later, the corridor ended in a solid steel door. Mortensen removed his mask and tucked it under his arm. Smooth gray skin covered a gaunt face with two slits and scar tissue in place of a nose. He met Skye's stare and said simply, "The change restores much of the body but not all. Steel yourselves; I am more fortunate than most."

"Are we about to become dinner now that we disarmed ourselves?" Skye asked.

Mortensen gave a wan smile. "We have developed other, more satisfying sources of nourishment this side of the Wall. While sand furies and wild Eddies might find you delectable, rest assured I and others like me do not."

"Oh, well, that's a load off my mind," Skye said with an eyeroll.

Cora shushed him. "We're not out of this yet."

Mortensen banged against the door and a hatch opened at its side. "Mortensen, plus three seeking an audience."

The hatch slid shut and the door rose into the ceiling with a grinding sound. Four guards stood with spears in hand as they were allowed into the darkened room. They were also unmasked, two with gray skin like Mortensen, though their wide shoulders and glowing eyes reminded her of the Eddie in the submarine. The other pair had no flesh at all — skeletons with empty eye sockets. Cora schooled herself not to react, though she had never seen such deaders before.

The chamber was filled with carpets, wooden furniture and tapestries on the stone walls, giving the place a softer look, though not a hospitable one. It had the sense of a beautiful throne room painting imagined by someone who had never lived in one. The ornate straight-backed chairs were orthopedic nightmares; they placed a table set with translucent china too close to a wall to be useful — all form, no function. The red carpet runner led to a sculpted granite throne, and before it stood a pale gray woman in a bustle dress of black satin with a small crown atop her head.

"Hail Her Majesty Queen Beatrice, defender of the free dead," a guard croaked. Mortensen went down to one knee, followed shortly thereafter by Cora and the others.

The queen's voice came out in a whisper. "You bring us these air-breathers, these quasi-living. Explain." Her face betrayed no emotion, but her pupilless eyes bore down on them all.

Mortensen bowed low. "Majesty, the change is on them. They hear the call."

"They may return after the change makes them suitable for our company."

Mortensen ducked his head lower. "They bring news from the other side you would wish to know. We may be in danger."

"The affairs of the living hold no interest to us. The free dead have nothing to fear, for we are strong."

Skye cleared his throat. "Begging Your Majesty's pardon—"

"Silence!" the queen hissed. "The living have no voice in this place." She turned to Cora and inclined her head. "Though you, Badlands born, we give permission to speak. Tell us this news my scout deems more important than decorum."

Skye mouthed to her. "Speak."

"Why me?" she whispered back.

"You know why."

"You're delusional."

The Blood Weeper coughed and glared at her from the corner of his eye. *Do it.*

She hated them both.

Cora nodded. "I am Cora Pierson of the Leppard Clan. How did you know I was Badlands born?"

"It is seeped into your pores as it was once with us, before the change. It is of no matter. Continue, 'claver girl."

Even here? Was there nowhere she could escape her upbringing? Cora waited for the usual flush of embarrassment on her face, but it did not come. Saved by the chamber's cool air, undoubtedly. She gave the queen a quick version of their escape, the sandcrawlers, and coming across the Imperial pathfinder.

"Few among the living possess the fortitude to penetrate the Wall," said Queen Beatrice with a wave. "We are well-equipped to deal with them."

Skye began whispering words in Cora's ear, which she repeated. "Your Majesty, this is no small force. It is a full battle group, well-equipped."

"Your living spark fans the embers of fear. We understand you and your companion are in the thrall of the body's change, but we expected better of the Blood Weeper. Even here beyond the Wall we have heard of the Blood Weeper's vendetta against the Creator's avatars."

The Blood Weeper bowed low. "The Blood Weeper died the day the Twins ascended. Only Kikuchiyo remains."

"And yet this self-styled emperor remains. Kikuchiyo is a coward."

The Blood Weeper choked. His limbs trembled and his head rose, revealing red sclera eyes. Cora's throat tightened around a building scream as her muscles froze like they had during the prison break. The

Blood Weeper's fist clenched and the guards around the room stepped forward, bringing weapons to bear. Sweat beaded on his forehead and his form became indistinct, fading from sight. Guards whirled, searching the room, and four more emerged from the shadows and took position around the queen with oversized handguns leveled. Seconds later, the Blood Weeper returned, still kneeling in place. He took several deep breaths as he regained substance, and tremors ran through him as he got his breath under control. When he at last raised his face to the queen, his eyes were clear. The tension washed through Cora, leaving an unexpected sliver of pity for the man in her heart.

"Coward? No," Kikuchiyo said. "An empty vessel, cracked."

Queen Beatrice gave a casual wave, and the guards relaxed. "Then of what use are you?"

"If I cannot hold water, then fill me with sand."

The queen was silent for many seconds. "We shall see," she said. She sat on the throne's edge, ramrod-straight, and placed her hands in her lap. "This upstart's incursion, this so-called emperor, will fail, as have all his other attempts to pierce the Wall. We shall watch this army flounder and help ourselves to its carcass before enjoying the feast from the emperor's second force approaching from the southwest."

Cora's jaw dropped. "A second group? And you're not worried?"

"Do you think our defenses begin at the barbican? The curtain wall? No. Our defenses begin with the Wall itself, then the desert you yourself have been hard-pressed to cross without our help. The dreaming desert will consume a sizable portion of their initial number and those remaining will be half-mad and low on supplies, assuming we are their target at all."

"There is no such thing as an impenetrable static defense," Skye said. "It's only a matter of attrition and the Empire has studied its math well."

"The air-breather dares speak?" A guard kicked the back of Skye's knees and sent him to the floor, then placed a boot on the small of his back.

Cora dropped to both knees. "Forgive him, majesty, he has... the passion of life."

"Indeed. He has not our patience."

Cora rushed on. "He is out of order, but it is the truth nevertheless.

These soldiers wear a new armor crafted specifically, I think, to block out the Wall's effects. The force we saw numbered in the thousands, certainly, in armored carriers with ornithopters strapped to their hulls like flies on a…" She faltered. "A corpse. The desert may not winnow as many as expected," she continued quickly. "Can this fortress stand against an army like that?"

"It could, and it will because it must." The queen sat statue-still for a minute before continuing. "In the beginning, we were few. The dead wandering from the Badlands, almost incapable of thought, drawn to this place by a compulsion stronger than hunger. Here we congregated and here we changed, restored to sanity. In time, more hungry dead found their way here, became neo-dead, and joined the community. We fortified, we thrived, we continued searching for more quasi-dead and guided them through the change, restoring their free will. We do this because those we miss, those caught too long in the dreaming desert, change in unpredictable ways, becoming mindless Eddies or worse. Believe that the strength of this fortress lies not in its walls. Once we assist you through the labyrinth, you will know the truth of our words."

"Whatever," Skye said, grunting as the guard pressed on his spine.

The Blood Weeper nodded.

"Well, I don't agree. I'd rather leave now, Your Majesty. I'll be fine," Cora said.

The queen turned her head and raised a perfect eyebrow. "You speak to us as if you have a choice in the matter."

Cora rose from the floor, but the guards were already there and their pikes glowed with electric crackles. Her muscles locked, and she collapsed, unable to move as they dragged her away with Skye and even Dog. It took three guards for the Blood Weeper, who sent one guard flying before he too fell.

"Separate them and place each at the Labyrinth's lesser entrances," Queen Beatrice said.

Hands picked her up and took her away.

10

———

Cora was locked inside her body; did they have to stick her in a cell too? She lay paralyzed on the floor, staring at a ceiling carved from pearlstone, and noted the differences between the razor-precise joints in the walls and the chipped gaps where the cell door had been shoehorned into the stone. Over the next half hour, she regained enough control over herself to push to her elbows and slide against the metal bars until she was more or less sitting up. When she got a good look at the cell, she discovered an archway on the far side. A trap? The queen mentioned a labyrinth. An entrance, then. That pull in her head urged her to run through and find the labyrinth's center, but she promised herself she would not run. She was not a mindless beast. She waited until the feeling had returned to her fingertips before she rose and dusted herself off.

Up close, she found symbols carved along the archway. Their meaning tickled at her memory, but the urge to move kept distracting her. She stepped through into a cavern whose ceiling was lost in darkness, its floor filled with towering monoliths erupting from the ground like teeth. She ran fingertips over the nearest monolith, its cool stone worn smooth as if sculpted by water or melted by fire.

Blue-tinged light flowed through the white stone in fist-sized blobs that flared when they jumped the tiny gap to the next stone and continued on. The path between the monoliths curved for several dozen steps before coming to a sharp turn, and as she took it, the sound of stone-on-stone grated behind her. She ran back to the archway too late; another monolith had risen from the ground and cut her off.

"Just follow the path, is that it?" she said out loud. No response, but she hadn't expected one. It made sense, though. If mindless deaders could find their way, she could too. But she didn't have time to wander around and get lost.

Think, Cora.

She leaned against the stone and laced her fingers on top of her head, then shut her eyes and mentally poked around. The deaders had to stumble about the maze seeking relief from the pressure in their heads, but that pressure surrounded her, no stronger in one direction than the other. Her fingers drummed on her skull. If this was truly a labyrinth, she should just pick a rule like "always turn left." She would eventually work her way out.

A tremor rumbled under her feet and she jumped as two monoliths shifted, closing one path and opening another.

"Oh, come on, be fair!" she said.

Fine, so she couldn't trust doubling back unless she marked each stone, and she didn't have any way of doing that. She shifted her weight and found herself stuck to the monolith, little veins of pearlescent stone penetrating into her skin and locking her arms in place. She pulled and wrenched from side to side but couldn't free herself.

No, no, no, no. Can't move. The thought grew louder in her head. She thrashed, kicking at the ground and crying out as her shoulders strained at their sockets. Her foot slipped and muscle tore within her, a white lance of pain that made her pause.

The pain means you're still alive, so stop thinking like a deader!

With effort, she pushed the panic down. The stone tendrils penetrating her skin were hair-fine, and her struggles had already chipped and broken a few. If she were smart about it, she might rock her arms free. A blue blob of light flowed through the monolith and into the tendrils, illuminating her body from the inside. The stuff was still growing, penetrating and coiling around her humerus, and would soon reach her shoulder, but there was an order to it. She could almost hear the light within her arm delivering orders to the tendrils. Then her view of the tendrils faded as the blue light jumped the gap to the next stone.

Her arm swelled as the rock burrowed further. In her shock she hadn't realized it, but the light's connection to the rock felt like a necro's connection with a deader. If she could catch another light mote and somehow subvert it... but the flow had changed, and lights detoured away from her.

Eaten by a rock. Where's a hammer and chisel when you need it? Not that her hands were free to swing any tools. Unless... she already had the tools within her.

Focus. Gonna need to block this deader static in your head.

She hummed a quick few measures from "You Spin Me Round," a song every necrosonic engineer learned in their first week. It was a primer piece, a warm-up often used for soothing a twitchy deader or assessing a broken one. To her surprise, the rock at her back resonated with each note. She kept the song going until a dim light formed and flowed from her arm into the rock, finding its way to the edge and jumping the gap to a neighboring monolith.

The tendrils retreated and flaked away, freeing her. A fading mental afterimage of the links between the surrounding monoliths tugged at her memory, bleary-eyed late nights cramming for exams at the academy, runic circuits and musical scales. She remembered having known all about it for the test, but also forgetting most of it a week later. Years later, almost nothing remained. If only she'd been paying attention.

Thought you had it all figured out, didn't you, Cora?

At least she had mastered the basics, and the basics could solve plenty of problems, even if the answers were a little brutish. She pressed a hand to the stone and sang out loud, running through the scales and testing resonances. In under an hour, she had it: a simple trip around a cycle of fourths and a bass line you could build just about any blues song around. Using that as her guide, she began finding patterns in the lights as they traveled from stone to stone, and discovered how they might tell a partic-ular monolith to rise, fall, or twist in concert to a more complex master plan. Armed with her new knowledge, she disengaged and stepped away from the monolith, her hand's glowing impression already fading.

She picked her way through the monoliths, pressing a hand against them and using her newfound trick to map each branch along her path, discovering which monoliths moved and which were fixed. She couldn't map the whole maze at once or predict when a monolith might open or close, but between the pull in her head and the general flow of the lights, she usually picked those paths leading towards the maze's center, and ran into few dead ends.

After the tenth dead end she noticed one light acting strangely. Instead of taking the predictable path to the next stone, it seemed to tunnel through the monolith and jump a sizable gap to the monoliths beyond. She reached out and connected to the stones and watched for several minutes as the lights flowed through until one made the odd jump again.

Aha.

She experimented with her voice until she found a note that caused the next few lights to take the unusual jump. This particular monolith wasn't pure barrier or gate, but a hybrid with some freedom of movement. An idea popped into her head. If she acted on it just so...

Dim light flowed from her palm into the rock and it shuddered as the gap between it and its neighbor widened enough for her to squeeze through. At the next dead end, she did the same, and again, until she found herself nearly at the labyrinth's center where she caught the scent of decay, not just the normal dustiness of a deader or the rust of oxidizing steel, but the putrid waft of decomposing flesh. Dread locked her in place, taking her voice away and numbing her legs as if they had turned to concrete. A monolith sank into the ground before her and she raised a hand against the blue glare shining through.

"Approach, child," said a creaking voice.

She twisted, attempting to turn around and escape, but her legs wouldn't respond. She couldn't breathe, and black spots crept in from the corners of her vision.

"The more you fight it, the worse it gets," the voice sing-songed. "Come, child."

The corruption filled her nostrils, crept behind her eyes and slithered down her throat into her lungs. She retched and collapsed to her hands and knees, where at least the stench was less horrid. She wanted to turn away, but the labyrinth's pull within her head surged and compelled her forward. As she crossed the stone, a huddled form in a mouldering brown robe sat poking a cane at the remains of a campfire. Flesh sloughed away from the hand and showed glimpses of the tendons and bones underneath.

"Welcome," the crone said. Matted gray hair poked from the cowl covering the crone's face in shadow. "The stones welcome you also, even if you cheated your way here." A viscous fluid dripped from her robes and darkened the ground beneath her.

Cora felt an urge to crawl closer, but she locked her arms out and shook her head.

"You won't make it to the center with that attitude," the crone said. "You'll be stuck with Old Martha until you go full-deader and shamble your way along an altered path through this damnable machine."

Cora opened her mouth, but no words came. She gasped and floundered.

Old Martha shook her head. "I give you permission to speak."

Her voice worked on the third try. "Are you trapped here?"

The crone laughed, a wet rattle. "Got lost in here, didn't I? Old Martha got cursed with knowing all the ways out except her own. Now I'm part of the tapestry, the system, the ecology of this place." She let out a gurgling sigh. "Sometimes, I think I'm just its janitor. Now stop being stubborn and come closer."

"You know the way out?"

"I know many paths, and how they might be unlocked." The crone pointed her gnarled cane at another gap bracketed by pointed stone obelisks. "The center is beyond, but there is a gate the living cannot pass." The miasma lessened, and though the urge to crawl closer to the crone grew, still Cora fought it. The crone shook her head and went back to poking at the ashes.

"Stubborn." She tapped her cane at her feet. "Approach."

Cora's body lurched, and she stumbled closer, against her will, fighting her limbs the whole way. She fell at the damp edges of the crone's puddle, and her cane reached out and forced Cora's chin up. Within Old Martha's cowl, shadows moved behind glimmers of wet stringy flesh. A black-lipped mouth opened with a stench that grabbed

Cora deep within her intestines, twisting them and causing her stomach to spasm.

"Don't know why I bother," Old Martha said. "You are almost full-deader, no mistake. But the stones, they seem to think you're something special, necro."

"I won't turn deader," Cora managed to whisper. "Necros can't turn."

A filmy blue eye opened in the cowl's darkness. "Who told you that nonsense? Another necro, I'll bet. Pride. Worst thing for a deader to have. Old Martha was prideful and look what happened to her. Would you like to stay and see what happens? You could be like me; wouldn't that be a treat? I should so much enjoy having someone to talk to."

A cold river ran down her spine at the thought. "What must I do?"

Old Martha withdrew a coin-sized pendant from her cloak.

"Wear this against your skin and sing to it, child."

"Sing?"

"The song etched into your bones, the one you cannot help but set free. In your new form, you will be allowed through the gate and onward to the machine's exit."

"Will it hurt?" she asked.

Old Martha's cane twisted and tapped twice against the ground. "You will endure it."

Cora reached out with a trembling hand and took the necklace. No corruption from Old Martha's sticky fingers clung to its silver chain or its etched copper pendant. She brought it closer, and it freshened the surrounding air and untwisted the knots in her stomach. Her mouth watered. She heard music. It would be so easy to surrender to it. The first note formed in her throat.

No.

She was still alive. This was just another test and like the problem of the moving monoliths, the answer was not to play by this place's rules. She wrapped the pendant's chain around her hand.

"You made a mistake," Cora said.

"And what's that, child?"

"You gave me a voice." Cora pounded her fists to the ground and began chanting the hymn of Saint Jett the Blackheart, the one used to stun wild deaders. Old Martha hissed and rose, bits of flesh swinging loosely from her arms as she reached out and sent a chilling numbness through Cora's limbs. Cora put more air behind her voice and launched into the chorus. Old Martha stumbled and Cora found the strength to run for the gap across the way, feet clumsy but more sure with each step.

"Stop, child!"

Cora ran through the gap between the obelisks and down a path terminating at an arch with glowing runes carved around the edges. She ran faster but smashed into an invisible barrier and then onto the ground. Cora picked herself up and pushed against the archway where the air gave like rubber to her touch, but only a few inches.

"Told you, willful brat," Old Martha said behind her. The crone leaned against one obelisk, a withered hand clutching at her chest. She stood with some effort and began shuffling closer, leaning on her cane. "Sing to the pendant, accept the change. Only then will the archway let you pass."

Rules. Rules, rules, rules. Her body was dying, and there were still rules. She began humming and rested her palm on the archway. The first rune glowed under her touch and she felt it reaching for the second. She cast her awareness into the stone, searching for how each rune connected to the larger whole, each a single instruction in a larger program. With time and some tools she might alter the sequence to let her through, but Martha would reach her in seconds.

No time for a scalpel, let's try a hammer.

Cora pitched her voice with a vocal cord-tearing distortion. The light under her hands turned a sickly green, and the stone beneath the runes flaked away. The archway vibrated and for a moment Cora thought it would explode. The archway flared, and she fell through to the other side.

"Cheat!" said Old Martha.

"I'm not turning deader," Cora said.

Old Martha hobbled forward but stopped short of the archway, her milky eye tracing the damage. "You've a notion of the machine but don't understand its purpose. Make the change, child."

"No."

Old Martha's cane stretched out and tapped at the damaged runes. The rock shards and dust rose from the ground and gathered at her direction. With a crack, the barrier returned and thickened the air between them. "The labyrinth cannot compel you, nor give you the sense to see reason. So be it. When the Badlands curse takes you, remember Old Martha gave you a way out and you threw it away."

"When I am dead, I will no longer care."

"We'll see," Martha said. She turned and shuffled away.

Cora followed the path into the heart of the maze. The path ended at a smooth altar-like stone that gave her a funny feeling it was used for human sacrifices. Light motes cascaded down the walls and flowed along the ground into the altar, which absorbed them. Other archways sat open to the maze, apart from one at the far end sealed with stone. This last one had a lever to the side, which refused to budge when pulled.

She approached the altar and laid a hand on it. Unlike the monoliths, the altar's stone was warm under her touch. She extended herself into it and the labyrinth unfolded in her mind. It was larger than she thought, and more complex. It had layers she couldn't comprehend, places within it both fearful and beautiful to behold, places no living mind could go without risking madness. If she were a deader, she might understand this more, but was that knowledge worth it? She felt like an ant crawling inside an engine, seeing how individual pieces worked but ignorant of the whole. No, it was not worth it. Life was more important than scratching that particular itch. She tore herself away and focused on the small part of the maze she occupied. She mentally drilled down layer by layer until she found the maze exit behind the sealed archway. She shifted her focus and with a mental nudge, forced open the latch holding the gate lever in place.

She ran from the altar and pulled the lever. The exit gate slid into the ground, and the stones beyond twisted in place, creating a straight path for her to follow. She hesitated and ran a thumb over Martha's pendant. It sang to her about which paths a deader might travel in the maze and which neo-dead form it would transform into at path's end. It sang to her about the maze patterns already imprinted on her bones and the Badlands curse flowing along their pathways. This was her map. If she could study it, if there was enough Twins-damned time left, maybe she could save herself. She dropped the pendant in her pocket and followed the path out.

11

Skye walked the maze, picking his way through cobbles and ankle-high ridges that would trip him if he wasn't careful, but otherwise paid no attention to the path he chose. Keep moving, that was what mattered. The stones rose high above him and the drifting ghost lights set his nerves on edge, so he gave himself more than enough time when squeezing between gaps. No telling what might happen. Sure, sometimes he missed an opening, but another came along eventually.

He wished he had a gun. The longer he walked, the more he wanted a gun. There was something hunting him, or was it haunting? He didn't know but he would love to put a bullet between its eyes when it appeared, left-handed aim or not. But he had only rocks — next to useless in a stand-up fight.

The stone fins growing across the paths grew taller as he traveled, now at chest height. His lungs worked as he high-stepped and vaulted one-armed over them. His body wasn't what it had been even a month ago, and he suspected this place would be what finally got him, when he'd always bet it'd be the drinking or a jealous husband.

He came to another dead end, but the gap between the stones wasn't too bad. He slipped through and his right hand brushed against the stones, sending agony washing along his arm. He hissed and gingerly pulled his arm in closer, curling his fingers into a loose fist. A light appeared at the stone's surface, and he started moving but it arced across before he could get out of the way.

His hand went cold and numb. He shimmied free of the rocks and swallowed hard at the sight, fingers clawed, flesh pale and bloodless. "Shit," he muttered and tried wiggling his fingers. There were only twitches. He pried the fingers straight with his other hand, but as soon as he let go, they curled back on themselves. He let the ruined hand drop and continued down the path. But hey, at least it didn't hurt anymore.

"You're gonna have to shoot lefty from now on," said a familiar voice.

"Shut up, Nicky," Skye said. It was the second time he heard his older brother's voice this past week. Nicky had been part of a phantasmagorical choir singing his fuck-ups when Cora led them through the Wall, but he ended that personal concert once he had the pathfinder's helmet. It seemed Nicky now had a solo act.

"Write, eat, play cards that way too. Gonna be hard to pull from the bottom of the deck, eh?" his brother asked.

Skye didn't think his dead brother was actually there, but he turned around anyway. Nope, just hallucinating. The rocks behind him groaned and sealed the gap, leaving him with a single path opening onto a clearing with no exit.

Skye shook his head. "This deal just keeps getting better and better."

The rocks pressed together to form a seamless wall so he couldn't see through or even guess what lay on the other side. The ghost lights to the left and right flowed ahead to the far wall where they cascaded up and over like a waterfall in reverse. The wall wasn't as high as the others either, perhaps twenty feet, with a rough and deeply pitted surface, unlike its smooth-faced neighbors. Under normal circumstances, it would be easily climbable.

Skye circled the clearing but could find no better way out. Up it was, then. He laced his boots together, slung them around his neck and began climbing. At first, it was manageable, though not easy. His right hand was useless, and he had to press a cheek against the cold stone as his left hand groped for his next hold. There were plenty of holds within reach, but they were tiny, never deep enough that he could set his feet and rest his arm. About two-thirds of the way up, his foot slipped and flailed, finding purchase only at the last second. His breath came in gasps and his heart thudded all the way into his throat. The malnourished and one-handed had no business climbing.

"You giving up so easily?" said Nicky's voice. "I had five bullets in me but kept firing."

"So I've been told, Nicky. Repeatedly."

He was stuck on tiptoes and fingertips with no way to go up and no way down unless he dropped, and at this height, a broken limb was almost certain. He searched around for any ledge he might yet make, finally discovering a crevice on his right.

His legs began quivering with strain. He reached out with his right arm and mashed his bad hand into the crevice, pressing and wiggling until it became wedged. He shifted his weight and pulled, wincing at snapping and popping sounds coming from his right as he twisted. He brought a leg up, then the other, and took the strain off his left arm. He gave himself a few minutes shaking life back into his good hand before resuming the climb and pointedly not looking at the damage to the other. When the next crevice opened on his right, he again jammed the bad hand into it and let it take up the load. What glimpses he had and crunches he heard, he put out of his mind and continued upward.

When he finally reached the top, he rolled himself over it and lay there for several minutes until his breathing came under control and he regained the strength to stand. Only then did he bring up his right hand and inspect it. The flesh had torn away in places and formed dark clumps in others. Tendons had snapped, as had bones, and his fingers turned in odd places, especially the thumb now flopping against his forearm. He expected to feel woozy at the sight, but it was so damaged, so alien, it didn't seem a part of him anymore. He wrapped his shirt around the thing and continued. What else could he do?

The stone's far side ramped down into a tighter maze in which he was soon lost again. He scratched marks onto the loose dirt near stones as he passed, discovering he kept coming back to the same starting point though he was certain he had taken differing paths: the always-left-turn strategy, the always-right, alternating left then right, or following a breeze. After following a ghost light around the maze, running to keep it in view and concentrating on it so as not to lose it among the swarm, he found himself once again at the beginning. His head ached, and after he snuck a peek at the ruined hand, he found his mouth watering and wondering what would happen if he bit into the blackened flesh. He re-wrapped the ruined thing and took another trip around the maze once again, though with no particular strategy in mind.

"I would have found my way out of here already," Nicky said.

"Yeah, you probably would've."

"They gave me a medal."

"They pinned it to your coffin."

Maybe it would have been better to wait in the prison camp for a better opportunity. He had rushed the escape, afraid he would turn deader and now look at him. At least at the camp he'd been starving slow, holding off the curse or at least keeping it to a snail's pace. Had it been so bad there? Lots of rest, just an hour or so dancing the pattern each day. He laughed to himself. He had traveled all this way and was still walking in circles.

Or was he? For the first time in a while, the surrounding stones looked different. Not wanting to jinx it, he let his feet carry him where they would. Several turns later, he found his feet walking the pattern Outpost 242 drilled into him. He closed his eyes, let his body do its thing, and by the end of the sequence, turned into a small garden featuring two plague doctor statues flanking a sealed gate.

"Huh. See anything like that before, Nicky?" he asked, but his brother didn't respond.

The statues stood ten feet tall, scarecrow-skinny and staring at a point on the ground between them. Skye stopped and wondered what the hell he was supposed to do. The one to his left held a long-handled spoon and pointed with it back the way he came while the one on his right pointed to the gate. Both statues pointed with their free hands to a cauldron set at their feet. The message seemed clear enough to him: make a donation or go home.

They ran deaders through here? But with the shifting stones the path had to be different for each one, so had some guiding hand led him here? He thought back to the first few obstacles, low brick walls little more than tripping hazards but insurmountable for a body that couldn't do more than limp along. Then the chest-high wall, and of course the one he had to scale, all while navigating the maze via instinct. Was he a deader already? The hand was the most damning evidence, perfectly ruined, but without pain and still somewhat functional. Would this place change him as much as a full-on deader? Did deaders become the same person they were before? Did they regain their old personalities or gain new ones?

Gurgling interrupted his thoughts as the cauldron filled with a noxious, cloudy fluid whose fumes singed his nostrils.

"You're kidding, right?" he said to the statues, who, of course, didn't answer.

Skye sprinkled loose sand on the cauldron's surface, which bubbled and hissed with a white froth. He then tossed a pebble in and watched it seethe as it fell to the bottom, shrinking and disappearing in a few minutes.

After another pebble dissolved, the stone doors groaned.

"Pay for play, huh? Gotta pay the toll? I don't have any money."

The statues with their long-beaked masks didn't seem the type that valued coins.

"An offering, then." He wondered if Mortensen's people had taken his gear away on purpose, knowing this was coming, or if walking another path might have presented a different challenge. He unwrapped his shirt from his hand and tossed it in the cauldron. The wretched thing disintegrated almost instantly, the buttons taking a few moments longer. The doors opened no more than a paper-width, but they had moved, pushing up dust at their base — Twins knew how long they'd been sealed shut.

Next were his pants, tricky to take off one-handed. Their canvas lasted longer, ten full seconds, and deposited a muddy brown sludge on the caldron's bottom. He tossed in his underwear followed by his socks. His boots lasted longest of all his offerings, taking some minutes before the leather dissolved and only the soles remained at the bottom, slowly bubbling.

The doors had opened all of three inches, not enough for him to squeeze through despite the wretched skinniness courtesy of Doctor Astbury's camp.

"I know the answer," Nicky said.

"Yeah?"

"But I'm not gonna give it to you, Johnny. Gotta figure it out yourself, for once in your life."

Nicky was always saying shit like that.

"I've got nothing left," he told the statues, who were indifferent to his nakedness. The cauldron bubbled and he spread his hands, a clumsy gesture with his right hand still refusing to open and remaining in a gnarled loose fist. He swore and sat on the hard ground, racking his brain for something else he could put in the cauldron. Anything.

Flesh was all he had left.

Now the statues seemed to mock him. Nicky sniggered.

"Bastards."

He acted before he could talk himself out of it and plunged his right hand into the caldron up to his ruined wrist. The numbness disappeared with the flesh and white-hot pain shot up his arm. He pulled back, dodging acidic splatters and drops that splashed towards his nakedness.

His hand's mangled bones remained, gleaming white and held together by Twins knew what. The acid capable of dissolving leather had only blackened the tendons and sealed the flesh at his wrist with a pebbled cap like grilled hamburger. Everything itched, but he dared not scratch it. He looked to the gate, wondering if the statues had accepted his offering.

The doors had opened further while he screamed, wide enough for his wretched body to squeeze through.

Keep moving. Gotta keep moving.

He mustered as much dignity as he could and headed for the gate and raised a middle finger at the statues as he passed.

"Been a pleasure, fellas."

HE DIDN'T HAVE much time to mourn the loss of his hand because his feet ached. He stepped gingerly down the path, trying to avoid the worst of the sharp pebbles and leaving bloody footprints anyway. He closed on the maze's center, and wondered if there was one last insult in store before it spat him out naked, bleeding, and broken. Maybe that's why Twisted Bluff's residents wore the full body suits and masks. Going through this place made them all hideous. Though they did all seem to have full use of their hands, so maybe he was special. Lucky him.

The center of the maze was a clearing where his and two other mouth-shaped arches met around a stone plinth, on top of which lay a bundle of folded clothes. He recognized the uniform and his first instinct was to leave them there, but then he saw the boots and decided he could play dress-up for a little while until he found something better.

"You can't seriously be thinking of putting it on," Nicky said. He was visible now, standing in an identical uniform with arms folded and a scowl on his big, punchable face. "You lost the right."

"The militia's long gone, Nicky. Besides, I can't stay naked forever."

He went to the uniform and paused when he found the weapon hidden underneath, one of those hand cannons he had seen the queen's guard carry. Dressing himself went well enough, despite a spasming right hand with no flesh for gripping. The buttons gave him the worst trouble, and he had to do them lefty. Once he was dressed with feet safely protected in boots, he picked up the gun.

It was a heavy bastard, like a revolver except with cowled gray metal fins and copper radiator coils jutting out where the cylinder should have been. Its wood grips were inlaid with that pearlescent stone in the shape of a smoking skull, and where the grips ended, the motif continued with wisps engraved along the frame and barrel. Its balance was terrible and his arm began shaking within moments. He had no idea how or if it worked, but damn, was it pretty. The uniform included an oiled leather holster customized for the weapon, except it was on his right side. The Twins must be laughing their asses off at him.

He re-gripped the gun and trapped it against his right arm as he slid it into the holster. The finger bones of his right hand brushed the inlay and it bit them. The gun thrummed and a wave of fatigue staggered him. After he recovered, he noticed a pale blue gem glowing near the trigger guard.

He was curious if that meant it was armed, loaded, safe, or what, but there was no easy way to draw it left-handed to try it out, and since his right was still a gnarled useless thing, he left the gun alone and hoped it wasn't about to explode.

Around him, blue lights swirled in the rocks and flowed into the plinth in ever-larger streams, bright enough at the nexus to sting his eyes.

Deciding this was a good time to leave, Skye pulled the lever at the far gate, revealing a straight path through the maze and hopefully an exit.

"Traitor," Nicky said.

Skye ran down the path and didn't stop to look back when the stone gate closed behind him.

12

Kikuchiyo walked the stones, which shuddered and moved aside as he approached. It was just as well, his muscles still ached from the fade. Weakness. Shameful weakness. The rage churned deep within, calling him to glory, not caring he had no soul anchoring his flesh to this world and so he kept the rage submerged. He focused on breathing, the nearby rocks, and his weight shifting with each step.

A dog's howl broke his concentration, and he spent the next few seconds motionless as he fought the anger channeling itself through the irritation. He tamped down the rage and followed the path but the dog bayed once again, giving the rage another handle. He took in a breath and held it until he regained control. He focused on making his mind like water, but forcing such a thing was impossible.

The Blood Weeper would have kept walking. Kikuchiyo should keep walking. Dog's howling was like the horn before an imminent crash. He turned and followed them.

The creature was wedged in a cleft between two stones, lurching and thrashing as soon as it saw him. Kikuchiyo grabbed the animal by its scruff and haunch. The unmatched eyes unnerved him, so he addressed the brown one only.

"Still."

Dog stopped thrashing and whined in the back of his throat.

"Quiet."

Good. He knelt and considered the animal's problem. There was no simple way to lift it free, and unlike the other stones, these did not part for him as he projected his *Ki*. The animal was well and truly stuck.

"You are very stupid," he said to Dog.

A light flared between the stones, raising the animal's black-and-white fur as it passed. Dog's body shuddered, and another whine escaped as it slid deeper between the stones. Its breathing became the laboring of slow suffocation.

What did he care for the animal, anyway? It was no use to him. It served no purpose. It was dirty, frail, and annoying. The rage swelled.

"Problems, Blood Weeper?" a woman's voice said. He turned and readied himself, balanced on the balls of his feet and one arm coiled to strike.

An apparition in a yellow dress sat on top of a stone monolith. She alighted and floated down, stopping well outside his reach. "You don't recognize me, do you?" she asked and patted blonde hair drawn up into a B-52.

It took him a moment. A familiar face from the Badlands. A girl stuck tight on the Creator's arm. A fortress ringed in fire, her face over a .50 cal spewing bullets at him and the swarming deaders. Her leaning out from a '69 Biscayne and shotgunning a motorcycle. His sword running her through and foot kicking her over an airship's railing.

"I remember you now."

"Good. I'd hate to think I hadn't made an impression." She snapped her gum and looked past his shoulder. "You going to help that poor thing?"

"It is not my dog."

"Isn't it? Looks like your dog to me. You know, they say animals look like their owners. Or was it the other way around? Both ways? Never mind. He looks like you, you look like him, you're twins. You should help him."

"If you are so concerned, you are free to assist him."

She held out an arm and pushed it through the rock. "Hello? Hello? Think, McFly. I'm a ghost here."

"Then you cannot help me or him. Of what use are you?"

The apparition's eyes narrowed and she swooped in. His punch passed through her and bothered her not a bit. "That bullshit doesn't work on me anymore, Kikuchiyo. Ghost. Specter. Incorporeal. I had to look that last word up, you know, which is a real bitch when you can't open a dictionary."

"Thesaurus."

"Fuck you." She flicked his forehead and sent an icicle-cold spike through his head. "Soulless B-movie knock-off motherfucker. You want my help or not?"

Kikuchiyo forced the rage down at her barb and instead rubbed at his forehead until the chill from her touch faded. "I do not need your help."

"The hell you don't. You're lost."

"Not lost. I am almost to the center."

She sniffed. "That's what you think, Magellan. You've been twirling around in figure-eights for the last half hour."

Had he really lost his way? Now that she had said it, he felt the truth of it. The rage kept him self-absorbed and circling within himself; his feet only followed. There was something about this place more subtle than the Wall's influence, and it had lulled him into complacence. "I see the truth of it," he said.

The ghost grinned at him. "He can be taught, folks! So you want out? Free the pooch."

"Why?"

"Maybe I'm a dog person. Move."

Kikuchiyo turned to the animal. What was it to him? Did it matter? No, it did not. Dog wagged his tail as he approached, then yelped as he tried lifting him free by his front legs.

"Don't make it worse!" the ghost said.

Kikuchiyo leaned over Dog and tried reaching under its hind legs but the gap was too narrow to fit his arms through. After thinking on the problem for a moment, he unraveled his sash and tied a small stone to one end. He leaned over and threaded the weighted end between Dog and the rock. Kikuchiyo flicked the weighted end under Dog and caught it in his other hand.

"Nice move," the ghost said.

Kikuchiyo fed some slack and tied the sash around Dog's hindquarters. The other end looped around its chest. He braced himself and grabbed both ends of the improvised sling and twisted his body as far into the gap as he could while keeping two feet planted on the ground. Dog whined.

Muscles and joints trained for delivering strikes from any angle strained and protested as he forced his contorted body to lift Dog and not hurt the animal further. His fade-weakened legs burned as Dog shifted, more so as the animal's legs flailed in the air and made the sling shake.

"Stay!" he said through clenched teeth. He twisted, weight shifting onto the leg that had never fully recovered from his battle with Jasmine and threatened to buckle under the load. The rage called to him, tempting him with a fuel that would make this effort trivial.

No. Letting the leash slip even a little would bring the fade, and he might not make it back. In this place he might end up like the girl in yellow, or he could disappear altogether. He would not do so while he still had promises to keep.

He groaned and twisted. Dog's hind leg brushed the stones and he pushed. Kikuchiyo overbalanced and something cracked inside his bad knee. Pain blossomed moments later, as bad as he had remembered it when Jasmine had first dealt the blow. The white-hot lance sucked the air from him and left him curled on the ground.

Something licked his face. He wanted to push Dog away but couldn't spare the effort.

"Damn, that didn't sound too good," the ghost said.

Kikuchiyo opened an eye. She floated nearby and stroked at the raw patches along Dog's flank. The animal didn't seem to mind, which gave him an idea.

"Put your hands on my knee," he said.

"I can't fix it. I'm no healer."

"Please."

His breath caught as her hands passed into his knee with an icy blast that numbed the pain. He straightened the leg and tightly wrapped his sash above and below the knee for support. After a few failed attempts, he managed to stand. White-hot needles shot through him as the joint crunched and popped under the weight, but he knew it would soon fix itself. Not as fast as the Blood Weeper might have managed, but he would be patient. It was only pain, after all.

"Let us go," he said.

"You sure? I've got all the time in the world if you wanna rest up," the ghost said.

"I am sure," he said. The ghost shrugged and floated down the path. Dog made a noise behind him and thumped a tail against the ground. "Very well." Kikuchiyo pointed with his chin and Dog trotted after the ghost, pausing to make sure he was following. He limped along and noted the rage had retreated, despite the pain. He wasn't foolish enough to think it had gone away and wouldn't test his control again, but for the moment he savored the reprieve.

The stones sank to the ground as the ghost flew through them and Kikuchiyo found himself outside the maze's center, judging by the converging lights. The ghost hesitated before taking them along a side path as she counted stones.

"That spooky bitch Martha would have a conniption if she knew what I was doing, so don't say nothing," the ghost said.

Kikuchiyo nodded.

"Right." She stopped at a stone and plunged an arm into it. Her tongue poked out from the corner of her mouth as she fidgeted and the rock slid into the ground. "Hang a right and follow on to the exit."

He stepped through with Dog, then turned and bowed. "*Domo arigato,* Cally."

"Tell me one thing? Is he really gone?" She bit her lower lip.

"He is."

The ghost's chin dropped, and she faded from sight. "Take care of that dog," she whispered.

13

———

Cora walked out of the maze, finding Skye and the Blood Weeper standing near Mortensen and Ross in a chamber whose chisel-scarred sandstone walls jarred her after the labyrinth's smooth monoliths. At the far end sat an iron-caged elevator car. Skye was dressed in a brass-buttoned officer's uniform from the defunct Paradise City militia and stood with one arm behind his back. The Blood Weeper seemed normal, whatever that meant, and was scraping his name in the dirt with one heel while Dog watched nearby.

Skye smiled at her as she approached. "You look like crap," he said.

Her step faltered. "Nice jacket. How's the hand?" she replied.

Skye scowled and turned away.

"Have you left with nothing?" Mortensen said. "No clothing, a tool, or some other object?"

"You mean the creepy zombie necklace from Old Martha?"

Mortensen inclined his head. "Old Martha manifested for you? That is rare."

"Good thing; she was disgusting."

Mortensen rocked as if she had slapped him. Cora pushed between Mortensen and Ross into the elevator cage, not caring if they would lock her up or not.

∽

THE QUEEN WAS NOT AMUSED. She sat statue-like, straight-backed, with her hands arranged on her lap. It was the same pose she had adopted after ordering them into the Labyrinth, and Cora wondered if the woman had moved at all since then.

"Miss Pierson, you are perilously close to letting chance decide your ultimate form. You are like the child that threatens to hold their breath until they get their way, except in this case the results are assuredly more dire."

"I'm trained in necrosonics," Cora said with more confidence than she felt. "I can stabilize the change and reverse it."

The queen clucked her tongue and waved her words away. "You necros learn a sliver of the world's secrets and believe you comprehend its entirety. As if the study of an elephant's toenail grants knowledge of the trunk. Necros say 'Deaders cannot think, deaders cannot feel, deaders are only tools for the living,' do they not? And yet here we are, listening to a necro denying her metamorphosis as a flower might the sun."

"I will conquer this or I will die," Cora said. "Majesty," she added.

"Indeed." The queen turned to Mortensen and gestured. "Fetch the device."

Skye leaned in as Mortensen exited through a side door. "You're like a mark that's convinced his two pair is gonna hit."

"Does it hurt when I do this?" She flicked a nail against his skeleton hand.

He placed the hand behind his back. "No. I don't feel anything."

"And you want me to do that to my whole body? No thanks."

"She's got a point, Your Majesty," he said.

"You also reject your evolution?"

"If that's what you want to call it. I mean, maybe I can make it hold a fork again, but it ain't the same as the original."

"May we inspect your weapon?" She rose and held out her hand to an Eddie who had collected Skye's gun at the chamber door. Queen Beatrice grasped the weapon in one hand and pointed it easily at the ceiling despite its bulk.

"Electro gun, isn't it?" Skye said. "The smallest one I've ever seen was mounted to a wagon and took two or more dead... uh..."

"Quasi-dead," Cora whispered.

"... quasi-dead to power it," Skye finished. "Begging your pardon, majesty."

The queen let the silence linger before replying. "It draws its power from your corpus. Many that undergo the change can use such weapons." She glanced at Cora. "Though miniaturized, the weapon compares favorably to the cruder cousins employed by Paradise City and the Empire. You will become more adept with practice, no doubt, Mister Skye. One prays that we survive in the interim."

Skye ducked his head. "Majesty."

"It will serve you well during the coming defense of the realm," she said.

"The what now?" Skye said.

"Your fanciful warnings have proven true. Despite our incredulity, the force you described broke through the Wall. Within the next twenty-four hours, it will besiege Twisted Bluff."

"Maybe they're just passing through, majesty," Skye said.

"We assure you they are not. The Empire needs our bodies to power their machines."

"With respect, you don't need our help."

"We have many warriors but few who can lead. We believe you were a captain in the Paradise City militia?"

"This isn't my fight."

"We would rather have you here willingly, but know we have already sealed the city so you are all here for the duration, regardless. It is in your own best interest to fight alongside the neo-dead."

"This is a shitty deal."

Queen Beatrice smiled, and a shiver ran down Cora's spine. "Play the cards we have dealt you, captain. Survive, and Providence may deal you a new hand."

Skye glanced at his skeleton hand and grimaced. He shut his mouth and gave a curt nod. Mortensen entered holding a metal hoop studded with small, evenly spaced boxes.

"Place the device on Miss Pierson."

Cora backed up but found herself in vice-like grips on either side by two Eddies. Skye rose, but another pair leveled pikes with glowing plasma balls at their tips.

"This is for the protection of all, Miss Pierson, since you refuse to undergo the transformation." Queen Beatrice gestured. "An explosive collar. Should you unexpectedly succumb to the curse and become... unmanageable, the device ensures our safety."

"That's barbaric," Skye said. "Why not let her go into the desert if she's so dangerous?"

"You have much to learn about the dreaming desert, captain. But should she take it in her head to run, know also that it will detonate automatically if she ventures beyond Twisted Bluff's gates."

Kikuchiyo remained kneeling the entire time, face placid and staring ahead. The guards, while nearby, couldn't possibly react in time should he decide to strike.

"Kikuchiyo," she said.

The Blood Weeper turned and regarded her silent plea. His eyes darted around from Mortensen approaching with the collar, to the guards, the queen. His hands flexed, then relaxed against his thighs as he turned back. "It doesn't look heavy," he said.

The Eddies held her still while Mortensen locked the collar around her. She shivered at the metal's touch and felt as if she couldn't swallow. Mortensen murmured as he checked the charges. "It will explode if its tampered with, Cora. Please see me when you've come to your senses and the queen will have it removed."

Cora shook her head. "I think you'll only get it off my corpse, one way or another."

"I surely hope not," Mortensen said and stepped back.

"And you expect us to fight for you like this?" Skye said.

"We don't have time to discuss this in a committee," said the queen.

"This is a sight worse than—"

Kikuchiyo rose, closed the distance, and slapped Skye before the guards could react. "Pay your debts before running away."

Skye rubbed at his reddened face. "Easy for you to say, Blood Weeper."

Kikuchiyo's eyes narrowed. "It is. Everything else? Bullshit."

14

If there was an upside to having a bomb strapped to your neck, it was that it took the edge off the hunger pangs. Cora tagged along with Skye because the others shied away from her. Whether it was the collar's stigma or its explosive nature, she couldn't say.

Skye tugged at his uniform collar as they were ushered into one of the spire's sub-basements. where several gray-skinned neo-dead surrounded what at first appeared to be a sand table with a replica of Twisted Bluff modeled in the center. As she drew closer, individual sand figures no bigger than ants moved throughout the fort and surrounding city, driving thumper carts, taking strolls, patrolling the curtain wall, and going about their daily business.

General Haggart, a skeleton in a black cavalry uniform, turned away from the table and fixed two empty eye sockets on them. "Captain Skye, the queen says I am to make use of you," he said, and managed a derisive sniff despite having no nose or lungs. "So how useful are you, captain? Infantry? Air Corps? Intelligence?"

Skye lifted his chin. "Not exactly. I don't know how I'd fit into this hodgepodge you call an army. I was a logistics expert on what they called detached duty."

"You may address me as 'sir,'" Haggart said.

Skye pressed his lips together. "I was on detached duty, sir."

"Meaning?"

"I led a small logistical team getting what couldn't come through official channels."

Haggart's jaw clacked. "A smuggler."

Skye held up a finger. "A troubleshooter. Sir."

"A thief."

Skye shook his head and tapped his chest. "Not me. I had authorization for everything I appropriated."

"Of course you did." Haggart's skull turned and empty eye sockets locked on Cora. "Miss Pierson, in your condition, would you perhaps be more comfortable in a more… private room?"

Skye held up a hand. "She is serving as my attaché, general. I take full responsibility."

"Oh, you can be sure of that." Haggart clacked his jaw. "Very well, captain. If you'll join me at the table?"

"Thanks," Cora whispered.

"Just give me some warning if you feel anything coming on," he murmured.

The general swept a hand over the sand table. "Twisted Bluff, as it is now." He pressed a button and the sandcastle version of Twisted Bluff and all its little inhabitants collapsed and the sand piles began reforming. Twisted Bluff regrew on a smaller scale and Cora picked out the road leading from the curtain wall and to the tiny pickup truck at the crossroads.

"This is all in real time?" Skye asked.

"It's limited by visual range, in this case what our wraiths can see."

"So you don't have eyes on the approaching Imperials?"

"So sorry to disappoint you, *captain*, only reports from recon scouts."

Skye lifted his chin. "Apologies, sir."

Haggart manipulated the table controls and the sand sculptures collapsed, reforming moments later. Twisted Bluff was now a few inches high and Cora recognized the Bathtub among other areas Haggart and his aides had marked: an airport nestled in a deep canyon, a rocket launch pad, and several small villages to the west. To the east, halfway between the Wall and Twisted Bluff, a line of sand crawlers advanced in formations miles across.

"This is based on the last report, which came in while you were in the Labyrinth, captain. Doubtless, our intelligence is incomplete, but our best guess is they will reach us within the next few hours. I've deployed a few heavy weapons teams here and here," he said, pointing, "but they can delay the advance a few minutes more."

Haggart changed the table to show the immediate area around Twisted Bluff. "The wall cannon and main bombard are adequate for taking those beasts out at a distance, unless the Imperials are hiding their full potential. We'll have several squads of scrabblers on the wall minding our flanks and skin jobs manning the gate defenses, mostly smaller cannons scavenged from the Bathtub and some machine guns scavenged from around the dreaming and a few electros stolen from over the Wall and the Badlands. Would that we had more."

"You still have a defensible position and don't have to resupply. You can hold off ten times your numbers with what I saw outside," Skye said.

Haggart's fingers rattled as he drummed them on the table's stone corner. "I'm more concerned about their necros."

"I don't follow."

Haggart nodded at Cora. "She understands. You're still new to this and also mostly alive, captain, but the rest of us will be susceptible to their magics. Distraction, encharming, arresting, mesmerizing, all at a distance. The closer they get, the greater their effect on our minds. Should they get close enough, there is the possibility they could make entire platoons lay down their arms or even turn their guns on their comrades."

"Is there no defense?"

"We are ill-equipped to defend ourselves against sonic incursion outside the spire. It conducts through our bones, through the very ground we tread on."

"Are there no jammers, no counter incursion available?"

"Who could run such equipment? It would be like a surgeon operating on his or herself."

"What about me?" Cora asked quietly.

Haggart clacked his jaw twice. "What about you? Volunteering to charge a couple and take them out when your collar blows?"

Cora looked around the room as others turned to stare and seemed to shrink into herself, second-guessing.

"She knows necrosonics," Skye said.

She shook her head. "I was trained but—"

Skye leaned in. "If we're going to make it through this, I need you. I've never defended a base from Imperial assault either. I'm guessing it's the same with you and counter-sonics. These guys? They know even less. Do your best." He squeezed her shoulder and stepped back. "She's the only expert you've got, sir. You going to use the tools you're given or wait for something better to come along?"

Haggart's teeth rapid-tapped as he thought. "Very well, you're our sonic specialist."

Skye winked at Cora and turned to face the table. "General, if I were them, I'd have some crawlers ferry a few thopters or an airship through the Wall. They might have some pilots crazy enough to try flying despite the low ceiling."

"Skin job sharpshooters and scrabblers can keep those to a minimum. We can bring down any airship with the wall cannons."

Skye pursed his lips and shook his head. "Sir, you'll want at least four electros up on the spire. Small arms won't be enough if they're willing to risk thopters."

Haggart contemplated the table. "We'd be ceding them the middle ranges if we did that. Infantry and mechanized could maneuver unopposed while the big guns are busy. No."

"Then they'll just land behind your lines and run wild."

General Haggart squared up on Skye, arms akimbo. "Keep it up, air-breather, and you'll be advising from a cell."

Skye's nostrils flared, and he tucked his chin. "Sir, why not rig the electros closer to the curtain wall's edge and let them cover both areas?"

"It can't be done."

The engineer deep within her took offense and she spoke up. "I've rigged electros on airships before. I bet I can do it if you don't have anyone else."

Haggart's eyeless stare centered on her. "It's complicated."

The enclave woman in her joined the engineer and put an edge to her reply. "I'm well-qualified to handle complication." Skye gave her a subtle nod and eyebrow flash. She still wasn't sure about the rogue, but her opinion of him rose a notch as she smiled back.

Haggart waved over another deader skin job wearing a lightning bolt on his uniform collar, which she took to mean he was some kind of technical officer. "Hodgkins, explain."

"The emplacements topside won't fit electros. We set the mounts up with howitzers and mortars in mind, with wiring all hard-piped to a centralized fire control — indirect fire, not anti-air. It'd take weeks to tear it out and rework it all for direct-fire."

Cora tapped her fingers as she thought. "Tell me, how long would it take to get four stagecoaches up there?"

THE STAGECOACH ROSE into the light, suspended from a rusted gantry. To the other side, scrabblers threaded power cables up the inner walls. They reminded Cora of spiders, the way they crawled up the sheer cliff faces with limbs bending in all the wrong ways, but sure-footed with no apparent fear of falling. She could not say the same of Hodgkins, who stayed well back from the edge and flinched at every wind gust.

Below, the teamster shouted and brought his thumper team to a halt. The lead thumper rapped its belly tread against the ground and sent a sub-sonic pulse to another team coaxed onto the sandstone rim to take over the load. Another scrabbler crew scuttled over and swung the gantry around before signaling the upper team's mahout and lowering the stagecoach to the curtain wall's rim. When the ropes were clear, the crew pushed the coach over to the new gun emplacement and went to work with welding torches and plasma cutters, heedless of the abuse spewing from their foreman's mouth. Cora nodded and walked farther along the rim to the first emplacements, now almost complete. Soon the stagecoach was hardly recognizable with its spoked wheels tucked underneath the frame and the passenger compartment transformed into a cradle-like berth for the electro gun. A workman sat in the side-mounted gunner's seat and cranked through the gearing, bringing the electro's barrel up to nearly sixty degrees and back down almost thirty below the wall's lip. It wasn't a great field of fire, but it would do for keeping any thopters and ground troops busy.

"Where are we setting the stops?" a skin job called out to her.

"Just short of shooting off the noses of the emplacements on either side."

"What about sonic incursion?" Hodgkins asked.

The settlement had little in traditional sonic defense system components. A basic setup would start with a media player of some type — a cassette, turntable, or in a pinch a radio tuned to the phantom stations out of the Badlands. The feed would go through amplification and cleanup before being piped out through speakers or inducted directly into the deaders' ear canals. There were few radios in Twisted Bluff. The neo-dead were sensitive to music and merely humming a few notes in public was received as a loud fart might among the living. Residents took great pains to ensure they kept music volumes at a personal level. Walkmans and other portable decks were highly valued and in short supply. Protecting the community from a wide-scale attack required a larger system.

"We need something that reaches the entire population with power and coordination. The Imperials figured out how to use pearlstone as a resonator; how about the spire?"

Hodgkins looked up as he thought about it. "It's more of a sponge when it comes to incursion. We had to tunnel holes in it just so we could think straight inside it at first. The upside is the queen and the rest inside are safe from sonics, but it won't do anyone out here any good. Besides, how would you get something that massive to vibrate?"

"So could we line helmets with it?"

He shuddered and shook his head vehemently. "It makes us sick."

Cora recalled her own reaction to the pathfinder's helmet in the Wall, and nodded. "For necros, too." She tapped her foot as she thought. They might scavenge larger stereo and public address speakers from places like the Bathtub, though she wasn't sure if there was time.

"What about..." Hodgkins snapped repeatedly. "Whattya call them..." Snap-snap, point. "Walkie-talkies? I'm sure we have a few lying around."

"Their speakers won't project more than a few feet. That's assuming the static around here doesn't make them useless right off the bat."

"How about setting up a network of singers? Space them every twenty feet or move them around in groups."

Cora shook her head. "Lag." Propagation time between identifying a threat and deploying a counter-song would take too long. She tapped her foot. "Maybe we could modulate the power grid and change the pitch at which the lights hum."

Hodgkins winced. "Maybe. Tricky business, messing with the dynamos on the fly. How would we filter out feedback?"

"Are the dynamos set up with a load balancer?" Hodgkins held a fist to his head and swayed. "You okay?" She didn't think a neo-deader could look ill.

"Yeah, fine. Could you maybe stop doing that?"

"Doing what?"

"The foot thing. I think it's messing with my head."

"Oh. Right." Cora stopped. Made sense, really. Percussive tapping set up a rhythm that traveled through the stone and conducted through Hodgkins' bones and messed with his inner necrotic balance. Not unlike a necrosonic incursion, really.

Really.

"What?" Hodgkins said.

Cora took off her boots and peeled away her socks. The stone burned hot beneath her feet, but when she closed her eyes, she could feel the rhythms of Twisted Bluff. The nearby workers' footsteps were like whispers in the rock, punctuated with quick shouts as their hammers struck. Somewhere a pump churned. After a moment she found something she had unconsciously tuned out, a series of slow syncopated beats. A pause. An answering slow pulse, slower than a heartbeat.

"Thumpers," she said.

Within a few hours she had a simple network up and running, adapting the mahouts' existing system to her needs. Some mahouts balked, but fell into line after Cora recruited Kikuchiyo to stand behind her as she explained her plan. If they were skeptical, General Haggart and Skye were doubly so.

"We're going to trust our defenses to thumpers," Haggart said.

"Partially yes. Thumpers are the only means we have right now for sending broad messages. We'll set up a few pre-planned songs to counter the most likely attack vectors. Hodgkins is duping the tapes for everyone right now."

"Aren't the mahouts on the front lines vulnerable? What if the necros get them?"

Cora shrugged. "All the neo-dead will be affected; we can't get around that. The mahouts have the advantage of being at ground zero of the thumpers' calls. That should help block out incoming incursion. But look at it this way: the neo-dead instantly feel what works and what doesn't. We ought to be quick enough to offset any disadvantage."

"I don't hear a lot of confidence."

Cora spread her hands. "It's never been tried before as far as I know, general. If it helps, I'll be on the front lines too."

"Then let's hope you're right, necro. It'd be a shame if an incursion forced me to trigger your collar," Haggart said.

"I'll try not to lose my head."

Haggart clacked his jaw in a skeleton version of laughing.

SKYE APPROACHED the front gate where Kikuchiyo flowed through his exercises. The samurai moved with exaggerated slowness, punching invisible opponents and stepping through to place his feet precisely before launching another strike. Tiny footsteps approached and a furry head butted against Skye's good hand.

"Finally tolerating you, eh, boy?" he said as he scratched Dog's head.

Dog's tail thumped.

"Yeah, I don't know what he's doing either. They stuck me with finding a use for him, as if I could order him around, you know? Damned if I know what to do about it."

Kikuchiyo snapped out a front kick punctuated with a *kiai*. He held his foot out as he pivoted to Skye before settling back into a fighting stance. Icy fingers tapped at Skye's innards and he clamped down on the impulse to go for his gun. Instead, he smiled as he approached.

"Any problems with the stitches?" he called out.

Kikuchiyo launched a slow punch. "No."

"Haggart's through picking my brain so he put me in charge of some sharpshooters, since I had a little experience. I'm also stuck with you, it seems." Skye kept his smile plastered as the samurai pivoted and swept his trailing leg in an overhead arc.

"You're good in a fight, almost as good as me." He laughed, Kikuchiyo didn't. "I thought you'd be best kept as a reserve, you know, stay back until we know where best to send you and plug any gaps that appear?"

Kikuchiyo's punch ended with a snap, and he shifted to cover another angle. "I feel the Prime drawing closer every hour. When he arrives, I will meet him and liberate his head from his shoulders. When battle comes, that is where I will be."

Skye cocked his head. "The Prime? He's off in some floating palace appointing flunkies and sorting his courtesans by shoe size, not in a rolling hotbox in this Twins-forsaken place." Kikuchiyo ignored him as he grabbed and threw an invisible opponent. "Even if you were right, how would you even reach him?"

"When surrounded, charge in! Where the enemy thinks he is strong, show him he is weak. Do not hold back."

His movements quickened, firing strikes to the left and the right, faster and faster until Skye had problems tracking it all. Skye was no stranger to unarmed combat, albeit mostly in the taverns and alleyways of Paradise City's more colorful neighborhoods, and could hold his own, anticipating where the other guy's next punch, kick, or gouge would land next. Kikuchiyo's unpredictable strikes came from improbable angles while still seeming a natural conclusion of his body's contortions. Skye knew the man was deadly, but the fullness of his art on display turned his guts to water. In a straight-up fight, Captain John Skye would have no chance against Kikuchiyo, and he couldn't buffalo his monkey-and-reptile brain into believing otherwise.

Could he really be the Blood Weeper? No, the man was just a talented, lucky lunatic. Maybe his disappearing act was just some variation of the Badlands curse, a divine joke that had broken the man's sanity long ago. Someday reality would catch up with him and it would end in a bloody mess.

Just like you.

Dog whined, and Skye made himself relax. He ruffled the dog's fur with his good hand and gave him two hearty thumps to the ribs.

Kikuchiyo's whirlwind attack ceased. "Stop that. You will hurt him."

"I know how to pet a dog. And since when do you care?"

Kikuchiyo blinked, then resumed his *kata*.

"Must get hot under all that ego, eh, boy? 'Course, you're wearing a fur coat so you probably know all about it." Skye let out a breath. "Make a man cranky, heat will. Thank the Twins he didn't get a sword."

Kikuchiyo froze. He rose from his fighting stance and strode towards Skye with wide eyes and flared nostrils. Skye stepped back as the gun appeared in his skeletal hand, then sailed through the air before his brain registered Kikuchiyo slapping it away.

"Leave," Kikuchiyo said.

Skye's retort died as the monkey-and-reptile brain took control and prepped his body for flight. He swallowed. "Fine. Come on, Dog."

Dog looked between the two men, and his fur bristled.

"The dog remains here," Kikuchiyo said.

"You're scaring him."

"Dog is fine where he is."

"You don't even want him. Come on, boy." He held out his skeleton hand to Dog.

Dog growled and snapped at Skye's exposed bones. Kikuchiyo snapped his fingers and Dog retreated to his side, hackles still raised.

Skye took two steps back and retrieved his gun from the dirt. When he turned around, Dog was looking up expectantly to Kikuchiyo, who ignored him.

"You're doing it wrong, Blood Weeper, if you think you can just barrel out through the front gate and kill everyone in sight," Skye said. "You want to go out in some fool blaze of glory? Go right ahead. But if you ask me, it's the coward's way out."

"I do not expect you to understand."

"Oh, I understand plenty. In fact, I'll keep a shovel handy."

Kikuchiyo bowed. "I will ensure you have an opportunity to use it."

15

He was up on the curtain wall when the crawlers came, rifle in hand. The other sharpshooters and snipers carried an eclectic weapons collection ranging from heirloom-quality sporting rifles engraved with bucolic hunting scenes to humming tripod-mounted monstrosities of chrome and sizzling power cables scavenged from the Utopian warbots. Most fell in-between: an assortment of military rifles from all eras prized for their accuracy and range above all else. They issued Skye a rather pedestrian .308 equipped with a scope and a bipod, which suited him just fine. Pedestrian was simple. Pedestrian was reliable. His job was to ensure the necros didn't get close enough to overwhelm Cora and her nascent sonic defense. He would not fail.

The shooters in what could loosely be called "his" squad were mostly scrabblers with a few skin jobs and a bone-boy. They had worked through the night setting up sheltered firing positions and blinds so they could cover the ground effectively. If this group held any animosity towards him for not being one hundred percent dead, they hid it well, or else his skeletal right hand was good enough for them.

The fortress heavy cannons opened fire, shaking the ground and sending Skye to his knees. Vehicle-sized shells smashed into the distant crawlers and sent glittering metal high into the air with each impact. A cheer went up; skeletal and leather-clad fists punched the air. Skye's brightened spirit faded as the cannons took agonizing minutes reloading while the Imperial crawlers advanced. Skye counted an even dozen coming for them at full speed, save for the lagging crawler that took the brunt of the first cannonade. High dust clouds rose behind the machines, and Skye worried at what might hide within them.

Another salvo boomed, and this time Skye tracked a shell as it soared past its target, sending up an impressive column of sand and stone. Another shell glanced off a crawler's sloped front, ringing the crawler like a bell and making it shudder in its advance. The dread in Skye's stomach compacted further, and he distracted himself by checking his spare magazines for the thousandth time.

The Imperials began breaking into smaller groups of three, fanning out and zigzagging, presenting the gunners with harder targets. Motors whined beneath him as massive barrels tracked back and forth. One crawler tried its luck with its own weapons, sending a whistling shell arcing high through the air, momentarily lost in the low clouds. Skye knew there was nowhere to go if it landed on top of the curtain wall, and dread's weight settled on his shoulders as the shell's whistle filled his ears. He would just have to trust his luck. A lifetime later, the shell tore through the last cloud layer and exploded a scant few hundred yards from the front gate.

He had no business being here.

Someone shouted, "Hope you brought your umbrellas, boys. It's gonna rain!"

"The hell you know about rain, Leeroy? You were born in the Badlands, same as the rest of us." Several snorts and guffaws followed.

"Fuck you, Porter," Leeroy said to more laughter.

Skye's dread turned to anger but he caught himself in time before shouting something stupid like other officers that had irritated him over his career. The fortress cannons boomed again, effectively shutting the others up for him. A crawler rocked as it caught a shell square-on and began smoking. The air filled with return fire as the Imperials closed in. One salvo went high and Skye found himself face-down on the ground, shielding himself from rock and dust raining down on his head. The fortress's smaller cannons opened up along the line, many having no hope of penetrating the crawlers' heavy armor, and instead targeted the weaker treads. The electros opened up, sending roiling plasma globes into the chaos. Skye crawled forward and scanned the field through his scope. Several crawlers had opened their rear assault ramps and began spewing out troops on runabouts and on foot.

"Snipers forward!" he shouted. He kept an eye on the crawlers at the flanks, but he couldn't do anything about them for now. He swept the battlefield through his scope, looking for a suitable target. The soldiers all wore Astbury's pearlescent melted-stone armor, with no insignia and featureless face screens. He lined up on one likely-looking candidate, an armored figure directing others from the back of a runabout.

He released his breath and squeezed the trigger. The figure collapsed and Skye moved on. Later he would wonder if it was someone he knew from the old militia. He settled in a rhythm of scanning, acquiring, breathing, and firing, missing sometimes, but rarely. Some part of him noted the machine guns had opened up and some Imperial on the ground was smart enough to start sending suppressing fire their way. It was only a matter of time before counter-sniper teams came forward and, if the Imperials were smart, the necros with their sonics.

Lightning crackled, and a burning ornithopter fell from the clouds.

"Contact! Look alive!"

The sky came alive with lightning strikes that turned black clouds purple and outlined an incoming thopter wave and monstrous ovoid shadow. The sortie descended, the airship revealed as its shields attracted and flared with each lightning strike.

"Who thought that was a good idea?" Leeroy said.

Skye smiled. "Sometimes generals think just because they have a tool they must then use it. Let's all give thanks for our enemy's mistakes. Light 'em up, Leeroy."

The electros fired, sending plasma into the airship's ornithopter screen. The thopters scattered, machine guns twinkling from their noses and tracers streaking. The return fire sent everyone's head down, but the crews kept firing even as bullets began chewing through the sandbags and ricocheting from metal shields. The first wave passed over them and began taking fire from the queen's palace atop the twisted spire.

"Force 'em high or force 'em low!" Skye called. Let the pilots decide if they'd rather face the gate cannons or the lightning and gusting currents in the clouds.

The crews began zeroing in on the airship, and it became enveloped in a glowing cocoon as its shields took hit after hit. The airship opened up with its own cannonade, focusing not on the curtain wall but the front gate. Shells rained down on the gate, and Skye frowned as the barrage began blowing it apart.

A burst from a passing thopter stitched across the ground a few feet away and Skye dove into his bunker. He dropped his rifle and pulled the electro gun from his holster, lining up the passing thopter. He tracked it for a moment until he had the lead, then pulled the trigger. Several miniature suns leapt from the barrel, singeing his face and leaving purple afterimages. His vision cleared in time to see the thopter pull up too late and explode.

The gate cannons continued their duel with the oncoming crawlers and the bombard roared again, flinging a car-sized shell into a crawler's path. The crawler slewed as it tried avoiding the resulting crater, but too late and toppled sideways into it.

Two ornithopters shot over the gates and bombs tumbled from them along the wide pathway, tearing the Cadillacs loose and sending defenders scurrying. Three larger thopters followed, a gunship and two troop carriers. The gunship continued down the main avenue, strafing everything in sight while the carriers landed and disgorged small teams that fled to the alleyways. Electros from the queen's palace guard rained down on them from above, making Skye wince as stray shots landed among the buildings, adding to the carnage. One troop carrier lost its wing as it lifted off and careened into the curtain wall. Its wreckage landed in some poor bastard's front yard.

The airship bore down on the damaged gate. It looked like its captain either had balls of steel or rocks for brains, lining up his craft to pass straight through the curtain wall's gap just as the thopters had.

"Force that big bastard down!" he yelled. He didn't want to think about how many troopers it could land behind the defenses.

The electros poured fire into the airship's shields and they flickered and flared under the pounding. The craft dipped and began taking fire from the gate cannons as well. The airship shuddered as the fire began to tell, and then its shields collapsed. The ship's silver envelope disintegrated and its air cells soon followed. The airship fell in slow motion and, to Skye's horror, crashed just behind the gate. An enormous explosion erupted a moment later, taking out the gate and the artificial Cadillac switchbacks with it.

The runabouts converged, flowing through the gap and maneuvering around the wreckage. Machine guns along the walls buzzed and RPGs streaked as the neo-dead poured fire into the runabouts, Imperial troops firing back and tossing grenades as they zipped through. One runabout overturned as a tire was shot off and another slowed to a halt, belching thick black smoke from its dynamo. The dismounted troopers scrambled and took cover behind their ruined machines and began firing back at the neo-dead. The defenders were well-situated, but their few numbers weren't stemming the flow. More runabouts made it through the gauntlet at the gate and began navigating through the wreckage into town. "Captain!"

A skin job slid to the ground next to him. "Crawlers on the north side have stopped, and something's not right." Skye followed the deader at a running crouch, trusting to luck he wouldn't buy it from a stray bullet.

The crawlers in question sat with their ramps open, outside the fortress's main guns and only taking small-arms fire from rock-clinging scrabblers charged with protecting the flanks. Squads of armored troops with oversized backpacks formed up behind the crawlers. What sane commander would order his troops to assault up a rock face over a hundred feet with defenders taking pot shots the entire way, let alone carrying everything but the kitchen sink on their backs? They couldn't be that stupid. Then again, Skye knew a few of the commanders on the other side and yes, they could indeed be that stupid. A high-pitched keening reached him and he realized the Imperials weren't carrying backpacks.

"Tell the electros we have incoming from the north," he said to the skin job.

Skye turned around as light flared behind the crawlers and the armored soldiers shot into the air on rocket plumes. They arced high into the air ahead of the electros' first volley. There was no time to organize his squad, and Skye could only react as the jump troops landed and began firing. He fired his rifle, cursing its cyclic. He didn't need accuracy right now; he needed to shoot more bullets.

A purple beam from a Utopian beam cannon caught a jump trooper in the chest and left a hand-sized hole burned through-and-through. The beam cut out as a grenade exploded and took out its crew. A scrabbler with a clunky bolt action huddled behind sandbags, pinned on both sides by automatic weapons fire, caught in a crossfire as the jump troops advanced. An electro gun lost its crew to a grenade, and a second gun stopped firing as its gunner slumped and then tumbled from its seat before another took its place.

Skye fired at the closest jump troopers, missing them but forcing them to retreat for the moment. He reached for a new magazine and came up empty. He glanced back and found the jump troopers sprinting towards him. His skeleton hand came up gripping his sidearm and squeezed out four shots. Four miniature suns raced out and caught the troopers in the open, sending them sprawling. His arm swung and fired on another cluster of jump troops, sending two more plasma balls before the gun ran dry. A jump trooper shouted and Skye dove as gunfire focused on his tiny sandbag bunker. Skye's right arm tingled on pins and needles in time with the gun's blinking charge indicator. Too slow! Any moment a grenade would come sailing overhead and that would be it.

A guttural yell cut through the din. Skye poked his head up as Kikuchiyo raced past, weaving his way through the weapons fire into the thickest concentration of jump troops and drawing his machete. The blade flashed, and a trooper fell, then another. Skye picked himself up and dashed over to a nearby gun crew.

"The Blood Weeper has 'em close. Take out the others!" He didn't wait for a response, but started running from deader to deader, some of whom were already shifting their fire and halting the trooper advance. Skye found himself back at his first firing position with his extra staged magazines. Somehow his rifle was still clutched in his left hand and while he reloaded, he took in the situation.

The Blood Weeper dispatched his initial foes and crouched low, looking for new targets. The electros filled the sky with plasma as fresh waves of jump troops arced in. It wouldn't be enough. More would land not only on the curtain wall but also within the town and link up with the force below.

A ripple went through the neo-dead around him, and Skye's skeleton hand spasmed. A chaotic rhythm thrummed in his bones and while it was just another irritation to him, his squad began shaking and convulsing. The defenders' gunfire went wide of their targets or stopped altogether. Sonic incursion. Somewhere, the Imperial necros had set up their sonics and pumped discord through the air. Skye turned away from the firefight around him and swept his scope across the larger battlefield.

Nausea passed through Cora and she steadied herself against the thumper's pebbled shoulder. Moses, she corrected herself. Hodgkins introduced her to the mahout, Rog Cuddahay, and his thumper Moses.

"Miss Cora?" Hodgkins said.

"I'm fine," she lied. She concentrated on the rhythms and chords coming through the air and tried to think of the correct counterrhythm.

"Pattern five," she said.

Rog clucked his tongue and rapped Moses behind an ear. The thumper lowered himself to the ground and his neck bladders swelled so full that the skin went translucent. Rog placed his hands on Moses' skull and the thumper's belly began hammering the ground in time to Rog's drumming fingers. The vibrations reached the next mahout barely visible near the gates, who took a moment to decipher the pattern and relay it.

Soon boomboxes, tape decks, and Walkmans with the volume turned up blared Van Halen throughout Twisted Bluff. The nausea eased in degrees as more players added to the effort, stabilizing at a point where Cora still felt queasy but could push through it. She ran through the playlist in her head, wondering if some other song or style would work better, but afraid she might make the situation worse by complementing the incursion's tune rather than countering it. She had been lucky and hoped it would hold when the Imperial necros adjusted. She didn't have long to wait.

The sickening rhythm changed, fading before coming back with a new syncopation and redoubled effect. She couldn't identify the song and each moment made concentration harder. She clutched at her head and signaled a pattern change to Rog. The music within Twisted Bluff changed to Whitesnake but with little effect. The cannon fire from the walls slackened and her thoughts became as thick as syrup. She couldn't remember her playlist and fumbled at a folded piece of paper where she had written it down. She blinked at the list and held two fingers up to Rog before sinking to her knees as the necro's song pulled at her, urging her to sleep. Rog tapped his fingers and Moses, oblivious to the music around him, thumped out the message.

The opening chorus of Don't Stop Believin' began and strength returned. She *hated* this song, but today she didn't care how bad the medicine tasted, so long as it worked.

Gunfire erupted around her. Her weaponless hands opened and closed as Imperials in pearlstone armor rushed into the streets with guns blazing. Rog coughed and fell with a gaping hole in his chest. Cora rushed to him and pulled him close to Moses, placing a hand over the wound and realizing there wasn't any blood coming out.

"S'okay," Rog wheezed. "Cracked my spine though. Help me up?"

Rog's limbs worked well enough, but his broken spine made him about as easy to move as a sack of jello. She got Rog's arm over her shoulder and with help from Moses, headed away from the fighting. The cannon fire picked up as did the syncopation of the necro's sonics but her luck held and they had not yet cracked her counter.

They turned a corner and headed to a gritterpillar stable. "The mounts are gone. We can hold here, and keep Moses safe." Rog said.

Her vision blurred and she had to kneel to keep from passing out. "The sonics are changing," she said.

"Good thing I'm lying down," said Rog. "This one's like a kick in the gut. What's your counter?"

Cora tried to identify the song but still had problems placing it. It was punk, it was metal, but it was slower than it ought to be. As the sound leeched the energy from her body she realized the familiar musical phrases and riffs of Badlands songs were missing and had been replaced by something murkier.

"Pattern seven," she called to Rog, who began tapping. Moses's thumping shook the stable and cast dust through the air with each percussive beat. The vibrations soaked into her bones and pushed the fatigue away, and after more thumpers picked up the rhythm she found her feet.

"It's still affecting me," Rog said.

"I know, me too. It's hard countering what I've never heard before."

"I thought you were trained." He pulled himself up and sat up against Moses's scaly flank.

Cora went to the window. She couldn't see what was going on but the explosions and gunfire were coming closer, which if there was a bright side, meant the sonics would be less effective. "You don't understand, Rog."

"I understand more of us are going to die."

Boots clattered outside. The door opened a crack and something egg-sized sailed through the gap.

Cora hit the deck and pulled at Rog. "Down!"

The device exploded with a deafening thump and blinding light. The world rang and she blinked purple after-images from her eyes as she felt Moses howl and surge to his feet beside her. The thumper bolted for the door, knocking down the incoming Imperials. Rog recovered enough to put a shot into one armored torso and Cora's questing hand closed around a wooden handle. She swung at an incoming trooper, who rocked under the shovel's impact but quickly recovered and swung his weapon around. Cora threw herself to the side as the burst went off, knowing there was no way the trooper could miss. Instead, Rog's torso danced under the bulletstorm, then slumped. The trooper's weapons swung to her. One figure shouldered his way to the front and crouched so his blank-faced helmet was inches from her face.

"Miss Pierson. I should have known," said the familiar voice.

THE THOPTERS and jump troopers kept coming, taking staggering losses to the electro guns, but what few made it through kept his squad busy covering the gun crews instead of searching the battlefield for necros. Skye learned to alternate between his electro pistol and conventional rifle as the sonic incursion ebbed and flowed around him. After the landing's initial shock, the neo-dead rallied and began pushing the Imperials back. At some point, the Blood Weeper had rushed after a four-squad rocketing from the curtain wall into town, leaving Skye and his sharpshooters to clear the last jump troops from the rim.

When the last trooper bugged out back to the crawlers, and with no necros to snipe, Skye turned his attention to the town. A mass of troopers had worked their way through the switchbacks, clearing the obstacles and exploiting a blind spot in the neo-dead fields of fire to organize their assault. Skye cursed. He told Haggart about that dead spot, but the bone boy hadn't listened.

"Shooters to me!" he called. He wished he had some grenades or a mortar team or two to use on the close-packed enemy below. Instead, he had nothing but bullets and bad shooting angles, but he would give the troopers below something to worry about. He lined up a quick shot and missed, the ricochet flashing against the red sandstone wall followed by the trooper's head swinging around and a gloved hand pointing back at him. More helmets turned his way and rifles rose. The return fire wasn't particularly accurate, but made up for it with volume. Skye ducked back as his squad came to the rim and took their own shots. The deaders might get a few, Skye reasoned, but if he were the Imperial commander, he'd start the assault now.

He didn't have long to wait. The counterfire ebbed and he lined up a shot in time to see the troopers rise and scramble into town, flowing down the avenue and moving to take the first buildings.

"Where are our guys?" someone said.

"I don't know," said Skye, and he began racking his brain for an escape plan that didn't involve shooting his way through an invading army or jumping from a cliff.

A rumbling came down the main avenue and moments later, a mass of tentacles and pedipalps appeared as the collected gritterpillar herds were released and driven down Twisted Bluff's streets. The Imperial troops poured fire into the stampede to no effect as the bullets pinged off the creatures' toughened carapaces. From the alleyways and side streets, a cohort of neo-dead emerged on their own gritterpillar mounts and let loose an RPG volley.

The rockets exploded among the troops and released a deadly mix of

fragmented steel and pheromone-laced gas. The troopers' stone armor
protected them from the former but not the latter as mouthparts
designed for shredding the titanium-doped cases of desert beetles scissored through as if it wasn't there. The gritterpillars nearest the troops
tore into them with a frenzy and proceeded trampling and driving the
survivors back to their wrecked runabout.

The Imperial troops gave up hundreds of yards before a knot at the
center stood firm and began organizing a defense. The Imperials closed
ranks and began fighting with a discipline that kept them from being
overrun. As the crazed gritterpillars crashed against the Imperial line, a
figure emerged on a gritterpillar and charged into the fray.

Kikuchiyo rode low, using his mount's natural armor to his advantage
and staying out of sight from those on the ground until he was upon
them. His gritterpillar plowed into the center knot and he lashed out with
his machete.

Skye shouted to his squad, "Whatever you do, don't hit the Blood
Weeper. It'll just piss him off."

Skye sighted in on a trooper working to flank Kikuchiyo, who was
engaged with a particularly large officer wielding a pistol and powered
tomahawk. Skye dropped the flanking trooper and searched for an open
shot on the Blood Weeper's foe. The two circled, Kikuchiyo feinting with
his blade only to roll aside as the officer's pistol fired. The tomahawk
swept down after Kikuchiyo's trailing leg, missing by a fraction, and the
officer leapt backwards, somehow anticipating the Blood Weeper's counterstrike that would have shattered bones had it landed. Kikuchiyo rolled
to his feet and shouted a mighty *kiai*, stunning his opponent.

In that instant, Skye lined up on the officer's helmet. His skeleton
finger pulled the trigger as sonics washed over him, making his dead
finger spasm and sending the shot wide. The bullet pinged off the
helmet's edge, and the officer came to a decision, retreating and signaling
his men to do the same. They sprinted into a runabout and turned it back
to the gate, leaving behind those too slow to the grinding mouthparts of
the frenzied gritterpillars.

A larger retreat followed, the few surviving transport thopters
launching and taking shallow angles back over Twisted Bluff the electro
guns struggled to match. Skye fired two rounds at the retreating trans-

ports before cursing as his skeleton hand went numb and started twitching. He tried reloading his rifle left-handed, but the thopters were already out of range. His squad's attention shifted to the battlefield where the remaining crawlers covered the retreating runabouts. Seven sand crawlers remained immobile and smoking along with the abandoned one lying on its side. One crawler limped on damaged treads, and Skye only gave it even odds it could get out of range before the bombard and other big guns tagged it, but its commander used the carcasses of other ruined crawlers to cover his escape and joined the other anvil-heads on the horizon.

Skye made his way down from the rim and found Kikuchiyo and Dog standing in the gate's ruins with thumbs tucked into his sash. The samurai's head turned a fraction at Skye's approach, then he hawked and spat over the ruined gate.

"You got that right," Skye said. "Looks like they're going to sit out there and wait us out."

"Until the second army arrives," Kikuchiyo said. "Then all will be plowed under."

Skye wanted to argue, but kept his mouth shut. He wasn't sure if they could have held if the Imperials had pressed the attack further.

"You fought well," Kikuchiyo said.

"I did what I could." Skye closed his skeleton hand to keep it from shaking. "Nothing like you, though."

"It was a good fight."

"We should leave while we still can, anywhere but here," Skye said.

"Is that where your honor lies?"

Skye checked the charge on his gun. "This honor thing you keep spouting is complete bullshit. I don't know where you picked it up, but I don't think it means what you think it means."

Kikuchiyo spoke in a low voice. "In the beginning, there was nothing. The people were but grains of sand in darkness. Then the Creator came with a flash of light and shaped the land as he saw fit. He brought the people forth from the ground so they would know and share his joy. Thus the Badlands were born."

"I know my scripture, thank you," Skye said.

"Then you know what it says about me."

"I know what it says about the Blood Weeper."

"Close enough." Kikuchiyo scratched at his beard. "I was formed apart. A splinter of a god's soul. My honor is separate from the people of the sand, as I was created separately. I have memories of places I've never been, places that have their echoes here — carryovers from the Creator's birthworld. You people of the sand are free to make something new of your lives, but I am bound to only one purpose now that the gods have left."

"Listen to yourself. Do you really believe your own bullshit?"

Kikuchiyo shrugged. "I hunt the other splinters of the Creator. Of all my half-brothers, only the emperor remains and those are his heralds." Kikuchiyo's finger pointed to the anvil-heads on the horizon. "He approaches, I can feel it. So you ask where my honor lies, why I stay? It is to meet him here. In battle. I will succeed or fail."

"You'll fail."

"That may be, but if I run away, what purpose have I served? What life can I live if it has no meaning?"

"You're overthinking it, Kikuchiyo. Life is under no obligation to make sense to you."

16

Kikuchiyo followed him up the slope where the Cadillac barriers once stood. General Haggart and his staff had emerged from their bunker and paced through the wreckage, surveying the damage. As Skye reported to the general, he noted a certain set to the skeleton's stance that made him uneasy. If Haggart were flesh and blood, he would have searched the man's face for some hint. As his report wound down, with grunting asides by Kikuchiyo, he noticed a tension in the staff officers as well.

His eyes narrowed. "What is it?" he asked.

Haggart's jawbone ground from side to side for several moments before replying. "The Imperials captured your companion and several others."

Icy fingers closed around his chest. "And the device?" Would he have heard the explosion when she went out of range? What was one more out of dozens going on all around him?

"It did not go off."

"How do you know..." Realization set in. "You sneaky bastards. There was no range limit setting."

Haggart's jaw clacked. "A necessary fiction to keep her from running off."

Don't argue with him; you're wasting time.

"Is there a rescue plan?" he asked. This seemed to take Haggart aback.

"No, captain. There are more important considerations, such as the survival of Twisted Bluff and all its inhabitants. Should the opportunity arise, we will attempt to retrieve our citizens and your friend, but I will not risk this fortress's security on a low-survival-probability mission."

"Then I'll get her myself." He pushed past Haggart, but the general's skeleton fingers closed on his arm.

"You will not. I need you here. I don't want to have to put a guard on you, captain, but I will."

"I'll make a piss-poor soldier."

"With men like you, it's no wonder Paradise City fell." Skye balled a fist but kept himself in check. Haggart's skull leaned in. "I think once the bullets fly, you'll do what you need to in order to save your skin. When we're secure, we'll go after our own and her. You have my word."

Skye glanced at Kikuchiyo, who just stared back at him. "Fine," Skye spat. "Your orders?"

"I'm giving you a squad of scouts to supplement your snipers. I want them deployed around the bluff, ready to warn us if the Imperials try to sneak in the back door. Dismissed."

Skye didn't bother saluting as he turned on his heel. The general started talking to Kikuchiyo, but the samurai ignored the skeleton and followed Skye into Twisted Bluff.

"What if he calls you back?" Skye said.

"I owe him no allegiance."

"But you're helping me?"

"I am simply waiting for the emperor."

Skye lowered his voice and tried to look as relaxed as possible as a crew of skin jobs on thumpers passed. "Look, they'll be expecting me to try helping Cora, but they can't stop me if I'm with you, right? We can bust her out together."

Kikuchiyo frowned and shook his head. "Your duty is here. With these people."

"And who broke us both out of the deader farm? Way I see it, she's got dibs. Wanna know something else? What Haggart forgets is without Cora holding off the sonics, we would have lost. Without her, we could very well lose next time. So either way, we should go after her."

"You must stop running from your obligations, John Skye." Kikuchiyo turned and walked away.

"I'm not running," Skye said to no one in particular.

SKYE WAITED until full dark and lost Haggart's minders in the twists and turns of the fortress. For all their ability to see in the dark, the neo-dead were still a little stiff in the joints and slow on the uptake at times. He stood on the northern rampart, picking his path down the bluff and tossing the rope over the edge. He felt a slight pang of guilt over that last part, since he would leave an easy way for some Imperial scout or commando to sneak into the fortress, but there was only a small chance that would happen before the sentries would find the rope and deal with it. He would be long gone by then.

He had one leg over the side when Kikuchiyo appeared from the shadows, Dog following close behind him.

"You should stay," Kikuchiyo said.

"I'm not abandoning her, orders or no."

"Your duty is to this place. You owe them that debt."

"Bullshit. I just paid it today."

Kikuchiyo spread his feet and hooked his thumbs into his sash. "They cured you of the hunger curse when you would have died from it. They set the bill, not you."

"I owe the same to her. Without her, we would still be in that camp roasting alive or screaming our deader heads off from the hunger. Seems to me she has the prior claim." He set his other leg over the side. "I won't make much difference here, not enough to really matter. Out there maybe I can."

"You're making excuses. Honor demands you stay."

Skye sniffed. "That word again."

"I would not expect you to understand."

"And it's all crap, Kikuchiyo, Blood Weeper, whatever you want to call yourself. You want to fight the Imperials? You have some grudge or score to settle? Just say so. Don't dress it up in mysticism."

"Not mysticism. Truth."

"Here's a truth for you. Honor's a leash you wear so you won't have to actually think for yourself. You're a pawn."

"I know when I am being controlled."

"Maybe you like it. I'm going, and so should you. She helped us both."

"And we helped her."

"Maybe she gets to set the price."

"Not the same thing."

"If you say so, Blood Weeper. Take up the rope after me, at least. Wouldn't want the wrong sort to find it."

Skye rappelled down the rope, mindful Kikuchiyo could call out, or cut the rope at any time.

KIKUCHIYO WALKED the spire's corridors at an easy pace, mindful of each step, sand grinding under his sandal as his weight shifted from toe to heel. Battle fatigue settled into his muscles and joints, but he would not let it affect his *zanshin*, total awareness. It expanded around him and he would react instantly to any attack breaching its bubble. The neo-dead around him pressed themselves against the walls as he passed, though he paid them no special attention. He centered himself in his body's awareness, the strength in his limbs, his single purpose. He didn't understand where his knowledge of *zanshin* came from, perhaps from Ryan the Creator or perhaps it had always been with him, but pondering such questions was an exercise in madness.

Dog yawned behind him, a lazy exhale ending with a quiet snap of the jaws. Irritation flowed through his chest as concentration wavered, allowing the subsumed rage a foothold in his thoughts, wanting him to grab the animal's mangy head and twist until its neck snapped and mongrel eyes clouded over. Honor stayed his hand, but the rage yet whispered. The creature mocked him, following him around and placing itself between him and any neo-dead that came too close, as if he were the one needing protection. He had shown weakness by first feeding the animal, then rescuing it at Cally's request. It wanted attention, craved attention, whether having rocks thrown at it or taking food from his hand. Therefore, he would ignore it.

He found himself before the doors to the throne room and did not pause as the guards hesitated before opening them. That they would bar his entry never occurred to him. Not even the dead were foolish enough to cross the Blood Weeper, even if he was a shadow of his former self.

Queen Beatrice sat on her throne like the pharaohs of old: back straight, head raised, and palms flat on thighs. She addressed a spectral woman wearing a blue dress with an outrageous hoop skirt right out of a famous movie.

Gone with the Wind.

Once again, the knowledge of a world he had never experienced. Movies he had never watched, lyrics to tunes he had never listened to, visions of a world that bore only a passing resemblance to his own. Kikuchiyo pushed his annoyance down. The detritus of Ryan the Creator. Another set of distractions that could appear at any moment without warning.

While Beatrice could not help but to see him through the specter, she kept her attention fixed. Kikuchiyo set his feet and hooked thumbs into his sash as he settled in to wait. Dog sat at his heels and chewed at a snarl in his black-and-gray coat. Shameful.

"You may approach us," Queen Beatrice said. The spectral woman had disappeared while he watched the stupid animal. Heat rose to his face. What if an attack had come just then? Doubly shameful.

He bowed to the queen and stood in silence while she regarded him. He was patient, as was she. Her guards were not so disciplined, fingers tightened around weapons, safeties checked and re-checked. Finally, she broke the silence.

"You bring us news."

"Captain Skye has gone off after Cora."

"We thought we had ordered him to remain, through our General Haggart."

"He felt his honor required otherwise."

"Indeed." Beatrice turned to a plague-masked skin job behind her. "Double the guards on the wall. Inform me if Captain Skye returns."

She turned back to Kikuchiyo and studied him. "You do not approve."

"It is not my place to say, majesty."

"Then I give you leave to speak plainly."

Kikuchiyo bowed. "He spreads his allegiances like a farmer sowing seed. He cannot help but be overwhelmed when they all sprout and require his attention at once."

"What would you do in our place?"

"I would seek him out and return him to his duty,"

"But he is undoubtedly close to the enemy now, if not within their lines. Why risk my people for a single deserter?"

Kikuchiyo shrugged. "If we abandon our duties because they are difficult, why bother pledging service?"

Queen Beatrice remained silent for several moments. "Would you have gone after Cora?"

"If honor demanded it."

"And if honor wasn't a factor? If you had no binding one way or another, samurai?"

"What would I breathe if there was no air? You put an impossible choice before me."

She came closer to him, well within his range. Her guards shifted and ozone drifted through the air. She leaned in and whispered, "I know you of old, Kikuchiyo. Before I was queen, before my first death and subsequent rebirth I knew you. I knew your maker. What a good little dog he's made you."

Kikuchiyo's nails dug into his palms. He could not give into the rage, he would not fade. He cast about for an anchor, wishing he could have devised a way to have his name etched on the wall. Something wet touched his hand. Dog's nose pushed under his palm and wiggled its way forward. His hand swept over coarse fur and came to rest behind the mutt's ears as the world became solid once again. Movement behind him. A shock lance ignited. Dog's fur puffed, and he snarled.

Beatrice held up a hand and stayed the approaching guard. Kikuchiyo kept his hand on Dog's head and settled the animal, though it still growled low in its throat.

"You're shaking, Kikuchiyo. You rage, but for what? They have pulled your teeth. Your link to the Creator lost, perhaps broken forever. Just your honor to fall back on, just... *human* like the rest of us." Her cold gray lips pulled back to reveal porcelain-white teeth.

The rage still called even as Kikuchiyo sought to bury it. He should strike out and take his chances. The fools hadn't taken his machete. Though a poor weapon, he would certainly take out the closest Eddies; they weren't used to working in concert. Could he take out the remaining half dozen?

No. He could not.

Too cramped, too many unprotected angles, and if by some miracle he got through them all, he would have the rest of Twisted Bluff to contend with. The rage subsided.

"What you feel is fear, Kikuchiyo. That is mortality tickling your soul," Beatrice said.

"You are wrong," he said. "I am an empty vessel. Created, not born."

Beatrice arched an eyebrow. "Interesting. We wonder if that is why the curse passed you by."

"I have only my honor left. One final duty to fulfill."

"And what is that duty?"

"Jasmine charged me to seek the remaining avatars and remove them."

"We knew her too, before we were reborn. You are doubly blessed."

"*Hai.*"

"How many avatars have you found?"

"All but one, and he approaches."

"The emperor?"

"*Hai.*"

"And you know he's coming here."

"We share an affinity."

Beatrice frowned. "Perhaps he comes because you are here."

"He has always declined to meet me on the field of honor and flees at every turn, sending lackeys and common assassins against me. This time, I have placed myself at the center of his ambitions. He cannot get what he wants without dealing also with me."

"And what does he want?"

"What does any ruler want?"

"Power. The neo-dead of Twisted Bluff would provide power for several armadas. We cannot let this happen. You see why Captain Skye's actions jeopardize us."

Kikuchiyo shrugged. "His distractions may benefit you."

"Regardless, Blood Weeper, I make this pact with you: defend this city and we will do all in our power to arrange your meeting with the emperor."

Kikuchiyo bowed. "Majesty."

～

THE ROILING clouds above Twisted Bluff glowed purple in the night, covering the sands in oozing shadows. The specter in the blue dress floated high overhead, speaking with another ghost dressed in a top hat and stained apron. They separated and took off into the desert, their blue luminescence fading into the clouds until Kikuchiyo's eyes, sharper than most, lost them little more than a mile away.

The day's battle echoed on the wind, and he pulled in a mighty breath to better savor the smoke and cordite. At last, the emperor was coming. He could not escape this time; ambition and lust for power would not let him. It was his weakness, and Kikuchiyo would exploit it. They would meet, and only one of them would walk away. Duty satisfied.

Dog whined. He put his paws up on a rock and searched the night, ears swiveling and nose working. Dog barked and looked at him, then back into the night.

Kikuchiyo rose and peered into the shadows. He could detect no movement, no signs of Imperials creeping up for a night assault. The runabouts made too much noise to be stealthy and the neo-dead's spectral pickets were numerous enough to warn of any approach.

"There's nothing there," he said to Dog.

Dog made a noise, turned a circle, and put his front paws back up on the rock, looking between Kikuchiyo and whining into the night.

"They are not coming," he said.

Dog jumped onto the rock and circled again.

"Get down before you fall."

Dog sniffed the air and sneezed.

"I'm not going after them," he said. As if he had to justify himself to this animal. There was nothing to do. Duty was duty. Besides, it would be folly to even try locating Skye and Cora in the vast dreaming desert, never mind the sand crawlers filled with troopers also standing in his way.

Dog sniffed again and pointed its muzzle back over the wall. Could he have picked up their scent? Impossible. "You don't know that."

Dog jumped down and sat at his feet. Its blue eye stared into his.

"You think I should go after them."

Dog's tongue lolled out.

"Impossible. I have promised to remain here." Hadn't he? He had promised to defend the city, which implied he stay behind its walls. Remaining within the fortress and waiting for the emperor to arrive was the safest, easiest course. His companions' mistakes wouldn't distract him, not when he was so close.

Dog cocked his head.

"No. I promised Jasmine I would defeat the emperor."

Though his actual promise was to protect the people the Twins left behind. His campaign against the former avatars had been his first idea, and he followed it, but was it the best choice? Jasmine wasn't around to command him anymore, so where did his duty lie?

"Which would she have me do, Dog?"

Dog circled and pointed at the far crawler with his muzzle. Or perhaps the mutt pointed the direction from which the emperor would arrive and circling was his way of telling him to remain within the fortress walls?

"Bah, why am I listening to an animal?"

Were that Jasmine was here. What would she do? He knew too little about her, even though volumes had been written on her since she left. Her acts, her miracles, her journey through the Badlands to the sea. Depending on the source, she was an angel, a demon, a martyr, or a terrorist. He knew she was not wholly any of these things. The little he knew first-hand made him an expert on Jasmine Shaw by comparison, and yet he could not fathom what she would have him do.

His ribs still ached and knitted flesh pulled oddly if he deigned to notice it. He was no longer invincible. He was barely competent anymore, his form atrocious, feet slipping out of position, letting himself get distracted with minor scrapes and bruises. The divine rage was denied him; he was soulless and broken. A samurai had pride, yes, but must also subsume himself to better serve his master, or so he had once thought.

His knowledge of the warrior's way lacked the nuances of his creator's other memories, and he no longer found comfort in its simplicity.

"You think I need them to defeat the emperor, don't you?" he asked Dog.

Dog wagged his tail. Kikuchiyo withdrew a hefty chunk of dried meat from his pocket and tossed it to Dog, who caught it in midair.

"Fine, have it your way. But if we miss the fight, it will be your fault!"

Dog growled as he gnawed.

17

———

Her explosive collar sat on a nearby table in two halves, explosives removed. This was done not only because it had posed a danger to her captors but also had impeded fitting her with a new collar restraint, which also matched the cuffs at her wrists, midriff, and ankles. The whole idea was overkill, in her opinion, because they also locked her in the laboratory's holding cell, a clear box just big enough to lie down in if she curled into a ball. The only other choice was standing, and her body refused anything so strenuous anymore.

Her skin had taken on a disheartening gray tone where it chafed against the cuffs, and it seemed to be spreading. She would die here, perhaps, but her ultimate act of spite to these idiots would be a leaving a mundane corpse and not the deader slave they expected.

The laboratory's heavy steel doorlock wheeled, and Colonel Astbury entered, tossed his arcane embroidered leather duster on a nearby hook, and took up a white lab coat from another. He doffed his hat and placed it on a table before regarding her with a smile.

"Cora, here I had thought I lost you and you turn up along the road, so to speak." He ran fingers through his hair and scratched at his scalp, combing at his blond hair with a sigh of relief. "It's not the heat in these rolling metal boxes that gets you. It's the constant damp, don't you think?"

"I hadn't noticed," Cora said.

"Well, I envy you that. Some small adaptation of the curse, or a function of necromorphosis, do you think?"

"I'm dying, Einstein. We can't turn deader."

"Hmm, maybe," Astbury said, rummaging around through a locker. "That's the common wisdom, but I think we've just been missing the obvious for so long it's become something "everyone" knows and never questions. It's a hypothesis that makes me wish I studied information theory and meme propagation, but there's only so much time in the day for all my interests." He withdrew a carton of syringes and began arranging them on a tray.

"It's been documented, Ian: necros just die. You don't mind if I call you Ian, do you? I feel we've reached that stage in our relationship."

Astbury smiled as he glanced at her. He began whistling as he brought the tray to the cell. Cora didn't recognize the tune, though she felt as if she should have. She pushed herself to her knees and used the restraints to pull herself upright. She tilted her head to better catch the song. Was he whistling the lyrics or the lead guitar? It wasn't Aerosmith, Black Sabbath, or Iron Maiden. She closed her eyes and listened, body swaying with weakness, which wasn't helping, nor soothing the pins and needles radiating through her arm. It galled her she couldn't name the tune, but she wouldn't give Astbury the satisfaction of thinking her an ignorant 'claver.

The music stopped, and Astbury was exiting the cell, flipping its latches behind him. The syringes on his tray were filled with blood dark as motor oil. Tiny punctures along her forearm oozed black droplets. Had she blacked out?

"Surprised? I pride myself on selecting the correct song for my subjects," Astbury said. "I wasn't entirely sure if I should go with a more obscure sonic cascade, or if one of the old standbys would suffice."

Cora shook her head. "No. This can't happen. It's never happened."

Astbury winked. "Thank you for your cooperation, Cora."

"You gutless punk," Cora said as he left with his samples. He chuckled as the door closed.

Punk. Billy Idol. Of course.

∼

THE PICKET WAS good but his buddy was an idiot, and idiots get you killed. Skye crawled on his elbows into a shadowed depression within a few yards of the two soldiers in their listening post. Skye had been waiting a half hour to sneak by. Three times the idiot had lost his focus and glanced back at his own lines or leaned in to share a comment or joke with his buddy, who was just vigilant enough to keep Skye pinned down. Skye scanned the darkness, wary of approaching patrols. He figured he had about another hour before sunrise, such as it was in this forsaken place, would reveal him.

Stay calm. Trust your luck.

Idiot's gaze drifted back into his camp and something caught his attention, causing him to nudge his buddy, who rounded on Idiot and pushed him back. A muffled argument erupted and Skye took his chance. He crept quickly but quietly to the listening post, knife in hand.

"... on report, dumbass."

Idiot spread his hands and shook his head. "You need to look around, Lars. Take in the big picture. Astbury's crawler is packed with special operators. The camp's set up like we're getting reinforced and we're not digging in. We're in the middle of some big action here."

"I don't care, Newstead. If sarge sees you rubbernecking, I'll catch hell too."

Newstead was doubtlessly composing a clever response, but Skye rose from the ground and drove the knife through a gap between the armor's gorget and the helmet. Lars fumbled for his weapon and Skye tackled him. They rolled and Skye came up on top, pushing the trooper's head back and laying a forearm across the exposed neck. Armored limbs pounded at him with fading strength before going limp.

Skye spent the next several seconds gasping for air before tying the unconscious guard's hands.

"You should have killed them both," a voice said.

Skye whirled and drew his sidearm. Kikuchiyo squatted on his haunches, paying no special attention to the gun. Dog stood a few feet away, tail wagging.

"Not all of us are the Blood Weeper," Skye said and holstered his gun. "Decided to help out after all? What about honor and duty?"

"There are many paths one can follow to the same place."

"Right," Skye said. "Well, I'm glad to have you. Help me with this one and then get the armor off the other one."

"Do you know where Cora is?" Kikuchiyo asked.

"No, but Astbury from the deader farm is in one of these crawlers. I expect he might be able to tell us." Skye picked up the dead picket's helmet. "You have any objection to wearing a disguise?"

The corner of Kikuchiyo's mouth twisted up. He turned to Dog and said, "Stay."

It was a truism that in any large military operation, egos clashed. It was also a truism that in the aftermath of any large action, chaos rippled through the usual military order as the machine rearranged itself to tend the wounded, bury the dead, re-supply, and cater to the whims of officers giving orders for no other reason but to justify their participation and rank. As these orders flowed downhill and rubbed against each other, a certain number of mutually exclusive edicts and commands at cross-purposes would begin wreaking havoc. Skye's whole military career had been based on exploiting such opportunities.

Soldiers getting cut off in battle and looking to re-link with their units was common enough not only to be unremarkable, but worthy of tasking a junior officer to coordinate herding the lost knuckle-draggers back to their proper units. Skye did his best noncom impression and looked at the map the lieutenant was using to direct him to the 51st Hussars.

"That's all well and good, but we're linking up with the Fourth Dragoons," Skye said, picking a unit on the camp's far side. "Sir," he added after a moment.

"Where did you say you came from?" the lieutenant asked again. It had been the third time for the kid, who undoubtedly had bought his commission.

"Eleventh Infantry, on detachment to the quartermaster corps."

"That's not on my map, soldier."

As if anything not on the map could not possibly exist in reality. He wanted to yell at the kid, shake him a bit until his head dislodged itself from his ass. He translated the thoughts into noncom. "Yes, sir."

"Eleventh Infantry is over there," the lieutenant said, pointing at the far edge of camp opposite the Fourth Dragoons, which was also why Skye had picked it.

"Yes, sir."

"So go there, soldier."

"Sorry, sir, but my XO told us to find the Fourth Dragoons."

"But you're infantry."

"Yes, sir."

"Not dragoons."

"Affirmative. Detached to quartermaster corps," he added in a helpful tone that he knew would blow the lieutenant's mental fuses.

"The quartermaster corps are not listed on my map. And why would they need infantrymen, anyway?"

Why had Skye ever become an officer? He should have stayed a noncom and wound lieutenants up all the live-long day. Kikuchiyo shifted in his armor, impatient.

"The quartermasters need grunts to escort high-value items to where they're needed, and dragoons don't take grunt jobs," Skye said.

"You sure about that?"

Skye shrugged. "That's what the XO told us. Quartermaster said the Fourth Dragoons have a high-value package for Colonel Astbury, and the dragoons won't play postman, so you're it. He told us to find you and get that package delivered before dawn."

The lieutenant perked up at Astbury's name and nodded. "Yes, yes. I'm sure the XO is right."

Because your superiors are never wrong, right? I'm almost glad to be out.

The lieutenant nodded to himself and pointed out the Fourth Dragoons and a crawler.

"There's where they're bivouacked, and then you'll head to this crawler here for the colonel."

"Thank you, sir," Skye said and saluted, followed by Kikuchiyo.

The lieutenant snapped off a jaunty salute. "Glad to be of help, boys." It would have come off better if the lieutenant's voice hadn't quavered.

Skye and Kikuchiyo trotted off towards the dragoon camp, then cut to

Astbury's crawler as soon as they were clear of the lieutenant. Up close, the crawlers rose big as buildings with mammoth treads wrapping around roadwheels and drive sprockets taller than a man. Skye shuddered to think what they would do to the unlucky sod falling beneath them. The windowed control bridge on the top story was empty at the moment, though there was plenty of other activity as a maintenance crew worked over the cannons and mechanics shuttled parts down the rear assault ramp to parked runabouts illuminated by the cargo bay's bright floods. Skye counted four guards with rifles patrolling with two more stationed within the bay itself, and unlike the picket and his idiot buddy, these soldiers looked alert and moved with a grace the usual conscripts lacked.

"Got any ideas?" he asked Kikuchiyo. "I don't think bluffing our way in will work."

"Get close, charge in. Speed and skill defeat superior numbers."

"Because that worked so well at the deader farm, right?"

"We are here, are we not?" Kikuchiyo's teeth gleamed in the darkness.

"Was that a joke? The Blood Weeper is human after all."

"Sometimes."

Skye chuckled and shook his head. "Seriously, there's bound to be more inside."

Kikuchiyo's fingers pointed between the roving guards. "They are vigilant, but they still believe themselves safe and it shows. There is a flaw in their pattern. When I give the signal, we run under the beast's belly."

"Then what?"

"Find a hatch or deal with the guards in the cargo bay."

"That's a shitty plan."

Kikuchiyo nodded. "Get ready."

Skye tensed and filled his lungs with air, ready to burst into a sprint on the samurai's signal.

Stupid. This is so stupid.

Kikuchiyo's hand shot out and caught Skye before he could launch himself.

"Wait."

Kikuchiyo sniffed and tapped Skye's shoulder. At his questioning glance, the samurai stepped aside to reveal a spectral woman in a blue dress.

"You air-breathers shouldn't be here," she said. "You're inhibiting my mission."

"We're on one of our own. Didn't expect to see you here," Skye said.

"Yeah, right. You're lucky it's nighttime. That one," she indicated Kikuchiyo, "has blood smeared down his back."

"It's not mine," Kikuchiyo said.

"We're here for our friend who was captured today," Skye said.

"The deadlocked girl? She's in there with the yellow-haired colonel."

"Is she alive?"

"More's the pity; her collar must have malfunctioned. I couldn't get inside — there's a barrier preventing me from penetrating the walls, a pearlstone weave same as their body armor. Otherwise, I would have tripped the override and taken yellow-hair out too."

"We're going after her."

The specter's pale eyes narrowed. "What makes her so special? You should go back to Twisted Bluff and do your duty."

Skye glanced at Kikuchiyo at the mention of duty, and there was the slightest tremor at the corner of his eye.

"We will rescue Cora and bring her back to the queen," Kikuchiyo said.

The specter folded her arms and backed into the boulder until only her head was visible. "Suit yourselves, but I will report your actions."

"Do what you have to," Skye said.

The specter held a finger to her lips, then pointed at the crawler. "It's powering up."

Colored lights flickered through the bridge windows, outlining the crew settling into their seats. A dynamo whined for several seconds before the main engines caught with a deep basso rumble. The crews on the guns scrambled and queued up around a rooftop hatch while the guards on the ground jogged to the runabouts and drove them up the assault ramp.

"Heading out to link up with other elements, maybe? Whatever your plan is for getting on that crawler, better make it fast," the specter said. "And get back to the queen with any intel you find, savvy?"

"Wanna come with us?" Skye asked.

She shook her head. "I drift through the world at a pace slower than you walk, air-breather. Even that lumbering behemoth is too fast for me."

"Then we'll do what we can," Skye said.

"Twins be with you." The specter faded and disappeared.

Kikuchiyo had them wait until the crew boarded and the assault ramp was lifting.

"Now what?" Skye asked.

"I am reminded of a movie Ryan watched in his youth. Within it lies our answer."

"What?" Ryan said. The crawler's doors closed, pivoted about on its treads, and pointed its nose east.

Kikuchiyo smiled. "You will not like it."

Of that, Skye had no doubt.

18

Her head rocked from side to side as the crawler moved across the sands. Blackened veins and gray skin covered her arms and legs now, with dark tendrils snaking along hips and shoulders, advancing towards her heart and possibly her brain too. It felt as if it were happening to someone else as she wondered with morbid interest which tendril would kill her first. She wasn't the only one.

Astbury sat in a chair across from the cell, glancing at her and scratching observations in a journal every five minutes between noodling on a keyboard synthesizer surrounded by a messy pile of hand-printed music.

"Answer a question, Ian?"

He leaned over the keyboard and scribbled a note on the music. "If I can."

"How'd you get kicked out from the fleet and then come back at a higher rank? Who'd you bribe? Was it blackmail, or did you trade some kind of kinky sex thing?"

Astbury blinked and put the pen down. "Did you ever wonder why we're stuck with the same music? Our vocation is steeped in the broadcasts from WBAD's radio towers and their effects on the cursed." He launched into a quick sequence on the keyboard that sent her muscles twitching.

Eurythmics. Sweet dreams indeed. She hummed a little Mellencamp to counteract the effect and regain control.

Astbury nodded in appreciation. "The perfect counter, of course. So I switch to punk, and you respond with country, and we go 'round and 'round. Therein lies the problem, Cora. Sonics are just a big game of rock-paper-scissors and any rabble with a modestly trained necro can stand against the Empire. But if I do this," he played a familiar passage that made her go limp, "what then, eh? You understand?"

"Bite me," Cora said and immediately regretted it. The hunger had returned and her stomach rumbled as she watched Astbury stand and stretch. She could smell him, tantalizing as fresh-baked bread with melted butter, morning coffee, and bacon, all wrapped up in a single scent that made her dry mouth sting.

"A shame, really," Astbury said with a shake of his head. He picked up Martha's pendant and dangled it before her. "Tell me more about this. Clearly you're attuned, or at least it resonates with your system, and it's unlike anything from the Badlands, Utopia, or Paradise City. An heirloom, perhaps?" He dropped the pendant into a glass dish at her silence. "No matter. When the change takes you, I'll just extract the information from your memories."

Cora's laugh disintegrated into a coughing fit. "Deaders don't talk."

Astbury perked up. "Do they not? You should know better, Cora, given where I found you."

"Twisted Bluff? I'm not going to tell you anything about that place."

Astbury waved the statement away. "Really, you're acting as if this is some big secret. We've known about Twisted Bluff for some time now."

She turned that over in her mind, then laughed to herself. "Your necros were ready, along with jump troops, sand crawlers, pearlstone armor. Perfectly adapted for the task, you said."

Astbury smirked. "I knew you'd get there."

"How'd you get the pearlstone to resonate?"

Astbury laid a finger aside his nose. "Trade secret."

"Those thopters and airship weren't the brightest idea."

Astbury's smile faded. "I told them it was moronic, and as usual, I was right. But despite all that and the Imperial reputation for inefficiency and ham-handedness, the Prime's reforms I suggested have borne fruit."

"And Prime? Is that what the emperor is calling himself these days?"

"It was the shedding of the last vestments of the caliphate. People need to be brought slowly to new ideas if they're to change at all." He grinned at her. "Most people, that is."

"Seems like a lot of work just to get your hands on a few hundred deaders. The Empire's shortage must be worse than I thought."

"You would think so, wouldn't you? All these armored boxes punching through the Wall, specialized kit, laying siege to deaders with guns and the wits to use them. Hardly seems worth it."

He peered at her expectantly with that smug smile back on his face. He wanted her to ask another question just so he could tell her the answer, the prick. She sagged against the floor and closed her eyes. It was a petty rebellion, to be sure, but it made her feel a little better. She wished she had some magical ability to just punch him in the face with telekinesis or make her eyes shoot lasers that would make his head explode. As she pictured it, her stomach gurgled and her mouth tingled.

"Suit yourself," Astbury said. "We have a long trip before us. I wonder if you'll still be altogether with us when we get there. I'd love to show you to the Prime."

"I'll be dead, Ian."

"Keep telling yourself that, if it helps. I'm just going to say 'I told you so' now since you won't appreciate it as a deader."

"I won't appreciate anything because I'll be dead!"

Astbury just smiled at her and made a note in the journal.

RATTLE, *rattle, clank, thump-thump.*

Kikuchiyo was right, this sucked. Sand and rock plinked against Skye's back and shoulders, thrown up from the gap between the crawler's middle and rear treads. His shoulders and neck ached from being wedged into a crevice between the middle and rear motors on the crawler's underside. To the left and right, driveshafts, hydraulic tubes, and rubber hoses rattled, clanked, and gurgled as the crawler trundled along. Sweat stung his eyes, and Skye carefully wiped it away, minding the spinning machinery just in front of his nose along with the sand and

146

grease coating his arm. If he lost his grip or slipped from here, odds were he'd end up as a stain on the rear treads.

Rattle, rattle, clank, thump-thump.

Two hours heading Twins knew where. And when they arrived, Skye didn't know what kind of fighting shape he would be in. With only two body positions, the cramped back or the numb left arm, he would probably emerge hunched, decrepit, and as likely to fall to a muscle spasm as a bullet once they got inside.

A ladderway ran the length of the crawler's underbelly, parallel to the driveshaft and ending at a hatch locked from the inside. Skye would have preferred waiting the journey out on the ladderway, hard, exposed, and uncomfortable as it was, but Kikuchiyo had other ideas. He directed Skye to maneuver around the whirling gears (watch your fingers and toes) and ball up into a crevice by the hydraulics leading to the crawler's right treads, while the samurai went left. Kikuchiyo did something to a hydraulic line, then closed his eyes. Skye shouted at him, but couldn't be heard over the din of the treads and the thrum of the engines.

Rattle, rattle, clank, thump-thump.

Skye tried to emulate the samurai, but couldn't. He tried entertaining himself but he was bored. Bored, cramped, and pissed. Kikuchiyo was sleeping, meditating, or whatever, and even the green fluid leaking from the lines above him onto his face didn't faze him. Anything could be happening to Cora above him and the longer they waited, the situation could only get worse.

Rattle, rattle, clank, thump-thump. Bang!

Kikuchiyo's eyes flew open and his body tensed. He held a hand out to Skye, imploring him to stay put as the ladderway shook and the new banging sound approached. A toolbox appeared, followed by a tech shining a flashlight along the hydraulic lines. Kikuchiyo swung from the crevice and contorted around to strike the tech feet-first. Kikuchiyo's feet pummeled the flailing tech's head and shoulders, and then with a final kick pushed him over the side. The man's brief scream ended with a crunch and red-tinged sand stuck to the treads. Kikuchiyo rolled out his neck and gestured for Skye to follow him.

Kikuchiyo paused at the hatch, then shimmied through in an eye blink. Skye took longer, stifling each yelp as his body pointed out where his back, hips, shoulders, and elbows were scraped, bruised, or otherwise locked in one position for too long. He crawled over the unconscious body of another tech and Kikuchiyo offered a hand up. He clasped it and Kikuchiyo pulled him through as if he weighed nothing at all.

They were in a small room filled with dials and knobs. One dial labeled ENGINE 3 RETURN read lower than the others and a yellow light blinked above it.

"Your doing?" Skye asked Kikuchiyo.

"Slow leak, serious enough to require attention but not raise suspicion."

"What is your plan?"

"You had all this time to think of one, and you're asking me?" Kikuchiyo shook his head. "I was content to stay within Twisted Bluff, but you convinced me otherwise. This is your rescue."

Skye's cheeks puffed as he let out a long breath. "All right. Someone's going to notice these guys missing soon, so we don't have a lot of time. We find Cora, steal a runabout, and bug out." Simple. He liked simple plans.

Kikuchiyo sucked his tooth. "Thin plan."

"You got a better one?

"Sabotage the engines, kill everyone in sight."

"And when they start shooting?"

"Bullets never bothered me."

"You mean they never used to. Let's try stealth for a change. Less samurai, more ninja."

Kikuchiyo shrugged and picked up a wrench.

Cora's eyes opened as the hatchway creaked open. Had she fallen asleep, or lost consciousness? Did it matter anymore? She pulled at her shirt and found gray skin now covered her torso. She imagined dark root-like tendrils underneath the skin tickling at her heart. Not long now. Astbury had sent in two soldiers, one who flinched at the sight of her, the other locking the hatch and standing to the side. She wanted to say something pithy, maybe hiss at them and see what happened. The startled guard removed his helmet to reveal Skye's ashen face.

"Cora," he said. "Can you move? We're getting you out of here."

What a beautiful idiot. "You shouldn't have come." Skye began unlatching the cell door and his scent hit her. Cora's mouth watered and something stirred within her. "Stop," she said.

Skye opened the door, and before she could stop herself, she lunged at him. Her teeth clacked against his armored forearm and slid down to the thinner covering around the wrist. Skye tried pushing her away, but she latched on and gnawed at his wrist. Skye struggled, then stumbled back as he broke her hold, eyes wide and breath fluttering. Like prey. She surged against the restraints once more, then sagged with legs too wobbly to stand.

"Sorry," she whispered. "Did I hurt you?"

Skye pulled off his armored glove and wiggled his skeleton hand. "I've always been lucky," he said with a smile. "Is there any hope?"

"I don't know. There's my pendant from the maze, but maybe it's too late."

"Could it hurt to try?"

Could it? Or would it be better to just end it now?

"I don't know. Moot anyway. Astbury has it."

"Do you know where he is?"

The hatch clicked. A speaker squawked. "Oh, don't worry, Captain Skye. We'll meet shortly."

Footsteps clanged outside the hatch. Kikuchiyo cracked his neck and set himself next to the hatchway. Skye drew his gun and took cover behind a lab table.

"That won't be necessary, Captain Skye. I'm actually impressed you're still functioning," said the voice.

Skye blinked, then searched the walls. "Gas!" He readied his gun. "Crack it," he said to Kikuchiyo.

Kikuchiyo set himself before the lock wheel and heaved, but it wouldn't budge. He heaved again and Skye joined him, but no luck. Skye's head dropped and the rest of him followed soon afterwards, slumping to the floor. Kikuchiyo's face turned red, then blue. Minutes went by, but the door did not open, and finally Kikuchiyo gasped. He fell to his knees before the hatchway, eyes squeezed shut and bloodstained wrench in hand.

Cora smelled nothing, didn't feel any weaker or more tired than before. Why didn't the gas affect her?

Kikuchiyo toppled over sideways and let out a long breath. After a few seconds, the lock wheel spun and a full squad entered and cuffed the unconscious men. Astbury strode in wearing a respirator mask and spent a moment with hands on hips as he surveyed the lab.

"Make sure they're disarmed and bring them over to the *Highlander*," he said. "Prime will want to see the Blood Weeper right away. Pretty boy can go into containment along with the deader."

She was about to protest that she wasn't a deader and realized she had no air in her lungs. In fact, she hadn't breathed in quite some time. Her chest rose and fell out of habit, but little if any air entered or left her. The gas didn't affect her because she didn't need to breathe. She was already dead.

19

They strapped her on a dolly and moved her with the others onto the emperor's craft. She had caught only a glimpse of the dreadnaught's armed and armored exterior, a war machine dwarfing the nearby sandcrawlers and whose engines rumbled with the arrogance of untapped power. Inside the hallways, crewmen and troopers moved with purpose, and although saluting as Astbury passed, seemed more concerned with their own business than appeasing his ego.

They took Cora to a new laboratory and left her in a cell next door to the unconscious Skye. He lay tied to the bunk, bloodied from the beating he had taken after the gas had cleared. It hadn't seemed personal, more like an assigned chore carried out with indifference. Their batons rose and fell, no questions asked, no reasons given. It made no sense. The same had not happened to Kikuchiyo, who was thrown in a cage with thick bars and rolled away under heavy guard.

Would she trade places with either of them? She couldn't feel her hands or feet now. Light and sound dimmed; no hunger, no pain, no sensation at all. She was trapped, awaiting the end.

Whether by unfortunate coincidence or cruel design, a mirror on the far wall showed her perfectly. The thing in the mirror hung slack in its restraints, as if it couldn't stand on its own. It wore her clothes and had the same general features, it moved as she moved, but it wasn't her. Its skin was ashy and gray, long dark hair falling out in patches and eyes too mindless and hungry, glassy and unfocused.

No, she wouldn't trade places with Skye or Kikuchiyo. This would be too cruel a fate to lay on them.

Astbury stormed into the lab, muttering under his breath. He ignored Cora and stood before Skye's cell with folded arms, still muttering for several minutes before he shook his head and, with a clap of the hands and a deep exhale, relaxed and pulled Martha's pendant from a jacket pocket.

He strode over to Cora's cell and tapped the pendant against its door. "Still with us, Cora?"

Her head rocked on her neck and talking seemed like too much work, so she tapped her finger against the wall twice.

"Good."

She pointed at Skye and waggled her finger from side to side.

"I know, it wasn't my idea, you realize, but something Prime wanted done. I believe in finishing the experiment at hand before jumping into new protocols, but Prime wants quick results so there you go. Now about this token."

Cora rolled her eyes.

"I think I've gotten all I can from its study, and I believe it's time for a live test, so to speak. Or at least Prime does. Have you ever worked with someone like that? I mean, I can't complain too much, he's usually so patient, but we are in a bit of a crunch, Cora, and the time for patience is over." He bounced the pendant in his palm. "From what I have divined, this device resonates with necrotic flesh and is highly attuned to you. It's not too far a leap to conclude it's meant for you. So, we're going to try it out and see what it does."

"Too late," she said.

"I'm uncertain if it's willful delusion or you truly can't see it?" Astbury took the mirror from the wall and brought it closer. "Here you go. You tell me, Pierson. Is the subject still human?"

The image blurred.

"What do you think?" Astbury asked. "You believe it's too late, but I assure you there's still time. I would stake any amount you'd care to name that your crossover isn't for another thirty minutes. So, with that in mind..." He opened the cell and approached. Cora tried to hurl herself at him but managed only a weak lurch.

"Refuse," she said as he easily leaned back from her attack.

"Now, now, this is for science." Astbury held the necklace out and the pendant hummed as he brought it closer. Cora strained, but her body barely quivered as he placed it around her neck and re-latched her cell. The pendant warmed her numb chest and music filled her ears, a melody unlike the one it played in the labyrinth or any other she had encountered before, yet felt as if she had always known it. She formed the first sound in the back of her throat and forced air from her lungs. The note came out in a whisper and the pendant responded and began sending hair-fine tendrils through her skin, like the monoliths in the labyrinth. Within the pendant, a switch turned on.

No! She caught herself just in time and flipped the switch off, bearing the ache as the pendant retracted its tendrils.

And Astbury hadn't noticed! He stared at her for several minutes as the pendant cooled before shaking his head in disgust. She savored what she suspected were her last moments of joy, even if they came from a petty place.

"Maybe you are too far gone, Cora. How you disappoint me." A buzzer sounded, and Astbury held up a finger. "Hold that thought." He picked up a nearby handset and carried out a quick conversation ending with "Yes, Prime." He hung up and began gathering his notebook and papers. "Where were we?"

"Going to kill you," Cora said.

Astbury knelt at the cell door and nodded. "I'm sure you think so, but you're quite too far gone to follow through. The curse will hit your brain and that will be that. I'd slow it down, but there's so much on my plate right now. I suppose this is goodbye, Cora Pierson. You've been a fascinating subject. I'll make sure they put your body to good use, powering the Prime's new war machine, perhaps? It would be such a letdown to be relegated to an auxiliary system or backup generator. Though I should warn you that where we're going, we may have no further use for deaders. When your service is complete, I'll end it quickly." He left the mirror propped on the workbench before leaving.

In the mirror, Skye twitched, and the movement set off the curse within her. Without thinking, she brought her wrist to her mouth. The cuff's leather was sour and her teeth kept slipping off its slick finish. She went slow, pressing canines together, and leather yielded millimeter by millimeter as her mouth filled with the leather's acrid tang that also was oddly comforting. She ripped at it, teeth slipping and clacking together, and she tried again. And again. Before long, she gnawed a morsel free. Hunger hit her with a pick axe to the gut. She forced herself to spit the leather out, the tiniest bit of wet brown no bigger than a grain of rice, but still so tantalizing.

The thing in the mirror had drool stringing from blackened lips, crazed yellow eyes, a pink tongue turning black at the edges. Its mouth latched back onto the cuff and gnawed like a wild deader caught in a trap. The curse's hunger was in control now, and she could only watch, locked away in her own head.

Redeemer help me, I've been a complete ass. Redeemer take mercy on me and get me the hell out of here. Redeemer forgive me, I couldn't help myself.

There was no divine response, and she hadn't expected one. Her own grandmother had known the Redeemer, witnessed one of her miracles, though hadn't elaborated no matter how much Cora begged. When Grandma Tee lay on her deathbed, she prayed for the Redeemer's forgiveness with tears in her eyes. "Of course she forgives you," Cora said.

Grandma Tee shook her head. "She forgave her brother, but she didn't forgive the rest of us. She left us here, child, as punishment."

"Then why pray?"

"There's always the chance she'll change her mind."

Grandma Tee died the next day, and they lit her pyre within the hour. The enclave didn't take chances with the dead.

Cora's chest itched. She looked down at her chest, pendant swinging free and leaving an oval of smooth healthy skin already shrinking as the necrosis retook lost territory. Was there still time?

Her deader self pulled another leather chunk free and chewed. The pendant swung back and lay against her breastbone.

This will not be fun.

Old Martha had said as much. She reached within and turned the pendant on, surrendering to the song and singing along with a raspy voice. The tingling started immediately, and from the pendant's edges flaking gray skin changed to a smooth warm sepia. Then the tingling became a burning, a fire front spreading through her at a snail's pace. The song within grew and seized control. It changed keys, and her flesh twisted. She writhed in the restraints and clenched her jaw shut.

She would not scream.

She would not scream.

20

———————

Skye opened his eyes and immediately shut them. Damn, what had he been drinking the night before? Dry mouth, aching joints, and he hurt all over. And how many kinds of stupid was he to have left the lights on? If the noncoms saw lights on in his bedroom, they might come knocking and expect him to do stuff, and he was not up to doing anything, let alone stuff.

He ran a dry tongue around to clear the cotton mouth, and tasted blood. A fight as well. Had he won? The fog in his brain refused to clear. Not a good sign. He had probably lost.

Some sick bastard was singing. He tried rolling over and couldn't. After some experimentation, he determined he was tied to the bed and not in the good way. Someone must have had taken him home from the pub and pranked him. Hopefully, it was just the tying up and no drawing on the face. He cracked open his eyelids a sliver and endured the spike to the brain as he adjusted to the light. After a few seconds he risked opening up a bit more and was oddly grateful for the tears taking the edge off the light and soothing his dried-out eyeballs. The tears pooled, then trickled into his ears.

"Gah!" He shook his head and almost puked as his vision swam. He took it slow and tried again. Metal walls, bucket toilet, and a mirror showing the deader in the cell next door. The fog instantly cleared, and he remembered. He had let her down.

"Damn."

Cora twitched in her restraints and sang? He had seen plenty of deaders before and even the neo-dead at Twisted Bluff hadn't bothered him any, but seeing Cora like this gutted him. A feverish wave swept through him, leaving nausea and cold sweat behind. He had failed her, and this was his punishment. Thank goodness he couldn't see her face; he didn't think he could bear it.

You just had to get involved.

But he had done the right thing for once, hadn't he?

Lot of good it did you too.

He winced and looked away. It was a small comfort to be the good guy for once. He didn't know if he ever would again, even if he somehow made it out of this, which didn't seem likely.

Cora's hoarse cry cut through his thoughts.

"Cora?" he said, not really expecting a response.

"Ow," she said.

After a moment he asked, "You okay?"

"No. You?"

"No."

"Well, all right, then."

"Sorry I couldn't get to you sooner," he said, the words spilling out. "They didn't tell me about you until way after the battle, then there was Kikuchiyo, and I…"

She looked up. Gone was Cora's dried skin and hollowed eye sockets. Her face had regained its withered flesh, restored to wide cheekbones, full lips, and sculpted eyebrows over arresting brown eyes. Her skin glowed under the lights like smoked topaz and she ran fingers through dark curly hair which fluffed out like a cloud behind her. She gave him a confused look before her gaze shifted to the mirror and her breath caught. She pressed fingers against her face, then to the hollow of her neck. She pushed aside her pendant and traced out an egg-shaped patch of gray scar tissue. She pressed two fingers to her neck, then reached into her shirt to press over her left breast.

"I'm dead," she murmured. "No heartbeat. Deader."

"Neo-dead, though not an Eddie, skin job, or bone girl. You're more like Queen Beatrice."

"I've been so stupid."

Skye jerked at the restraints a few times. "Welcome to the club. We meet every other Tuesday. Bring donuts."

She smiled with porcelain-white teeth and shook her head. "You'll get cookies and you'll like them."

"Where's Kikuchiyo?" he asked.

"If I had to guess? With Astbury's boss."

It took him a moment to process it. "Oh shit."

She nodded. "Quite."

21

———————

A highway at night. High-beams stabbing the sky behind the hill. Jagged gravel points poking at the soles of his high-top sneakers. Headlights crest the hill, throwing his shadow over the highway, a highway littered with bloody high-top sneakers just like the ones he's wearing. The light is blinding and the bumper kisses him. He tumbles through the air.

He coughs blood and knows what comes next. It's not fair.

An awakening. A red mist descending over his eyes and with it, the rage.

The rage makes him strong, invincible. It eats him from the inside, but there will be no rest until the anger leaves him.

"This is what you must do," says the Creator's voice, "if you want the rest again."

When the killing is over, the red mist leaves and the Blood Weeper can sleep. Until the rage wakes him again.

Kikuchiyo awoke in a cage. Guards in their faceless armor surrounded him with weapons drawn. One stepped away and opened a door, speaking with someone outside. More guards entered, encased in blood-red armor and moving with the economy of worthy opponents. They formed up around the cage and pushed long handles built into the sides, maneuvering the cage while remaining out of reach. A squad fanned out ahead and behind them as they moved into a large room appointed with velvet banners, lacquered wood side tables, and a long ruby-red carpet leading to Astbury standing behind a man seated on a low golden throne.

The man had tea-dark skin and curly hair, with a handsome face framed by a short sharp-trimmed beard and dressed in an elegantly simple outfit of black pants and a white-collared shirt. He twirled a lock of hair and smiled at something Astbury said, revealing perfect teeth.

Kikuchiyo remembered the man preferring suits with metallic threads to better match his favored weapon, a nickel-plated automatic, though that had been on board the Caliphate of the Clouds. This man had been the Caliph's majordomo, running more and more of the caliphate's daily operations as the Caliph sunk into the pleasures of the flesh. He waved the guards to the side and leaned forward on the throne to regard Kikuchiyo with a smile.

"Ah, the Blood Weeper awakens," he said.

"Majordomo," Kikuchiyo said. Astbury stiffened and one of the red guards pushed a cattle prod through the bars and sent an electric sting into his lower back. He breathed through the pain and pushed the rage down as his back spasmed. Control. He would stay in control.

The emperor gestured, and the guards stood back. "You may address me as 'Prime,' Blood Weeper."

"Just Kikuchiyo," he replied, and after a moment added, "Brother."

Prime inclined his head and nodded. "Fair enough. I would like to talk to you about all I've experienced since our last meeting."

"Then talk. I cannot do else but listen," Kikuchiyo said, glancing at the surrounding bars.

"Ah, yes. That does put a dampener on things. Tell me, Kikuchiyo, is your honor intact?"

He would dare question? Kikuchiyo managed a tight nod.

"Then swear upon it, and I will release you. Swear no violence or attempt to escape, and it will be so."

A ripple ran through the guards. Astbury blanched and leaned closer to Prime. "Eminence, Blood Weeper or not, his capacity for violence is undiminished. He cut through squads of your loyal soldiers at Twisted Bluff, and I only caught him with a carefully prepared trap. Getting him out of the cage is easy, putting him back in will be more than difficult."

Prime gently pushed Astbury away. "I wouldn't expect you to understand, doctor." He turned to Kikuchiyo and waited with a smile tugging at the corners of his mouth.

Kikuchiyo's face burned, and he bowed his head both in sincerity and to hide his shame. "I pledge upon my honor that I will not harm or attempt to escape this day."

"And tomorrow?"

"We will see."

Prime nodded at his guards, and one unlocked the cage. The guards held weapons at the ready as he emerged. They were ready for violence, perhaps even dangerous, but his mind already had a plan to take them all down. He fixed each in turn with a cold stare before dismissing them from his thoughts.

"Leave us," Prime said.

"Eminence!" Astbury said.

"Now," Prime said with a coldness promising no mercy.

When the room cleared, Prime slumped back in his throne and threw a leg over the armrest.

"Thank God they're gone. It's so tedious, isn't it?"

Kikuchiyo shrugged.

Prime rose from his throne and gestured for Kikuchiyo to join him at the window. They moved through rocky terrain, the purple-dark sky of the Dreaming Desert yet overhead. Sandcrawlers by the dozen surrounded the Prime's mobile palace, which was itself several times wider than its escorts. Where the crawlers were simple boxy affairs, the Prime's crawler was akin to an armored catamaran with treads set out wide from the main body on stout bracing. Kikuchiyo's gaze ran along the armor's slope to cannon emplacements, machine gun blisters, anti-air electros, ornithopter catapults, and stowed airship mooring towers ready to be erected in a moment's notice. Runabouts swarmed like a shoal of fish.

"Impressive, isn't it?" Prime said.

"I had not known the Caliphate capable of producing so much."

"Oh, I beggared the economy and still had to scrounge for resources, but it's amazing what one can accomplish with a tireless workforce and a bit of imagination." Prime tapped his head. "In a way, you were my inspiration."

"Indeed." A lighting flash gave him a glimpse of the dreadnaught's main batteries, larger versions of those mounted on the sandcrawlers and paired in turrets behind a chiseled prow. The darkness returned, leaving only clawed shadows.

"This land, Kikuchiyo, is a fertile ground of ideas made manifest. The Creator squandered his time here trying to create a safe womb and only churned out a handful of failed utopias. I thought to myself if someone as weak-willed as the Creator could bring entire societies into being with a thought, could I not create a few paltry toys?"

Kikuchiyo took in the crawlers, the runabouts, the soldiers in armor negating the Wall's psychedelic effects, an army with equipment tailor-made for this place. When the Caliphate had defeated Paradise City through sheer numbers and heavy losses, it barely had the resources left to occupy its new territory. This army should have taken a generation to build, not a few years. Then he remembered the deader farm, Motorhead stripped of its metals, and he sensed the scale of the Empire's cannibalization, and the mind behind it.

"I had thought Ryan's avatar of ambition dead."

"Ah, Chevket. A useful tool, but always distracted by the carrot at the end of the stick."

"And you are different?"

Prime's face broke into a wide smile. "I am industry, freed from the mismanagement of a fat lecher and the unconscious desires of a man-child with a god complex. When I felt his soul depart, I rejoiced. I consolidated, sacrificed, and rebuilt the Empire into a more perfect form."

"For what purpose?"

"You will learn, Kikuchiyo. For now, it is enough to break free from this prison the Creator made for us. The world is ours again and we have the freedom to forge our own destiny. You are the embodiment of combat and slaughter, imbued with fighting techniques unparalleled in this forsaken reality, but is that what you want?

"We were all delegated jobs, whether we knew it or not. Yours was removing obstacles and enforcing his will. The Caliph let him indulge in those sybaritic taboos he could not openly enjoy even as supreme ruler. I kept it all running. But I ask you, was that fair? Who's ultimately responsible for this mess?"

"Ryan." The name was sour on his tongue.

"That's the bastard." Prime paced, gesticulating. "He made this place his little fantasy world, building it without thinking it through, and never cleaned up after himself. We leaked out. We're mental leakage, brother, emotional garbage he couldn't deal with. No wonder the Caliph got fat and whored around at the end. When Ryan lost focus, so did we. That's why we're dying. This land doesn't need us because it only existed to serve *him*. Without his will, this place is doomed."

"The people have survived without him or Jasmine," Kikuchiyo said.

Prime snorted. "That bitch. She could have fixed this all, but she left us to suffer."

"Emotions without souls."

Prime cocked an eyebrow. "Think so?"

"It must be so. When Ryan left, I felt it here." Kikuchiyo tapped his breastbone. "I am hollow. My swords died. Joyless metal."

Prime held up a finger. "What if I told you that you were wrong? That you could have it all back?" He went to his throne and opened a chest behind it. When he turned around, he held Kikuchiyo's *daisho*, the long and the short swords, in each hand. Kikuchiyo sucked in a breath as Prime held the swords out to him. "We can reclaim everything we lost and gain so much more."

Kikuchiyo set the swords in his sash, letting their familiar weight settle at his hip. Prime grinned and didn't flinch when Kikuchiyo pulled the katana from its sheath and let the room's light play over the waves of its tempered edge, the *hamon*. "I wonder at why you would need me at all, given what you have accomplished so far. You have your army, your velvet-lined war machines. What need have you for my swords? It would be easier for you to kill me."

Prime turned away and waved a hand. "I welcome your swords, but don't need them; I need what's in your head. Someone else who knows what the Creator knew. I can create all the machines, weapons, buildings, and tools one could ever want and more, but I cannot replicate memories.

"There's all these things in my head I know but can't share. I make a joke, or quote a movie line, and everyone just nods and smiles, but it's not genuine. Sometimes I just wait for someone to get it." He dropped his voice into a monotone. "Anyone... anyone..." He raised an expectant eyebrow.

"Bueller?" Kikuchiyo said.

Prime raised his arms to the ceiling. "Thank you! Yes!" He took a healthy swig from a nearby goblet and set it down with a crash. "What we hold in our heads is unique in the Badlands. When we are gone, it will leave with us. But it's all bullshit, isn't it? This stuff we inherited from him that no one else knows. But where did he learn it all from, eh? Who created the Creator?"

Ah. That is his plan.

Prime slowly nodded. "You see it too." Prime reached out and Kikuchiyo allowed him to grip his shoulder. "You called me brother. Did you mean it?"

"Such a thing is not possible," Kikuchiyo said.

"Say it was."

"What about my companions?"

"Free to go as soon as we get there."

Kikuchiyo said, "I must think on this."

"What is there to think over? Are you not your own man?"

"There is honor."

Prime balled a fist at his side. "You mean a naïve mentality meant to make you a better assassin."

"So I've been told."

"Then set aside this false honor implanted into you and become your own *daimyo,* man!"

Kikuchiyo sheathed the katana. "*Daimyo?* No. Merely the emperor's companion."

"Better that than Astbury's latest project. You've seen what he's done with your friend."

Kikuchiyo shook his head. "With your blessing."

Prime shrugged. "If it wasn't her, it would have been someone else. I made him the perfect researcher, and the investment paid off a thousand-fold. I'm willing to invest the same in you for both our benefits. Your swords can live again!"

Kikuchiyo's thumb traced the silk cording along the katana's hilt. The swords that once sang with joy as they channeled the battle anger, guiding his arm to parry gunfire and separate the heads from his enemies' necks. Could dead steel truly live again? Simmering anger trickled from his core and tried connecting with the weapon to make it sing again. It wasn't enough. It would take more, much more to replace what Ryan had taken away and make them live again. More anger, more blood, more souls than the Badlands could ever provide. He didn't doubt Prime, the former majordomo, would supply all that was needed.

Kikuchiyo spat. "I am a wicked man no longer."

Prime's mouth worked, and his hand flexed from palm to fist. "You who have spilled so much blood, killed thousands. The weak and innocent included. You dare judge me." Prime swung and Kikuchiyo allowed the slap across his face. He accepted the second and then the third even as the rage within threatened to boil over.

I must not fade.

Kikuchiyo stepped back and pulled the *daisho* from his sash, then gently put them down and sat in the cage. "We are finished, brother. It is a new day and when next we meet, I will take your head."

Prime strode to the cage, slammed the door shut, and shot the latch closed. "This is our last meeting, Blood Weeper, and as you can see, my head is exactly where it is supposed to be." He shouted for his guards, who wheeled him away. Kikuchiyo kept his eyes fixed on the Prime as he flopped on his throne and drained the last of his drink. As the doors closed, Kikuchiyo spared one last glance at his swords.

"Is this wise, Prime?" Astbury said. He cast a wary glance at the samurai being wheeled away, sitting placidly in his cage with eyes closed in meditation.

"I am the seat of wisdom here. It is for me to say and you to implement." Prime swirled and sniffed at his wine before taking a sip and grimacing. "The sooner we're out of this accursed machine, the better. The rust is already settling in, making every breath like sucking on a bad penny."

"Penny, your celestialness?"

Prime waved a hand. "You wouldn't understand the reference."

That Astbury did, or thought he did, he kept to himself. A penny was a coin made of copper, of that he was certain. He couldn't place its worth, but he was certain it wasn't much. Like so many of Prime's references lately, they only stirred half-remembered truths, like details from a dream. But the Prime demanded focus, not woolgathering. "I'm not certain it can be done, Prime," Astbury said.

"And I'm not certain I appreciate your attitude," Prime said. "Of all the tasks you've done without hesitation, I fail to see why this is any different."

Astbury twisted the brim of his cavalry hat and swallowed. "It is not the task itself, Prime, but the timetable. Installing such a system is a delicate operation, even under ideal circumstances. Would it not be better to delay one until we finish the other?"

Prime placed a hand on Astbury's shoulder. "You are my valued vassal," he said and squeezed, digging a thumb under Astbury's collarbone. "But you are not irreplaceable. You will do it. You will do it now."

Astbury hissed through his teeth. "Yes, Prime. It will be done."

"Excellent. See to it, then."

Astbury touched his forehead to the floor and left the throne room, reluctantly turning for the machine bay instead of his lab.

22

———————

The red-armored troopers brought Kikuchiyo's cage into the lab and maneuvered it into a second cell like a nesting doll, which seemed like paranoid overkill to Cora. The squad left, save one with "Horkins" stenciled on his chest plate who posted himself beside the door. When the clomping boots faded down the passageway, Horkins relaxed and locked the hatch, sparing a moment's glance at the other cells before heading over to Kikuchiyo's. He removed his helmet and rubbed fingers through his buzz-cut as he studied Kikuchiyo through the bars.

"So you're the big bad, huh? You don't look all that tough to me. Kinda scrawny, actually." Cora didn't think the kid was any specimen himself, though her younger, stupider self might have disagreed.

Kikuchiyo didn't respond and kept meditating.

"Oh, all mysterious, aren't you?"

Skye let out a slow breath and shook his head. "Son, you'd best go back to your post."

Horkins produced a knife and spun it in his hand before pointing it at Skye. "And I'd suggest you shut it, meat. How'd you like me to carve my name on the arch of your foot?" He turned back to Kikuchiyo. "Or how about you, Blood Weeper? The doc's gonna turn you deader too. Ain't that funny?"

Kikuchiyo let out a deep breath, but didn't open his eyes.

"Wanna know what it's like to be a deader? Here, I'll show you."

Horkins went to a rack and picked out a long metal rod with an insulated handle. He pressed his thumb to a button, and static crackled. "This is how we'll keep you in line when you're a walking battery. Has a nice pop to it, enough to get even the dumbest deader's attention." He jammed the button again and tiny blue lightnings danced along the tip.

"You don't want to do that, son," Skye said. Horkins ignored him and jammed the rod into Kikuchiyo's cage. The prod's tip discharged and Kikuchiyo's meditating form jerked. Kikuchiyo tumbled and his eyes opened. Horkins yanked the prod back, then with a tight grin thrust it back and delivered another series of shocks.

"Astbury's not the kind to let something like this slide," Cora said.

Horkins threw a glance her way with a faint grin. Kikuchiyo crawled closer to Horkins and stared balefully.

"Away from the cage, meat!" Horkins said, and thrust the prod into Kikuchiyo's stomach. Kikuchiyo shuddered and spasmed, but Horkins didn't let up. Kikuchiyo's form faded and his ghostly self fell through both sets of bars, regaining solidity on the deck.

Horkins gaped for a moment, then jabbed the prod forward. Electricity popped as Kikuchiyo jerked, then he grabbed the prod's end with one hand and pulled himself to his feet. Horkins cocked a fist, but Kikuchiyo's arm darted out quick as an adder and latched around Horkins's throat. The prod flew into the air as Horkins went over Kikuchiyo's hip and crashed to the deck with a sickening crunch. Kikuchiyo stood while Horkins remained on the floor, staring at the ceiling as blood pooled around his head. Kikuchiyo swayed and caught his balance against a lab table. He drifted in and out of existence and then with a grunt, solidified.

"You're not well," Cora said as he opened the cells.

"I lost control." Kikuchiyo nodded at a chemical locker. "Open that, if you would."

She rattled the locker's handles and frowned at the lock.

"We'll need to find the key," Skye said.

"Don't bother." Cora opened a drawer and took out Astbury's miniature tool set. "Shame to ruin precision instruments like this, but..." She selected two fine-tipped instruments and jammed them into the lock. After a few seconds tapping around, she twisted and the lock clicked. She opened the double doors and scanned rows of chemical labels. "What am I looking for?"

"It calls to me," Kikuchiyo said. "Bottom shelf."

She handed a worn belted pouch to Kikuchiyo, who opened it and cried out in anguish.

"What is it?" she asked.

He brought forth a vial half-filled with blood. "This is all that is left. The others are all gone."

"Other what?" Skye asked.

"She left them for me, almost a dozen," Kikuchiyo said. "Another failure."

"Redeemer," Cora whispered. "Is it really godsblood?"

"Bullshit," Skye said.

"Not bullshit," Kikuchiyo said. "Not entirely."

Cora wanted to take the vial from Kikuchiyo's hand. Imagine her, a 'claver girl, holding a piece of divinity. "Astbury must have taken them."

Kikuchiyo popped the top on the vial and downed its contents. He inhaled a sharp breath and color returned to his face.

"Better?" Cora asked.

Kikuchiyo nodded. "For now. Hold out your hand." Cora did so, and he shook out the last drop onto her fingertips. Warmth flowed through her as her stone flesh drank, softening to living tissue once again. The change lasted only moments before the blood vanished and her flesh slowly hardened. The heat in her veins left her better than energized; she could lift any weight, win any race, meet any challenge.

The blood of the goddess flows in me.

Kikuchiyo said, "We move."

"Not without our kit," Cora said, gathering up her hair and tying it out of her way. It had never been this thick before, she thought.

Skye nodded. "Agreed. Does us no good to escape if we die crossing the desert."

She gave her head a shake, satisfied her hair would stay out of her face. "It's going to be a bitch getting transportation. Any ideas?"

Kikuchiyo nodded. "An army prepares, drawing on lessons learned in its last battle. History lets us learn from our mistakes, if we have but the wisdom to see its true lesson. Come."

"Come where?"

Kikuchiyo selected several items from the cabinet. "Let us test what I suspect will be Prime's first-rate fire-suppression systems."

~

CORA COULDN'T STAND sloppy design. More so when some jackass couldn't see the design problems, made it standard, and propagated it throughout the fleet. The only thing worse would be for a conquering empire to blindly copy standard tech, assuming its superiority. From such cascades, massive failures were inevitable.

Whatever this war machine looked like on the outside, it used Paradise City's technology, which included design flaws like routing the primary control system wiring and the secondary in side-by-side conduits. The learned designers were late discovering the standardized flaw, and realized changing the standard would run afoul the cantankerous brigadier who wrote it, the same brigadier who wrote their promotion board evaluations. If one wanted to keep their career prospects alive, one went along with the standard. It was a minor flaw, anyway. Hardly worth the expense to change across the fleet. Yes, sir.

All to say that sabotage hadn't been high on the list of design considerations when developing the wiring standard. Cora picked out two conduits on the ceiling and followed them to a point where they almost touched. She brought out a piece of chalk and stepped into Skye's laced fingers to get a boost up. She marked each conduit with an X and dropped to the deck.

"You sure this will work?" Skye said, grunting as he gave Kikuchiyo a boost. "We're going to look stupid if we just knock out the air conditioning."

"If you think I spent hundreds of hours in the classroom and countless more skinning my knuckles on airships to get second-guessed by a gun monkey, you're sorely mistaken."

Skye rolled his eyes and took in deep breaths as his legs began quivering. Kikuchiyo took almost another minute before actinic light flared overhead. He dropped, and they ran back around the corner as Kikuchiyo's handiwork began hissing and glowing metal dripped from the ceiling. An alarm sounded and fire-suppressing foam began spraying moments before something rumbled deep within the cruiser's bowels and the lights went out. The whole vessel came to a shuddering halt and several seconds passed before emergency lights flickered back on and alarms resumed.

Around the corner, the hallway was a mess of soot, foam, and slag and her nostrils were filled with the stench of burnt metal. The severed conduits still sizzled and glowed, as did a hole in the decking below, but the edges were already greying as foam suppressant sputtered from the ceiling.

"Thermite is a wonderful thing," Skye said.

Cora smiled. "Yeah, and power plants don't like being suddenly stopped under a load. Probably broke something big. Okay, we're on the clock, gentlemen. When they see this, they'll come looking for us."

"This way," Kikuchiyo said, and took off running.

THE THRONE ROOM WAS EMPTY. Cora and Skye secured the doors, though they wouldn't hold for long if someone came knocking. Kikuchiyo pulled two swords from a chest and secured them through his sash. Cora and Skye found Skye's electro gun in an attached antechamber, but no sign of the missing blood vials. A second door in the antechamber revealed a ladder leading to an armored hatch.

"Any other ideas?" she asked. "We don't have time to search everywhere."

"The armory," Skye said.

"Personal chambers," said Cora.

Muffled shouting came from the other side of the throne room doors. They rocked but held as guards crashed into them.

"No time," Kikuchiyo said.

"But—"

The doors rocked on their hinges again and split a hand's-breadth apart. Something flew through the gap and landed on the floor.

"Grenade!" Kikuchiyo pushed Cora and Skye to the floor and the air cracked with a flash. Cora blinked at the smoke and her ears rang. She searched for targets but only caught glimpses of Skye blind-firing his electro gun into the smoke.

"Get back," Skye shouted, pointing to the antechamber.

"What about Kikuchiyo?"

Gunshots erupted at the throne room's entrance, followed by several screams. Kikuchiyo swept through the attacking squad with a sword in each hand, twisting and contorting his body as he dodged fire from one trooper and sent a sword tip slipping in the armor seam of another. As scary as he had been before, sword-wielding Kikuchiyo was Destruction's avatar. A trooper's head fell and Kikuchiyo rolled under the burst from another, the sword's edge reaching out in passing and severing the man's foot. The trooper fell onto Kikuchiyo's other sword as it pierced the armor's gap between the waist and chest plate.

The dying trooper fired a long burst and Kikuchiyo brought a free sword around to bat the gun away a fraction too late. The bullet took him through the abdomen and he doubled over. Cora rushed to him and added her hand to his as they both pressed against the wound.

"Stand up. More are coming," she said. "Skye, get that hatch open up top!"

She helped Kikuchiyo back to his feet and put her shoulder under his. More shouting echoed down the corridor, and bullets passed through the air behind them. She left Kikuchiyo leaning against the wall and picked up a fallen gun and sent a blind burst around the corner.

"Can you make it up the ladder?" Cora asked.

Kikuchiyo sheathed one sword and pointed at the other lying at her feet. She sent another burst around the corner before stooping and retrieving it for him.

"I can make it," he said.

Something hissed behind her and thunked to the floor. The grenade spewed a blue-white smoke that sent Kikuchiyo into labored coughing. Red seeped between his fingers with every convulsion.

Gas, then. They must still want them alive; too bad she was already

dead. She kicked the grenade back into the passage and grabbed
Kikuchiyo, who slumped into her with all his weight. Skye shouted at her
from the antechamber and latched the door behind them as she brought
Kikuchiyo through.

"The ladder leads to a thopter pad on the roof."

"Help me with him first," she said.

Skye laid Kikuchiyo out on the table while Cora snatched some linen
napkins and pressed them against the wound. She wrapped a folded
table runner around Kikuchiyo's torso to hold it in place.

"You go up there and make sure it's clear," she said to Skye. "I'll carry
him up."

"I'm stronger, I'll take him," Skye said.

"You're still weak."

He glanced away. "I'm fine."

"You're almost ready to collapse. What happens if it gets to be too
much halfway up?" She pointed at the ladder. "Go. Deaders never tire."

Skye turned on a heel and started up the ladder. He slipped on the
third rung and Cora pretended not to notice. Was he going to be a
problem later? Whatever, so long as he made it to the top. Embarrassed
and alive was better than heroic and dead.

The troopers crashed into the throne room and shouted orders at
each other. She grabbed Kikuchiyo in a fireman's carry and plodded to
the ladder. Her stomach fluttered. She could do this, she told herself.
Time to see if what she'd told Skye was actually true.

THE POCKET FLIGHT deck was nestled among armored gun turrets, giving
its single thopter cover from ground fire. With luck, they could jam the
hatch behind them and launch before anyone alerted the gunners. Their
sabotage had Prime's behemoth and accompanying crawlers stuck in a
narrow valley with high walls that would aid their escape once cleared.
Pursuing thopters and the low ceiling might be problems, but those could
wait.

"Hurry up!" he called down to Cora, who shouted an obscenity back.
He thought about how he could help her with the awkward load until the

first bullet whizzed overhead. He ducked and weathered the volley curled into a ball behind the ladder's tiny hatch, then rolled and snapped a shot at a trooper sneaking around a turret, trying to flank him. Skye's shots went wide but got the trooper to duck. Skye scrambled behind the thopter and took another shot, this time winging the trooper in the shoulder and sending him stumbling back behind cover.

Three shots, then reload. He didn't know if he had any reserve energy to give it; he was dog-tired. Maybe if he could dash out and grab one of their guns? He guessed Cora was just over halfway up the shaft.

Another burst went overhead, and he took aim at the trooper.

Fired.

Missed.

Two shots.

He kept his eye fixed over the sights. Where would the trooper pop out next? He guessed left.

The trooper went right and Skye dropped as bullets pinged off the thopter. Now the tables had turned, and the trooper was guessing where Skye would come out.

Damn, damn, damn.

Cora's boots clomped on the rungs and would soon poke her head into the line of fire. Skye made up his mind.

I've always been lucky.

He jerked up enough for his head to clear cover, then dived to the right and dashed left. The trooper was fast enough to track his first move but not the second and the burst passed over Skye's shoulder.

Skye didn't miss.

He helped Cora at the top with Kikuchiyo. Damn, but he forgot how heavy he was! Cora didn't seem winded, then he realized she wouldn't.

"Get him in the back. He'll have to sit on your lap," she said.

She went through a quick pre-flight as he tried maneuvering Kikuchiyo's dead weight in the cramped space. He caught movement from the corner of his eye.

"That turret's twisting our way," he said.

"I see it. I'll try avoiding it when we lift."

Skye got Kikuchiyo settled on his lap and found himself squished between the samurai and a hard seat, only an observer from here on out.

Voices echoed up the ladderway. Boots sounded on metal rungs.

The engines came to life with a banshee howl and Astbury's yellow-haired head popped up from the ladderway along with a rifle. Cora eased the stick back and grimaced as the canopy spiderwebbed around her. She thumbed the thopter's chin guns and bullets sprayed across the crawler's deck, sending Astbury diving for cover.

The turret gun boomed and its shell passed over their wing. The shockwave followed, rolling over the deck and rocking the thopter's landing gear into the deck, though the troopers got the worse end of it as they stumbled with hands over ears. She eased the throttle forward and the thopter tipped back and away. More turrets swung around from the escort crawlers on each flank, and Cora weaved from side to side in the narrow canyon. Skye, pressed down with Kikuchiyo's dead weight, could only watch twinkling small-arms fire trying to kill him as they raced for the canyon rim.

He only caught a second's glimpse, but the image etched itself in his brain. A dark mass trailed the sandcrawler formation, a sea of bodies swaying in the telltale shamble of deaders. Deaders in the hundreds, more than Skye had ever seen in one place. Enough to power fleets of airships and dozens of cities. Enough to double the population of Twisted Bluff.

The canyon walls suddenly disappeared, and they were clear. Cora leveled the thopter off and relaxed into her seat. "That was like dancing with your shoes tied together," she said over her shoulder. "What now?"

Kikuchiyo grunted. "We cannot allow him to take Twisted Bluff," he said. "He drained an empire and aimed its remains where the dreaming barrier is thinnest, and will invade from there."

"Invade what?"

"The same world that birthed the Twins and the dreamers."

"Martha called it a machine," Cora said. "He doesn't want Twisted Bluff, he wants the maze. We know it can remake deaders into neo-dead, among other things."

"He must know something else about it we don't," said Skye.

"Or Astbury does. He was quite smug about the attack. He'd need a large power source and killing the very people you need for batteries seems like a losing strategy," Cora said.

"Would a thousand deaders be enough?" Skye told her what he saw.

"Damn. So what now?" Cora asked.

Skye let out a long breath. "I guess we head back and face the music."

"You sure?" she asked.

"No, but I don't think we can run anymore."

23

Cora discovered being dead gave her an almost robot-like ability to control limbs and stay focused. No muscle jitters, fatigue, eyestrain, or bleary-fuzzy brain lock from concentrating too hard for too long. Meanwhile, Skye alternated between napping, unfocused staring through the canopy, and bitching about losing circulation and how Kikuchiyo was heavy and bony at the same time. Cora didn't envy them.

The approach to Twisted Bluff involved a delicate act of buzzing over the Imperial lines, then slowing and flashing the landing lights in a way she hoped wouldn't get them shot down. Guns tracked them from the mesa's walls, but whether it was Skye's famous luck or her own, they held their fire as she landed outside the gates. Scrabblers with welding rigs swarmed over the gate applying armor patches. Beyond the patched barrier, thumpers dragged wrecked Cadillacs and Eddies stacked sandbags, re-fortifying the road into town.

She cut the thopter's turbines and discovered death's downside as she rose from the pilot's seat and collapsed to the ground like a sack of dirt. Skye shouted her name, and she tried to tell him she was okay but her body refused to respond or make a sound.

Four skin jobs in plague doctor masks and tan dusters approached with weapons drawn. She had enough energy to move her eyeballs and watch them surround the thopter. One shouted through his mask at Skye, who struggled getting out from under Kikuchiyo. Another lifted an RPG to his shoulder.

A lone skin job emerged from the barricade, waving his arms at the others and shouting with a voice she recognized — Mortensen.

"Stand down!" The squad relaxed, the trigger-happy one reluctantly. From the shadow of a wrecked Cadillac, a mottled black-and-white shape emerged and began barking. Dog streaked towards them, overtaking the jogging Mortensen and snapping at the skin jobs as they brought down Kikuchiyo from the thopter. One skin job lashed out with a boot, making Dog leap back and snap. Skye rushed in, wrapping an arm around Dog and holding him back as the skin jobs laid the samurai on the sand.

Kikuchiyo opened an eye and reached out. Skye let Dog go and the animal came to the samurai's side and danced about, alternating between pushing his head into the samurai's outstretched hand and licking it. A pair of boots blocked the rest of the reunion, and she found Mortensen staring down at her.

"Welcome to dropping off the cliff. Here." He brought a finger-sized wood splinter from a belt pouch and placed it between her teeth. "Eat this. Dreamstuff, from one of the ships in the Bathtub."

Her body had enough strength left to work her jaw against the sun-bleached wood. It disintegrated into a smoky gunpowder-flavored paste under her teeth. Swallowing seemed more a reflex or custom than a need as her body absorbed it directly. She soon found the strength to stand and accepted another splinter from Mortensen's pouch while the squad sent for a stretcher for Kikuchiyo. Skye hobbled around in circles, windmilling his arms.

"Your body won't tell you when it's tired, so mind what you're doing and fuel accordingly. Congratulations on making the transition. You're all under arrest."

The sand fell from her stone-like skin as she rose. "Arrest? Prime himself is coming here, driving the largest mob of quasi- and wild dead you've ever seen. If you're going to throw us in a cell, fine, but hear us out first." She lowered her voice. "We need to make sure Prime stays out of the maze."

Mortensen considered for a minute, then turned to the squad. "Bring them to the queen. I'll get Haggart and meet you there."

"Thank you, Mortensen."

"The queen will decide what to do with you." He placed a hand on her arm and murmured, "Be persuasive."

THEY WERE NOT TAKEN to the throne room, but to General Haggart's map room deep within the spire's bowels. The queen sat on an industrial version of her usual throne, all gray metal and heavy cabling wrapped around lugs as big as her wrist. General Haggart stood with braced hands on his sand table displaying the Imperial encirclement. His shoulders hunched around where his ears would be, had he any.

Mortensen stood to Cora's left, ostensibly her guard, though he stood at ease. They brought Skye forward in manacles and Kikuchiyo warranted two Eddies with electro-pikes even when lying incapacitated on a stretcher, though one seemed more wary of Dog's raised hackles.

Cora and Skye knelt as they were announced. Kikuchiyo's head lifted from the cot and he tucked his chin in her direction. Beatrice nodded in return and he let his head fall back.

"You return to us at the eleventh hour when our army's commander counsels flight from the enemy." Haggart pushed from the table and folded his arms. "We are told you were within the Imperial host, on the Prime's own crawler. What more will he bring to our doorstep?"

"Your Majesty," Skye began, but Beatrice held out a palm.

"We have not given you permission to address us. Miss Pierson, it would appear you've come to your senses and are fully one of us. We would hear your news."

Cora wet her lips. The sensation left her surprised yet thankful turning deader hadn't taken this bit of humanity from her.

"Your Majesty, I must first thank Captain Skye and Kikuchiyo for rescuing me. You may be angry with them, but they delivered me from the Prime's laboratories."

"We have taken that into account, which is why they are not already staked out for excarnation via gritterpillar. Tell us this news."

"The Prime has gathered a quasi-dead host larger than any I have ever seen, or heard of for that matter. He's driving them with his army, likely for the Maze."

"To what end?"

"He wants to conquer a new world," Kikuchiyo said in an unsteady voice. "The first attack was a probe to assure them you have not fortified the Maze."

"Not to conquer and enslave us?"

"He has all he needs already. He doesn't need you to feed his war machines."

Beatrice turned to Haggart. He shook his head and pointed to the encirclement.

"If what you say is true, though I don't know why you're indulging the words of deserters and oath-breakers, all the more reason for us to slip away through this gap in their defenses."

"They're baiting you," Skye muttered, and an Eddie shoved from behind.

"Mind your place, captain," Queen Beatrice said.

Skye scowled and stared straight ahead. "Beat me if you must afterwards, but at least listen! We need to defend the Maze."

"With what?" General Haggart said. "You saw the damage, and if you had the wit, might realize we don't have gates thick enough or the firepower to hold out for more than a day."

"It's that or cede the Maze to the Imperials and aid whatever plan they have, which can't be good for Twisted Bluff or your people," Cora said. "If there are no more dreamers, then there will be no more dreamstuff. What will happen to Twisted Bluff then, majesty? Will you be forced to consume all you've built until nothing is left and you raid the Badlands for living flesh? How many of your subjects will collapse in the sands?"

"There is no guarantee Prime will cut us off from the dreamers. He would be a fool to seal off an escape route back to his power base," Haggart said.

"But he takes his power base with him! He gutted his empire and put it on treads and wheels and means not to return."

"So much the better," General Haggart said.

The queen leaned forward. "Can you say the Imperial plan will harm us? We do not see it. If Prime means to move on from this place, we should let him."

"And kick the problem to someone else?"

"We must look after our own first and foremost. We did not create this haven for the neo-dead only to dash it against the teeth of the Imperials in a futile gesture."

Kikuchiyo coughed. "*... and when the Bishop delivered the pilgrims from the Badlands into Paradise, he called up saying, 'Behold, I have brought the tired and hungry to their promised haven! Rejoice! Cast open the gates and embrace your new brothers and sisters!'*

The people of Paradise looked down on the multitudes and cried out to the Creator, 'We who harkened to your call obediently and abandoned all to follow You to Paradise have toiled long to earn our respite and comfort. These late multitudes following your Bishop spurned wisdom and embraced folly. Only now they come like locusts to strip away all we enjoy and reduce us to the basest existence. Send them away.'

The Creator withdrew in contemplation and wrestled mightily. On the third dawn, Bishop called up to the Creator, 'Lord, will you not open the gates?' The Creator looked down from his parapet and said, 'Nay, my palace is filled and will take no more."

General Haggart broke the room's silence muttering, "The Blood Weeper can cite Scripture for his purpose."

The queen held up a palm. "Thank you, general, that will be all while we consider this news. Take Kikuchiyo and the captain to suitable quarters close by under guard. Leave us but do not stray far. A moment, Miss Pierson." When the others had left, Cora approached at Queen Beatrice's indication. "We wanted to offer our congratulations on your transition into the neo-dead."

"Thank you, Your Majesty."

"Do you know your form's potential?"

Though the queen's marble-like face betrayed no emotion, Cora sensed a tension. "I have not had time to process much, majesty. I could carry the Blood Weeper more easily than when I was... prior to the change. The flight in the thopter was difficult but made easier by a steady hand and lack of fatigue, though I collapsed soon after landing."

"Yes, be mindful, Miss Pierson. Gauge well your effort's energy, for now you no longer have the crutch of biological hunger as warning. We ourselves ingest dreamstuff at regular intervals for precisely this reason."

"I see, Your Majesty."

"Do you? Have you not looked in a mirror and wondered about your place in our society?"

Cora spread her hands. "It's been a long day, Your Majesty. I worry for my friends."

"Pash! Those two, a relic and quasi-living turncoat. Your loyalty is admirable, though your judgement suspect."

"Without them, Your Majesty—"

"Oh yes, they're useful, but not to be trusted in the long term. They have no home here, unlike you."

"I'm not certain I follow."

Queen Beatrice clenched a fist at her side, then moments later spread her fingers. "We maintain this kingdom by exploiting our natural gifts to their utmost. Our population, the neo-dead, are segmented by their aspects. The skin jobs, the Eddies, scrabblers, specters, and skeletons all serve according to their adaptations. A scrabbler makes for an excellent scout in rough terrain, the Eddies apply brute strength for heavy labor, the adaptable skin jobs form the backbone of all our endeavors. Together we form a most formidable engine of progress and prosperity in this desolate place."

"I've noticed, majesty."

"Even ourselves, the queen, are cogs in the machine. We are diva."

Well, no sense of humility there. "You provide direction and vision, majesty."

"You misunderstand us." She motioned Cora over to a full-length mirror. "Look into the mirror. Stations aside, are we not alike?"

Cora studied their reflections and compared their similarities: sculpted features, brown eyes shot through with amber flecks, porcelain-smooth skin. Beatrice hooked a finger under her high collar and pulled, revealing a puckered oval of dry gray skin under the hollow of her throat. The queen's delicate eyebrow arched. "There is a resemblance, majesty," Cora said.

"We are diva. Where a skin job might power her rifle with a dozen shots, we provide enough for a company. Did you not wonder whence the electro guns on the battlements drew power? It was from us, on this throne. Below us lies one of the largest dynamos ever assembled."

Cora bent to study the throne, seeing now the contacts concealed in the arms and seat with thick cables emerging from the back and disappearing into the floor.

"Thus are we engaged during battle. Our person provides the batteries and the fortress at large its power."

"A literal seat of power," Cora said.

"Quite."

"You think I possess this same power?"

"Dear, we do not know. We would have you tested and brought into our retinue were there time."

"You sound as if you have decided, Your Majesty."

"Long have we known Kikuchiyo. In our first life the Blood Weeper was a feared demon, then during our quasi-dead life as the Creator's primal agent. In our third life as queen we see a man mortal, and for all his faults he reminds us that our responsibility is not only to the neo-dead but the quasi-dead horde. What queen are we if we fail serving destiny's fiat?"

"Fiat?"

The queen waved her hand. "Something like that. 'Mandate' seemed too common, and we are not common. No, we find ourselves on the horns of a dilemma. To leave this place and defend the Maze puts our land and people at risk. What good is rescuing the quasi-dead if there is no home to come back to? Neither can we risk losing the Maze and thereby consign our potential brothers and sisters to servitude, not to mention the added chaos wild Eddies and the like would wreak."

"Could we not gamble, Your Majesty?"

"One does not play dice, wagering a people."

Cora shook her head. "You wager either way, majesty. Acting boldly risks swift ruin, running could well condemn your people to slow decay."

Queen Beatrice leaned in. "You are too like your reckless friends, wishing death in some suitably noble way against impossible odds, stalwart of a lost cause to feed your ego."

"I don't wish to die, majesty. Surely there must be a way. Your people know this land's secrets better than any."

"Bah! Would that the Bathtub were still filled and the Prime could play with the straw man navy."

Cora tapped a finger against her tooth and paused. "Perhaps there is a way to bring more firepower to the conflict. Tell me, were any of those captured sand crawlers carrying airship bladders?"

"Yes, but airships are of no use in battle, you've seen that."

"We don't need them to fight, we just need them to float a load."

"Indeed."

"And I'll need to take my friends with me."

The queen's lips pursed. "You may take the Blood Weeper, but Captain Skye will remain here."

Where you can keep an eye on him, no doubt. And make sure I return.

Cora bowed. "As you will, majesty." In a strange way, she would rather be wearing the explosive collar.

<h1 style="text-align:center">24</h1>

"No, no, no! This goes here, that one goes there." Skye pointed with his skeleton hand, ungloved to remind the neo-dead around him he belonged here. He had borrowed a detachment of Eddies to place what few portable heavy guns they had where they could do the most good.

"You certain... sir?" said a hoarse voice like knife dragging across a whetstone. The Eddie, who went by Steelbender on account of the two massive arms jutting from his patched denim vest, stepped close enough to bump chests. Heads swiveled around and the sounds of hammers striking and tools turning died.

Skye stood straighter and forced himself to meet Steelbender's glowing eyes even if he had to crane his neck to do it. "Interlocking fields of fire, trooper, and we only have so many heavy guns to go around. I saw what's coming and we'll need each one placed exactly right, trust me."

"Trust you." The skeletal head tilted from side to side. Neck joints popped. "It's a good thing you went over the wall, then, wasn't it, sir? I mean instead of staying here at your post like the rest of us patching up the gate and busting ass to put speakers up everywhere. Got you a nice cozy look at the Imps and ran back here to tell us all about it. Makes it so we can trust you. Sir."

Skye wanted to back far away from Steelbender and those stone-pulverizing fists. His second instinct was to rest a hand on his sidearm and even the odds. Both were bad ideas. Command, someone once tried to tell him, was a balance of power and judgement, knowing how much to apply and where. Apply too little or too much and orders would be ignored or followed with feet dragging. Such failures lost battles and cost lives.

"Steelbender, you have to ask yourself one question: are you a betting man? Because ten bucks says I hold the line." He took a tenner from his wallet and stuffed it into Steelbender's lapel pocket. "I'll even let you hold the money."

"This a joke?"

"I never joke when it comes to a bet."

The Eddie stood statue-still and for a moment, Skye wondered if he had misjudged and would have to shoot this deader after all. The Eddie stepped back and picked up the launcher. "If you say so... sir."

"Carry on, trooper."

Skye continued down the line, resisting the urge to turn back and see if his orders were carried out. At the next stop, he inspected a machine gun emplacement and snuck a peek and Steelbender setting the launcher where he had been told. He still had them. Maybe there was hope yet, even under the distrustful eyes of both General Haggart and the troops around him, all waiting for him to make a mistake.

The curtain wall's defense had been reinforced with burnt-out car frames and Czech hedgehogs, man-high caltrops made from metal beams, scattered across the entrance, which would help against the crawlers but wouldn't do more than slow down Imperial infantry and the deader hordes. He placed the neo-dead defenders behind junked-out cars and overturned wagons staggered three layers deep, denying the Imperials a straight shot up the ramp. It could hold for a while, hopefully long enough until Cora and the Blood Weeper arrived. His skeleton hand itched, but no matter how much he scratched, it wouldn't go away.

Cora scratched the back of her hand as she fought the urge to scream. The "power throne," which she would rename as soon as she had the spare time, was wedged in the engine room next to the generator, which made the connections shorter, if cramped. The room shifted around her, shuddering and sending her bracing. Then the floor dropped, and she stumbled, scraping her forearm against a pipe coupling. Kikuchiyo's unnatural recovery took him from hobbling around that morning to removing his bandages and walking the decks by noon. His voice echoed through the vents as he shouted at the skin jobs struggling to secure the inflated cells.

She pushed to her feet and resisted stomping topside and supervising the skin jobs herself. Kikuchiyo could handle it; she needed to focus on the electrical systems. She dragged heavy cables from the throne to the diesel generators and began unbolting twisted copper coils trapped under fist-sized lugs. Her wrench didn't budge at first, but with a bit of undead strength and fitting a pipe over the wrench's handle to make a bigger lever, she worked the power feeds free and wired them to the throne.

Midway through the job, metal groaned and shuddered around her, dust cascading from nearby panels, pipes, and overhead conduits along with one tumbling screwdriver that missed skewering her thigh by inches. Then the cacophony stopped, and the room settled with a tiny sway. Minutes later, Kikuchiyo strode into her engine room, heralded by Dog's nails clicking on the metal decking. Dog stopped just inside the compartment, muzzle lifted as he sniffed. He snorted and shook his head as Kikuchiyo pushed past him. The samurai bowed to Cora, but remained silent.

"I'm hurrying as fast as I can," she said. Outside, someone shouted, and a whip cracked. The room pitched forward and Cora caught herself against the generator. "I'm not even sure breakers will hold; they're so corroded the entire system might short." She pointed at the other box wedged between the engines and tack-welded to the deck. "And that thing needs tuning, which is usually a week's job in dry dock with a complete necro tech team. After we power it up, there's no telling how long it'll last before it collapses. Got it?"

Dog glanced up at Kikuchiyo and yawned, punctuated with a tinny yelp. Kikuchiyo looked back at Dog and shrugged.

"I'll get it all working by the time we get there," she said.

Kikuchiyo bowed and turned for the hatch. Dog thumped his tail against the deck and followed.

"Slave driver," she muttered and went back to her tools.

25

The Imperials attacked after full dark, a wide chevron of
crawlers, screening the *Highlander* and its deader horde. The
bombard's traversing motors hummed and its cauldron barrel
swiveled as the first crawler came into range. The boom jostled Skye's
innards, reminding him his body was mostly Jello, and giving his organs a
squeeze in passing. He hadn't thought the first shot would hit anything,
and indeed it did not, as the spotter relayed through the specter network.
However, the shot had its intended effect, sending the crawlers into
evasive maneuvering, zigzagging across the sands and giving Cora more
precious time to arrive. She was close, he was sure, but would she make it
in time?

The crawlers gained as the bombard reloaded. Voices chattered
behind him and he turned to glare at a skin job and bone boy having an
argument over whether Bugs Bunny could win a fight against Optimus
Prime. He let it go.

"Sir, there's two breaking off," a skin job said. Skye scanned the left
flank through his binoculars where two crawlers had split off and angled
toward the curtain wall.

"More jump troops?" his runner asked. The specter introduced only
as "Candyman" wiped a dripping hand on his bloodstained apron before

adjusting his top hat's angle. Skye was certain the unnerving ghost's assignment to his unit was not coincidental.

"It's so obvious, it's got me bothered," Skye said. "They'd be smarter keeping them in reserve."

"Some people need be taught the same lesson a few times 'fore it sticks. We whipped 'em before, we'll do it again," Candyman said.

"Unless they know about the shipment and are going to intercept." That would scuttle the plan, but there wasn't anything he could do about it now. "RPGs to the left flank."

"Sir." The specter floated off to relay the order.

The bombard cannon was still reloading when the lead crawlers opened up with their own cannonade. The shells whistled through the air and hit the curtain wall's edge, sending a stone rain over the defenders. One shell followed a flat arc and blew through a weak spot on the gate's right side. A second shell arced over the gate and exploded against a Cadillac anchoring the leading barricade. The wreck's front end slewed, opening up a gap in the front barrier. Skin jobs scrambled from cover to push the wreck back in place, heedless of Sky's shouting at them to stop. Another cannonade came, and this time the gunners had found their marks exactly. Car frames lurched and rolled, crushing one skin job underneath. Another was blown a hundred feet to the side and didn't get back up.

The bombard fired again, shaking the ground and rattling his teeth. The shell passed over the horizon and another sand column rose, this time with glints of metal confetti.

"A hit," someone cried. "Eat that!"

"Glancing hit," Candyman whispered in his ear a moment later. "Minor damage to right treads."

Skye's right cross passed through Candyman's leering face. "Dammit, you did that on purpose!" He took a breath to compose himself and let his arms fall. "Very well. Signal the heavy weapons. Target the leading crawlers' treads first. Mobility kills, then the bombard can clean up. When that land cruiser comes in range, switch targets. *Highlander* is our highest priority." He checked the left flank where the two runaway crawlers were moving out of sight. "Send another observer to track those two crawlers. I want to know what they're up to." After Candyman disap-

peared through the rock, Skye let his shoulders relax and turned back to
the battle. More crawlers came into their ranges and cannon shells filled
the air.

Hurry up, Cora, we need you.

～

Dog poked into the engine room, cocking his head with that crazed look
the brown and blue eyes gave him. Cora threw a switch and grimaced.

She sat in the throne and made sure her palms rested on the metal
contacts built into the armrests. The metal warmed under her hands,
pulling with a weak magnetism as energy trickled from her palms and
the lights began glowing above. She relaxed, letting the trickle become a
tiny flow, and the room around her came alive with the buzz of fans spinning up, capacitor banks filling, and turrets spinning. The circuits felt like
aching muscles and she felt a little winded herself, as if taking a brisk
walk, but the systems needed more power. The box across from her
turned on but didn't have enough juice to activate. She poured more of
herself through the wires, and the box began humming. A green light lit
and the air crackled with ozone.

"Tell him it's ready."

26

The heavy guns opened up on the crawlers who responded in kind, filling the air with high explosive and plasma. Explosions shook the ground and soon the air filled with dust and smoke. Gunners caught glimpses of their targets moving in and out of concealment, tracking dark shapes and muzzle flashes in the dust. Wild shots from both sides sent sand geysering and gouged the curtain wall's thick stone as often as they found armored hulls and junked cars.

By some trick of the winds, a gap opened in the smoke and the *Highlander* appeared, bristling with guns and the deader horde fanned out behind it. The cruiser's forward batteries lit up with fire blossoms and shells whistled into the barricades, tossing metal, wood, sand, and bodies into the air.

"Focus fire!"

The bombard roared and sent a shell arcing into the dark clouds. The other cannon and electros swiveled and poured fire onto the cruiser, which shrugged off the hits as it picked up speed. The bombard's shell landed dead-center on the cruiser's forward turret and a split-second later, the turret split with a deafening boom and rose on a flame pillar lighting the entire battlefield. The cruiser's chiseled prow bounced and chattered, but the machine kept coming. Its smaller guns and turrets fired, but to Skye's thinking, only halfheartedly.

A flare from the left caught his eye. Skye glanced that way as more flares went up. RPGs sailed into the jump troop's staging area while electros on the walls spat plasma into those already airborne. The fire took care of a few jump troops, but the rest landed on top of the RPG squad.

"Send more riflemen to the rim," Skye said. The RPG squad fell under withering fire as they reloaded. The last of them managed the task and fired point-blank. Imperials went tumbling to the ground, a few over the side. A second wave landed and began assembling something behind a fold in the rock. Skye had a flash of recognition before the device powered up and his skeleton hand began twitching.

"Sonics! Get those thumpers countering."

A nearby mahout spurred his thumper into action and the creature's sounding tread began driving rhythms through the ground and into defenders' bones. More thumpers took up the beat and sent subsonics rumbling throughout the battlefield. Cora didn't have a ready answer to Astbury's alternative music, so they would rely on brute strength and Cora's mix tape of drum solos cribbed from the Badlands' greatest hits. The rifle squad approached the jump troops and began retaking the rim while the city's speakers played; his skeleton hand's tremors subsided but still ached.

He turned his attention back to the front gate and the advancing land cruiser. The bombard fired just as the *Highlander* tacked to the right. The shell hit the ground seconds later — a near miss. Skye looked around for a runner to tell the bombard crew the cruiser had their timing figured out, but there wasn't one available. He shouted it anyway, watching the *Highlander* bearing down on the gate, helpless to stop it.

A distant klaxon blared a shrill *whoop-whoop-whoop,* followed by cannon fire crashing from the right. A crawler covering the cruiser's flank rocked as the shells hit it, one penetrating and sending flame shooting through every window, port, and hatch.

A hazy blue ovoid rounded the curtain wall, shaped like an airship but hugging the ground with a shadow carpet before it. The craft fired again, fire blooms erupting from forward batteries and revealing its true form: an armored hull lashed to an airship's envelope, straining to keep the thing aloft — a man would have to duck to pass beneath it. Its glowing shield fizzled and popped, and gritterpillars fanned out before it, straining at tow lines while riders put lashes to chitin flanks. And standing in the bow, Kikuchiyo, resting a hand on Dog's head, both indifferent to the surrounding danger.

Skye cupped his hands and shouted at *Highlander*. "The Blood Weeper sends his regards!"

THE *LIBERATOR*'S engine room shook from the main turret's salvo, and in her throne she felt the shield generator's power fluctuate as it absorbed the return fire. Sweat beaded on her skin and brow, something she thought death might have spared her. The sweat sizzled as it hit the contacts, blistering her palms, though the sensation was more nuisance than pain. She double-checked her surroundings and prayed to Twins there wasn't anything that would react badly should she drip on it. The shield pulled power in little jerks, letting her know each time it absorbed a hit. The turrets buzzed like wasps above her, pausing only as they fired. The skeleton crew aboard (many of whom happened to be bone boys) was untrained, and she hoped they were making a difference, since surely they had enough firepower if they could put the shells on target.

The shield tugged one last time, then fizzled as it went out. The hull rang as a shell hit it like a sledgehammer, and it was as if someone had taken a baseball bat to her ribs. She grunted and told herself she was okay. She hoped Skye was still alive and wished she could scratch the itch on her right hand.

KIKUCHIYO WATCHED the wounded crawler slow to a stop, its final shots deflecting off *Liberator*'s shield. *Liberator* continued on with gritterpillars clawing at the ground as their riders drove them harder. *Highlander* emerged from behind the crawler's shadow and opened up with its powerful cannons and the ground exploded near *Liberator*'s flanks as the *Highlander*'s gunners began finding the range. Its shield flared, then fizzled, allowing a shell to penetrate and explode against the hull. The *Liberator* swayed and heaved at the gritterpillar's leads, sending several tumbling. The shields flickered back to life, though Kikuchiyo doubted they would survive another direct hit.

One gritterpillar broke free from its harness and scurried in circles, screaming. In the distance, a lower bellow answered. Kikuchiyo turned to the skin job next to him, who was swearing.

"Death cry," she said.

"The gritterpillar appears uninjured."

"No, that's a sand fury coming to defend a pup. We call it a death cry."

The gritterpillars began fighting their harnesses, caught between their handler's commands and triggered instincts. Machine gun fire twinkled against the shield. The *Liberator* listed closer to the curtain wall, losing momentum. Kikuchiyo grabbed the skin job, held out a straight arm aimed at the gate, and chopped through the air. "Stay on course. We will gather the mounts."

Kikuchiyo whistled at Dog and pointed to the gritterpillars. The two dropped over the railing, hitting the ground running.

"And if the sand fury appears?" the skin job called to him.

"Charge in!"

Dog raced out to the panicking gritterpillars and nipped at their legs, driving them back into position. Kikuchiyo ran to the screaming maverick 'pillar and leapt onto its back. His legs slid over the hard chitin and he wrapped the broken lead around his arm, then grasped a fistful of the stiff hairs separating the gritterpillar's segments. Weapons fire lit his way as he worked to the beast's head and dodged its snapping mandibles.

The beast thrashed as he clamped his legs behind its head and began squeezing. Its segments gathered, telegraphing its intent to roll on the ground. Kikuchiyo cinched the tether around his hand and squeezed his legs tighter.

"*Iie!*" he cried and punched the 'pillar between its compound eyes. The blow didn't crack the chitin, but the 'pillar suddenly froze and fell over as all its legs lost coordination. Curling instinctively, Kikuchiyo held on with both hands as they slammed into the sand. Air whooshed from him and warmth trickled down his hip as the bullet wound in his abdomen re-opened.

They lay there for a few seconds before the 'pillar shook itself and rose with a twist that rocked Kikuchiyo's head against hardened chitin.

The beast remained still, though its wide-open spiracles whistled as a ripple passed through its segments and began filling the air with a chemical stench. Kikuchiyo loosened his legs a fraction and tapped his heels to the beast. The 'pillar shuddered but crawled forward on shaky pedipalps, slowly gaining strength.

The *Liberator* had passed him by with Dog still herding the remaining 'pillars while the riders got them pulling in the same direction. The *Highlander* and *Liberator* traded shots as both raced for a breach in Twisted Bluff's gate. Behind the *Highlander*, deaders swarmed like a kicked-over anthill. Armored herdmasters on runabouts flanked and trailed the group, though there seemed little need now with the deaders fully in the labyrinth's thrall. Ranks of dismounted infantry followed, more than Twisted Bluff's defenses could possibly handle.

Another bellow emerged from the darkness. Closer. The 'pillar shivered under him and turned toward the sound. Kikuchiyo yanked on his makeshift lead and smiled as he kicked his mount into a full gallop.

A SCRABBLER JUMPED from the rocks and latched onto the necro who had looked up too late. Gangly arms and limbs grappled and contorted until the necro and scrabbler were hopelessly intertwined. A burly trooper advanced with a trench tomahawk and raised it high overhead. The scrabbler twisted as the tomahawk fell and continued rolling, still tangled up with the necro. The two went over the edge, separating as the necro lit his jump rockets, though the necro's freedom was short-lived as the rockets shot him into the curtain wall. The rocket pack sputtered as the necro tumbled from sight a moment before re-emerging bonelessly atop an orange blossom of flame.

The itching in Skye's hand stopped, and the neo-dead around him straightened as if someone had lifted a great weight from them.

Skye pointed to the top of the wall and shouted to the surrounding neo-dead. "That scrabbler just bought us some time! I want that rim cleared before they can bring up another necro!"

Rocket flares caught his eye. Another wave launched from the desert floor to the curtain wall, while those on the wall jumped for the labyrinth's entrance and engaged its defenses.

"Incoming!" Skye called out. He was already splitting his reserves, sending half to the maze entrance, the rest to defend the rim's electros. Gunners picked off a few jump troops in the air, but more landed where the gun emplacements couldn't reach. Soon bullets began zipping overhead.

"They got us in a crossfire!" said a skin job.

Skye slapped him on the shoulder. "No shit. Return fire and keep their heads down." He took up his rifle and searched for a target. "Hurry up, Cora," he muttered. "I'm shit outta luck here."

27

———

Cora hissed as the shields drained her once more. She needed to focus, but her vision went gray at the edges with each charge-discharge cycle and aching bones told her the batteries still traded salvos with something big outside. Somewhere, sonic incursion was making her teeth ache. On top of it all, her body needed energy. She reached into a nearby crate and crunched on a toy dump truck and a stuffed dog. The flavors came with names and memories attached.

She saw a world with no sand, where people in strange clothing gathered on a grass field and stood in lines to ride on machines that spun around, tilted, and glowed with neon light. Children squealed as the rushing air tickled their sweat-slick skin and roared in their ears. No one carried guns. No one walked around with hollow cheeks or checked over their shoulders. She discovered hot dogs, little sausages on a bun with a red and yellow sauce called ketchup and mustard. Cotton candy was a sticky fluffy sugar that melted in your mouth and made you sick minutes later, but you didn't care. At the end of the night you'd fall asleep in the car's backseat and wake up the next morning in your bed, wondering if it had happened at all. And there, tucked in next to you, the stuffed dog you won for popping all those balloons.

Cora came back into herself, the pain-free dream evaporating under the ache of reality. She felt lesser, a smaller and pathetic echo of the dreaming girl. She already missed the wind on her skin, something the change had stolen from her, but she hadn't noticed until now. She hardly had any sense of touch left, really.

The scent of fried food faded, replaced by diesel fumes and the acrid smoke of burning metal. The shield was back to full strength, and her fatigue disappeared. Another shell hit the screen and set her body shaking. She shook off the fugue and focused on powering the screen, but in the back of her mind she wondered if there was any more of that stuffed dog.

~

On the canyon rim, scrabblers rose and laid suppressing fire into the Imperials crouching against the rocks. RPGs headed for a sand crawler assembling a third wave of jump troops. The rockets arced down in lazy corkscrews, some missing entirely and others exploding harmlessly against the crawler's armored flanks.

Of the ten RPGs fired, two landed in the jump troopers' midst, sending molten copper boring through armor and in one case, holing a fuel tank. Hydrazine spewed, found a glowing ember, and the hapless trooper became the epicenter of an incendiary event igniting the whole formation. Secondary explosions erupted as more fuel hoses ruptured and ignited, causing a chain reaction of burning fuel and oxidizers snaking through an open hatch and blowing the crawler apart some fifteen seconds later.

The cheers of the scrabblers were cut short as the jump troops on the rim took their revenge on the exposed grenadiers. The remaining crawler backed away from the conflagration, its own jump troopers already deployed. For now, there would be no new Imperials rocketing over the curtain wall.

The jump troops at the labyrinth's entrance began pouring fire into the defenders. Skye grabbed the dirt and shouted orders, trying to rally the neo-dead as the crossfire boxed them in. The *Liberator* was lumbering into place and would easily cut off the crawlers, but the cruiser would be a near-thing.

"Come on, Cora, block that gate."

Though the Prime's cruiser might already be in trouble. Its guns were slow to traverse, and its main batteries had not fired in some time. Whatever the cause, he'd take what luck provided. The gritterpillar team was crossing the gate, *Liberator* only a few hundred feet behind. Dog was among them, snapping at feet and keeping them moving. The gritterpillar's tough carapaces made them hard to kill, but the machine guns and cannon bursts had a more telling effect on the 'pillar's weaker pedipalps, slowing the team as ichor-splattered 'pillars lost limbs in twos and threes.

A great wrenching sound erupted from *Highlander* as its nose swung to a new course, aiming for the open gate's far corner. Its hull shuddered and its treads chattered as its main batteries fired with a simultaneous belch of flame. The shells screamed into *Liberator*, obliterating the shield and sending up an explosion so bright, it made the destroyer's silhouette indistinct around the edges and threw Skye to the ground. The airship envelope disintegrated and *Liberator* went crashing into the sand, plowing a great furrow across the gateway. The destroyer lay on its side, underbelly facing Twisted Bluff and prow a dozen feet short of sealing the gate's far edge.

In slow-motion horror, *Highlander* plowed into *Liberator* with a crash that threatened to rattle the teeth from Skye's jaw. Metal screamed as it buckled and tore, followed by an explosion sending twisted gun barrels pinwheeling through the air, along with smaller shapes Skye's brain refused to recognize. Then everything was covered by a great cloud of smoke and sand. As it washed across the field, the battle paused and Skye could see nothing, not even the hand in front of his face.

"Cora," he said, wondering if she could have somehow survived. His skeleton hand warmed. A phantom squeeze. She was alive. He knew it.

The haze lifted and he could make out his outstretched skeleton hand.

"Steelbender!"

A dark form shuffled to him.

"Redeploy the machine guns to cover the right-side gap in the gate and mow down whatever comes through it. Have someone find Nash and Mungo, and send them to the ass-end of the *Liberator*." Skye hopped over the barricade.

"Where are you going?"

"Rescue op! Cora's in there and I'm getting her out. Until I'm back, you're in charge."

"Me? I don't know anything about leading a squad. I'm not even regular army, I'm just a drummer!"

"Just fake it until you believe your own bullshit. Keep fire on the gaps and if the Blood Weeper shows up, for Twins' sake, don't get in his way." As Skye took off, he called over his shoulder, "And I'm coming back for that tenner!"

28

The gritterpillar's oily musk seeped into Kikuchiyo's clothes and skin, coating him in a rancid black film. Behind him, the ground shook and furrowed as the sand fury closed. Kikuchiyo shouted at the gritterpillar to go faster, fly if it could. Ahead, the deader horde's leading edge crashed against the wreck of the *Highlander* and *Liberator* in dark waves, some climbing, others pushing along the hull's edges, all heading for the labyrinth's entrance. To them, Kikuchiyo and his mount were of no importance. Their armed wranglers, however, had noticed.

Whoever was in charge was no fool; the runabouts formed up in an inverse wedge before charging at him. Gunfire twinkled and bullets buzzed past his ears as he turned the 'pillar and charged. Kikuchiyo crouched low and put the beast's flesh between him and the oncoming runabouts. The sand fury's roar rumbled closer. A bullet ricocheted off the gritterpillar's tough chitin and whizzed into the night, followed by another. The gritterpillar squealed under the impacts and fought Kikuchiyo's control. He wrestled the beast and aimed them at a gap between runabouts even as he began sliding farther down the 'pillar's flank, almost touching the ground. As the runabouts' headlights grew bright enough to outshine the gunners' muzzle flashes, the furrow trailing him disappeared.

The sand fury erupted from the sand, front segments rearing high as a building and a great scoop-like mouth unfurling and emitting a deafening bellow. The fury's legs rippled as it descended, pinning a runabout with its ebony claws while its great mouth engulfed another. The other runabouts scattered, bullets sparking off the fury's bony plates.

The fury released an obscene form of the gritterpillar musk, a miasma like a skunk dipped in ammonia. Kikuchiyo's mount lost all sense of itself as the odor hit it, and it ducked its head between its legs, coiling into a ball and throwing Kikuchiyo to the ground. He rolled with the impact and came up spitting sand and blood as he took in the scene.

The runabouts ignored him and focused on the sand fury lunging at one of their own. The fury's body rose and fell on the runabout, pancaking it. Its tail-end whipped around and sent another tumbling. Gunfire ceased and one runabout peeled away into the desert while the last two sped back to Twisted Bluff. The fury's maw turned to Kikuchiyo, and he rested one hand on his sword, judging the timing of a roll to the side and planning the cuts he would have to make if he guessed wrong and were swallowed whole. The fury inhaled, then roared and chased after the machines, leaving Kikuchiyo alone for the moment.

Perhaps smelling like a gritterpillar had its advantages after all.

He followed the fury's trail at a jog, and Dog's mottled white shape ran to him from the darkness. If the gritterpillar's odor offended the mutt, he gave no notice and kept his tail wagging.

When they caught up to the fury, the *Highlander*'s main batteries had depressed as far as they could and fired over the fury with little result other than further enraging the beast. The side batteries, designed for anti-personnel and point defense, distracted the fury from the runabouts but focused the creature on themselves. Doubtless the remaining crew would have been able to bring more firepower to bear, but only one turret in three appeared to be working. The others were pointed away and battle damaged from the slugfest with the *Liberator,* either inoperable or lacking gunners to fire them. The fury's claws were useless against the turret's heavy armor but the gunners found themselves trapped inside while the creature began probing weak points. Gun barrels bent, deck vents spewing smoke crumpled, and hapless crewmen caught on deck were eviscerated and devoured. A few of the braver troopers attempted to rally, bringing up a tripod-mounted heavy rifle, focusing on the creature's joints.

As Kikuchiyo reached the *Highlander* the deaders still ignored him, more interested in climbing over each other and reaching the labyrinth. By some herd sense, those deaders on the left side found and surged through the gap between *Highlander* and the curtain wall, heedless of the bullets tearing into their flesh. Kikuchiyo made his way around the *Highlander*'s armored hull and snatched his hand away from a hatch's searing handle. A fire raged on the other side and he paused, wondering how close it might be to an ammo locker and how large the resulting explosion might be.

Metal-on-metal clanged weakly from another hatchway. Dog ran to it and began barking, where the metal clanking took on a panicked tempo. Kikuchiyo ran to the powder-blackened hatch, which had taken a beating from a glancing hit. He cleared the metal jamming the handle — cool — and slapped the hatch twice. The handle turned, and a crewman tumbled out, soot-coated as if he had been dipped in ink.

"The fires cut me off, thanks..." His eyes shone all the whiter as he recognized his rescuer. His hands came up. "No, no, no! I'm just an engine tech! I never wanted to be here!"

"Where is the Prime?" Kikuchiyo said.

The crewman shook his head. "I — I don't know. The bridge? The assault bay?"

Kikuchiyo thumbed his sword out a fraction from its sheath. "Which one?"

"The assault bay. There's something the red suits — his guards — wouldn't let anyone near."

"A vehicle?"

"Maybe?" He flinched as Kikuchiyo cleared more steel from the sheath. "It was behind a screen, but about the right size for a thopter."

"Where is the assault bay?"

"Down the hatchway, left, then the third right, but you can't make it! The fire's cut everything off!"

Kikuchiyo eased the katana back and kicked the crewman to the deck. "Run. Don't let the deaders get you." He cocked an ear and took in the sounds of battle around them. "And if the sand fury sees you, freeze.

It's attracted to movement." He entered the cruiser and paused. "Dog, come."

Dog sniffed the crewman, then jumped through the hatch.

"You're lucky he likes you," Kikuchiyo said to the crewman, who only nodded.

Skye barked his shin against the hatchway as he crawled through. The pitch of *Liberator*'s decks required him to half-climb, half-crawl and sent him sliding when his skeleton hand lost its grip on the slick metal holds. The scrabblers ahead of him, Mungo and Nash, had fewer problems with the off-kilter footing and called out potential obstacles as they scuttled for the engine room. Muffled explosions boomed outside the hull and machine guns chattered and buzzed at the deaders swarming through the gap. Closer in, the horde scratched and banged above them as they swarmed the *Liberator*'s top deck, and every few seconds something would scrape overhead as another deader lost its hold and fell to the sand below.

Nash went crabwise to a down ladder and latched on with all four hands. "Careful," he said. "There's broken conduit and some unsecured boxes all mashed together down there."

"Can we make it through?"

Nash shrugged with both sets of shoulders. "Maybe, assuming the damage isn't worse farther along."

"See if there's another route. Mungo, you're with me."

They slid down the ladder and he saw a sweat-slicked Cora through the hatchway, sitting on an iron throne wedged between a scorched shield generator and humming dynamo, hands clawed around the armrests. He called out to her, and her head slowly turned. Her eyes shone with amber light and stared through him. She shuddered and the light dimmed until her iris and pupils returned to normal, though the amber flecks still smoldered. Her eyebrows drew together.

"What are you doing here?" she asked.

"I'm trying to rescue you. Again."

Before she could reply, metal screeched as a shell punched through the hull and exploded. Skye was thrown into Mungo and the world went silent for several seconds. He tapped at his ears with fingertips that came back bloody. Mungo grabbed his arm and said something. Skye shook his head and pulled away, stumbling into the engine room.

The shell had hit the dynamo dead center and turned its toroid shape inside out, less like a donut and more like a metal flower with jagged misshapen petals. Cora's iron throne was missing its heavy back, which had saved her from the blast but now pinned her to the deck. She struggled face-down on the floor, shouting at him. He couldn't understand her words any better than Mungo's but he knew she was angry and somehow it was his fault.

That's what you get for getting involved.

He set his legs and heaved at a corner of debris. Cora got an arm out and twisted her torso, scooting free as Mungo put his shoulder to the pile and lifted. Skye backed off and let the junk drop to the deck, relieved his ears heard its crash.

"From now on, no rescues," Cora said. "You're gonna get killed!"

"You didn't abandon ship," he said. "I thought you might have been, you know, trapped somehow."

They mounted the ladder and climbed.

"Nobody told me!" she said. "If you haven't noticed, the intercoms don't work. It's easy to get lost when you're linked to the grid. I was doing my job, how about you?"

Skye swallowed. "You're not wrong, but bitch at me later when we're out of here, okay?"

Her mouth pursed, but she nodded. "Where's Kikuchiyo?"

"I thought you might know. There's a whole crapload of deaders coming through a gap between the wall and this ship, with more fixing to overrun the decks."

"How many?"

Skye checked the hatch leading out and swore. "See for yourself."

The barricades had been abandoned, and the fighting now centered on the labyrinth's entrance, where Imperials had broken through. Scores of deaders shambled through the entrance, stepping on their twitching and disabled brothers and unmoving neo-dead cousins. A figure emerged from the mob, black duster billowing as he strode forward and pivoted on a silver-runed cowboy boot. The portable speaker slung over his shoulder came to life with a feedback squeal, and he raised a microphone to his lips. A note half primal scream, half operatic aria sounded, and the mob shivered.

As the song continued, the mob began moving in time to the beat, stretching itself out and taking on a ragged order. The first rank entered the labyrinths' gate led by an Imperial necro and the tiny circulating lights in the stone flared, as they did again when the next rank went through, and the next. The tiny lights multiplied and became a continuous greenish glow that spread as the deaders advanced.

"That's not good," Skye said.

"No crap," Cora agreed. "We need to take Astbury and his team out."

Skye brought up his sidearm, but shook his head. "I can't hit him from here. Let's get a turret working and we'll let him play catch with a five-inch shell."

"Power's out, Skye. Give me an hour and maybe I could rig something, but we don't have time. Aren't you a good shot? I bet the Blood Weeper could do it."

Skye let the comment slide. "I'm no miracle worker and Kikuchiyo ain't here."

"We'll need to get closer, then."

"He's already inside the gateway with a whole lotta deaders blocking the way."

Cora smiled, just a twitch. "I've got an idea, but I'll need someone to cover my back for a minute while I work. Know anyone who's up to it?"

He smiled back. "Reckon so. Mungo, you find the Blood Weeper and tell him the fight's moved to the Labyrinth."

29

The *Highlander's* interior was a chaos of smoke, klaxons, damage control teams, and soldiers making ready to abandon ship. It was a tune Kikuchiyo knew well. He moved along the passages at a relaxed pace with Dog beside him, pausing only once to loot useful things from an open weapons locker. Visibility was terrible, so he evaded the crew, or in those rare cases where he couldn't, he gave them the chance to run away. Those few who didn't realized their folly too late. Their deaths brought him no comfort as they once would have, not even the pride of a master craftsman executing his vocation. For the first time in his life, he was weary of battle.

He turned the corner and found the door labeled ASSAULT BAY 01. Prime was on the other side, he could feel it. He turned to Dog and pointed to the deck. "This is no place for you. Stay." Dog's brown and blue eyes didn't leave his as he whined and thumped his tail. He leaned forward as if straining against an invisible leash and pushed a wet nose against Kikuchiyo's outstretched hand.

Kikuchiyo clenched his fist and Dog shied away. "Stay," he said to Dog. The animal's lips pulled back in the beginnings of a snarl, but he sat.

"Good boy." Kikuchiyo sketched out his name on the wall with some grease. "So they remember," he said to Dog. He took in a breath and squeezed his fist until he felt utterly solid and in the moment. He would not fade away. With that, the Blood Weeper kicked open the door and shouted into the room.

"Prime, your account comes due! Face me with a blade or forever be known a coward!" He took in the room at a glance, marking obstacles, angles of attack and defense, and machinery that would provide cover. These he committed to memory, and he knew that should he choose, he could run full-speed through the room blindfolded and end up precisely where he intended without a stumble or bump.

A dozen troopers in red armor surrounded Prime, who was fitting himself into a metal contraption suspended from overhead chains. The troopers brought up weapons, and red laser dots swarmed across the Blood Weeper's chest. Prime wore a puzzled expression and held up a hand.

"Kikuchiyo, I thought you had left us altogether, but I am happy to see you back in my moment of emancipation."

The Blood Weeper shook his head and slapped the katana's tip against the decking.

"Must we really, Kikuchiyo? You have to know I won't indulge you with any kind of antiquated duel. Will you not reconsider my offer? It's not too late."

The Blood Weeper settled into his stance with eyes unfocused. "I will not."

Prime's shoulders dropped as he let out a sigh. "So stubborn. It always was our failing, brother."

"Will you hide behind your guards, coward?"

"As if I care what you think of me. I'm no hero, I'm an emperor. Heroes die for their glories, emperors create dynasties for theirs. So die well, hero."

Prime's hand dropped, and a hail of bullets flew. The Blood Weeper had already dropped and rolled, coming up behind a disassembled runabout. He tucked his legs in against the ricochets and pulled two canisters from his kimono, pulling their pins and tossing them overhead as they began spewing yellow smoke.

He would have preferred honorable combat, but he would take what they offered. He closed his eyes and adjusted his grip on the katana, then with his off-hand drew the wakizashi, the smaller sword of the *daisho*, and charged in. Yellow smoke filled the room and to the credit of the Prime's red guards, they did not panic and fire blindly. He would test their mettle. Quiet as the void, the Blood Weeper swept through the room. A trio stood backs-together, guns out. The Blood Weeper dropped and rolled, stabbing his blade three times between armor seams and driving forward. As the group fell, one triggered a burst that ricocheted across the room and the other soldiers opened up.

The Blood Weeper kept the fallen guards between himself and the incoming fire as he finished them off in the confusion. The last one got an elbow past his guard and he blinked stars away even as he ran the wakizashi across an armor seam and let the life spill out. He sheathed the wakizashi and grabbed a gun as he kept moving, rising from a crouch and sprinting as the bullets zipped closer in the thinning smoke.

He ducked behind a support beam and brought up his gun. The muzzle blasts clustered in two areas, so he emptied the gun into the closer group and drew the katana as he charged, angling to avoid the rolling tool chest the group was likely using for cover. He leaped and pivoted as the chest's edges became visible and put his momentum behind a flat swing. The katana passed under a red trooper's helmet and sent it bouncing along to the floor along with its owner's head.

The Blood Weeper landed and skewered a second trooper while ducking under a third's point-blank burst. Fortune was with him as the remaining trooper took several hits from friendly fire across the room before collapsing.

A hatch opened and a deep rumble filled the space as two long gouts of flame erupted. The Blood Weeper dropped to the floor and let the heat wash over him, gritting his teeth as the exposed skin on his neck seared. Voices screamed and for a moment, the Blood Weeper thought he would be roasted alive. Then something passed overhead, sucking the air from the bay and leaving only the smell of fuel, exhaust, and burnt flesh behind. The roaring echoed away, and the room quieted save for a few moans coming from the far corner. The Blood Weeper stood and when the smoke cleared, there was no sign of Prime, just dead guards on the deck and empty chains hanging from the ceiling.

Kikuchiyo whistled and Dog padded in, nails clicking. "Our quarry has flown," he said. "Come."

30

———————

Cora ran at Skye's side. They skirted the main entrance to the maze and made for its exit. A pearlescent blue glowed along the maze's outer walls, and wild deaders murmured and rasped over the sporadic gunfire and electros hissing through the air. They came around the last curve and skidded to a halt as a pair of jump troopers came into view. Skye snapped off three shots and pushed her aside as the troopers returned fire.

"We don't have time for this," she said.

"I'm open to suggestions," Skye said and fired twice more. One of the plasma balls winged a trooper. "One shot left, then I have to recharge."

"Give it here," she said and grabbed its muzzle before he could argue. Her flesh sizzled, but she felt no pain. The gun was heavier than it looked, and felt alive in her hand, a thirsty animal. A second's thought, and the power flowed through her to quench the gun's thirst.

"Full charge, give it a go."

Skye snatched the gun and braced himself against the wall. He ignored a bullet whipping past them and fired four measured shots. The first plasma round went high, but the other three connected and the troopers went down.

"Hurry, there might be more coming," Skye said.

Cora picked up a fallen weapon and a spare magazine before

sprinting to the gate. Skye reached it first and lowered his shoulder, living flesh passing through with no problem, but jerked short as his skeleton hand met the barrier.

"Did you think that was going to work?" she asked.

Skye shrugged and gave her a wry grin. "Worth a shot, but it was like hitting a damn wall."

"Get out of there and let me work," Cora said.

She placed her palm on the stone, and the world faded. The stones recognized her, revealing structured layers she hadn't sensed before, though their runes still barred the gateway. She searched for the links between the symbols and routed the power around those responsible for detecting the neo-dead. She split her focus and partially retreated from the Labyrinth's embrace. As she did, she noticed bullets passing nearby and Skye's pistol returning fire.

"Ready," she said.

"About time. I'm down to one shot before I have to throw this thing at them."

"Hold on to me and pull me through when the barrier goes down. I can spoof it for a few seconds at most."

Skye's living hand gripped her arm. The Labyrinth discovered her meddling and reacted, altering its flow through the stones as her arm jerked. She severed the link as she tumbled, pulling herself back to the real world and landing on something soft and warm. Amber light faded from her eyes and she found herself on top of Skye and suddenly her skin wasn't so numb.

She quickly pushed herself off and offered a hand up. "You okay?" she asked.

"Don't take this the wrong way, but you're a lot denser than you look."

"That makes two of us, I guess." She pulled him up.

He opened his mouth, then closed it and shook his head. "We should go."

"Yes, let's." They jogged down the straight path leading to the maze's center. When they reached the altar, Martha was already there, contemplating its glowing surface, which showed the maze's outer pathways filling in with green light behind the deader advance. Skye, seeing

Martha for the first time, reached for his gun but stopped when Cora placed a hand on his shoulder and shook her head.

"The virus starts, children," Martha said.

"You don't seem surprised to see us," Cora said.

She tapped the maze exit. "I saw what you did, naughty girl. Took you long enough."

Skye's finger hovered over the maze as he traced its pathways. "How long until they reach the center?"

The crone tapped her cane. "Difficult to say. They are not moving as deaders move. Something has perverted their instinct. They break apart, go against the flow, into unused backwaters, then come together again. It upsets the machine. It is rebelling even against its oldest friend."

"Is it because there are so many?" Cora asked.

"The first settlers were such as these and the machine converted them in the hundreds as easily as the loners and singletons."

"What will happen with this lot?" Skye asked.

"I do not know," said Martha.

"All the more reason to stop Astbury," Skye said.

"Astbury?"

"The Prime's right-hand man and also the necro who force-farmed all these quasi-dead," Cora said.

Martha tapped a dot at the head of the green wave, and it turned red. "That is him, the one who perverts the machine. Stop him, children. Martha yet has a measure of control over the machine and will open a way for you. But be swift; my control weakens with every footstep taken by these cultivated deaders."

She held a withered palm to the walls and hummed low. A door rumbled open, and beyond, several others followed suit. The music from Astbury's speaker reached them, tinny and discordant. Cora ran through, knowing without looking that Skye would follow. The door to the central chamber closed behind her and fear began dancing its way down her spine.

"He won't stop just because we ask nicely," Skye said.

"I know."

~

THEY SNEAKED up on an Imperial necro singing with his eyes closed as the deader horde danced around him with limbs held in familiar patterns. Cora ducked back behind the wall and chewed at her lip. The stones had taken on a greenish hue and the light motes twisted about each other as they jumped the gaps. Skye drew his gun but paused as Cora held up a hand.

"What?" Skye said.

"What he's singing. Notice it isn't affecting us?"

Skye cocked an ear and shook his head several seconds later. "It must be obscure."

"No, it's in Astbury's alt-style, and it's causing the stones to turn green."

"Does it matter? I can take the shot from here."

"I don't like it. Martha calls this the machine, right?"

"For turning deaders into the neo-dead."

"I think Astbury figured out how to make it do something else."

"Then let's take him out," he said.

"Unless killing him would break the machine and do Twins-know-what to anyone stuck inside it. When you throw a wrench in a running machine, everything turns to scrap metal, including the wrench."

"The alternative is letting him keep on doing what he's doing. Think that'll end well for us?"

She took in a breath her body didn't need and let it out. "Guess not. Let's hope your luck holds and this doesn't blow up around us."

Skye winked. "It'll be fine."

Her lips thinned. "It better be."

Skye braced himself against the stone and brought his gun up in a two-handed grip. The shot was not insignificant, but he would make it. The gun's iron sights lined up on the necro's head. The necro's eyes were closed as he sang and swayed in time to his own music, a tune that came across to Skye as nihilistic and morose compared to the Badlands standards he grew up on. Skye slowed his breathing and brought it into synch with Astbury's tune, trusting his instincts to squeeze the trigger at the right moment. A thousand nuances arranged themselves in the back of his mind until everything aligned.

Now.

He squeezed the trigger. A miniature sun erupted from the gun barrel and streaked towards the necro's skull. It couldn't miss. The projectile and target were on a collision course, simple physics the necro couldn't change even if he saw it coming.

Then a hundred deaders jumped in unison and landed facing him, all but one, who collapsed at his master's feet minus a head. The necro opened his eyes and shouted a command. As one, the deaders raised a clenched fist overhead and charged. Cora pulled Skye back and slapped the stone beside them. She closed her eyes for a moment and the green lights swirling in the stone turned white under her hand.

"Slow them down for a few seconds," she said.

The deaders stumbled and lurched in their lockstep and Skye sighted in on one wearing a tattered Paradise City uniform. As he reached for the trigger, he wondered how the militiaman had wound up in a deader farm. He pulled the trigger and the former soldier fell face-first as the shot mangled his leg below the knee.

There but for a bit of luck, go I.

The fallen deader hampered the others just enough so that when the stones shifted and began pivoting to close the gap, none made it through. Skye picked up a severed arm and placed it in the grasping hand of a deader pinned between the rocks. Nearby, floating lights took on a purplish cast that swirled and interfered with the green streams.

Cora grabbed his hand and pulled him down the path. "I have a better idea of what they're trying," she said. "Each of these deaders is like an individual electron in a circuit, and—"

"The short version?" he said, sensing he wouldn't understand it anyway.

"They're using the deaders to configure the maze into a different mode. Instead of giving deaders their minds back, the Labyrinth is directing its energy somewhere else."

"Where?" he asked and followed her gaze up. Green motes swirled on the ceiling, forming a ring that crackled with blue lightning. A wind swirled around them, and mist leaked from within the ring, thickening cloud-like.

"Portal?" Skye asked.

"Likely."

"How do we shut it down?"

"We could kill all the deaders, or we could try closing off the flows and route everything back out through the entrance."

"How long do we have?"

She shrugged. "Ten minutes, maybe?"

"Gonna be hard shooting deaders in this giant hide-and-seek. You sure?"

"Forgive me if I'm not an expert on weird-ass artifacts already. I got here the same time you did!"

"Fine. So what about the other option?"

"We need to get ahead of them, find a choke point, and reconfigure the maze."

"Martha?"

She shook her head. "She's too busy keeping the machine together."

"Can you get them rerouted?"

"If we're quicker than Astbury."

"So how do we cut him off?"

She smiled. "Easy. We cheat."

31

Stone flowed and changed its texture under her touch, rippling from base to tip with ridges and divots. Cora's eyes opened, and she stepped back. "It's not the best ladder, but it'll have to do," she said.

Skye looked at it and ground his jaw from side to side.

"What?" she asked.

"Nothing." Skye holstered his gun and flexed his skeleton hand before climbing. "Let's hope we don't come across a gap we can't jump or a door we can't open."

They ran across the monoliths and Skye cursed as the maze twisted back on itself while the green glow spread through its walls, creeping steadily towards the center. They caught up to Astbury and his team of necros surrounded by a deader mob standing shoulder to shoulder. Astbury scrawled sigils on the monoliths while the deaders swayed in time to the necros' depressing music that gave her a headache. Cora lay on her stomach next to him, and they both crept to peer over the edge.

"Got any idea what he's up to?"

"Those sigils are all wrong. It's like he's trying to turn this clearing into a dynamo, but the output forms aren't coherent. The power will just circulate and… Shit."

"What?"

"He's routing power from here to another part of the maze. I think it's where Prime wants to break through."

"Can you shut it down?"

"Most of the sigils are on that skinny monolith. I can try subverting it, but it'll take time," she said.

He nodded. "I'll get you the time you need."

Skye crept forward with gun in hand. He glanced back, and she nodded. His first shot went wide. Astbury flattened himself to the ground behind the deaders, and the other necros split duties between returning fire and keeping the deaders under control. Bullets and plasma filled the air, super-heating it and sparking against the stones. Skye fired shot after shot into the clearing and shouted something about cutting off his other hand for a Twins-damned grenade or two.

Cora pressed herself flat against the stone, sending her consciousness deep within the monoliths. The green-tinged currents resisted her as she pushed where she could, corrupting or reversing Astbury's new sigils, blunting their effect. It was a dangerous game. For all she knew, she could be turning the whole machine into a giant bomb. She had also attracted attention, as another presence entered and began correcting her sabotage. She pushed against it, and it pushed back with a cold amusement. It had to be Astbury.

Astbury's changes were frustratingly subtle, like a thousand tendrils creeping in from all sides, distracting her and fixing errors faster than she could create them. She changed tactics and encoded bulwarks around the thickest clusters of tendrils, enforcing her will over Astbury's with brute strength. And yet, she was still losing. Astbury's subversion flowed around her blocks, coming in from subsystems and subroutines, circling around and weakening her control with a thousand tiny incursions. Power flowed into the portal above. The stones groaned under the stress.

Cora scrambled. She searched farther out, trying to use what her new senses could reveal. She felt Astbury and his quasi-dead churning through the maze's guts, twisting it into a new configuration that chewed at the barrier between worlds. She felt the stones around her, the pearl-stone spire above, resonating with sonic incursions but shielding those within, shunting the debilitating effects deep into the earth like a lightning rod where they would surface miles away and join the Wall's mental static. If she wasn't careful, she could see how it could easily flow along the surface, coating the town and surrounding mesa like a flood.

Let's not do that.

She found the part of the machine controlling Haggart's sand table, and realized he hadn't scratched the surface of what it could do. The machine saw the neo-dead like dim versions of the motes within Labyrinth's stone circuits, the living flesh of thumpers and gritterpillars glowing a vibrant green, the Imperials' ghostly images in their pearlstone body armor and armored crawlers, flickering as the machine tried making sense of their out-of-phase echoes.

Resonating out of phase. Wearing armor with built-in sound systems.

She got a bad idea.

She threw a reckless attack at Astbury, sacrificing part of her bulwark. Astbury countered and struck deep within her defenses, driving for the Labyrinth's core. Cora sidestepped Astbury's dash and reached for an area he had just abandoned, taking control of the spire's incursion shunt and giving it an inverted twist.

Either this works, or I've just doomed us all.

The sonic incursion's flow changed direction, flowing up from the bedrock and through the spire. The tower hummed as the incursion flowed counter to the pearlstone's natural twist, pitch rising as pressure built until the flow erupted from the spire's crown. Fighting in the town came to a standstill as thumpers bellowed, their mahouts clumsy and slow to react. Skin jobs and Eddies fouled shots and weapons slipped from hands. Scrabblers fell from the rocks, some to their permanent deaths. The mighty bombard and curtain wall guns went silent as Twisted Bluff screamed.

For the living, it was worse.

Bodies encased in resonating pearlstone began thrashing as ultrasonic waves produced bubbles in their bloodstreams that acted like tiny bombs as they began cavitating and destroying flesh from the inside out. Those nearest the spire dropped instantly, those at the gates seconds later. Within the crawlers the sonics sent steel hulls howling in sympathy with their pearlstone lattices at levels that ruptured the eardrums and soft tissues of the crews inside. Bodies stumbled and crashed to the deck with senses overwhelmed. Deader-powered dynamos failed as the incursion knocked out necros in the engine rooms and electricity surged through the control circuits, immobilizing crawler after crawler, though the deaders inside their powered sarcophagi remained unaffected and would have enjoyed the rest had they minds to appreciate it.

The colonel in charge of the reserve crawler squadron, farthest from the action and least affected, screamed over the cacophony to his crew, who turned the crawler around and fled, and the rest of the squadron and a few survivors on runabouts followed while their brothers and sisters' brains slowly succumbed to madness.

Cora watched the Imperial echoes fade, and hardened her heart against what she had just done. The shock of it seemed to have distracted Astbury as well, as she felt his confusion in the machine, a pause in the storm overhead. It had been worth it, hadn't it?

Then a pain lanced through her shoulder, and her control disintegrated.

THE DEADERS FLOWED into the labyrinth's entrance, spreading an eerie green light throughout its passages. Outside, Imperials fought the neo-dead in isolated firefights, little side-fires igniting from the greater conflagration. There was no order to it, no direction, no purpose. It was that place in battle where all the plans had succumbed to chaos. Kikuchiyo made himself a stone and let the chaos flow and eddy around him. Deaders parted before him and closed ranks as he passed.

The Labyrinth pressed against his mind, but whether because he was not dead or because of Cally's earlier meddling with the rules, he and Dog slowed only briefly crossing the gateway's threshold. Once inside, the pressure eased, and he sensed Prime's presence nearby. A miniature storm swirled high overhead, lightning crackling and thunder echoing throughout the maze. Kikuchiyo recognized it for what it was, the beginnings of another Maelstrom between worlds.

Dog sprinted to an intersection and turned away from the river of dead onto another path. Kikuchiyo considered for a moment and followed. The green light deepened the farther he went, and he came upon Dog, digging between two monoliths, one with a misshapen base like a chipped tooth. He joined Dog in digging, exposing a hole between the stones wide enough for him to wiggle through.

The passageway dead-ended at an emerald stone ring emerging knee high from the ground. A dust devil swirled within it, its dancing tip setting each marker stone aglow with its touch. The Labyrinth's light streams avoided the surrounding walls, and the air hung thick and humid. Dog raised his nose and followed it several paces to the left before returning and scenting the air to the right. His head swung from side to side and he whined.

Kikuchiyo laid a hand on Dog's head and quieted the animal. He patted at it as he considered.

"He's not here," he said to Dog.

Dog gave him a look saying he did not agree.

"Very well, but we had better be right about this."

Something screamed through the air and landed with a ground-jarring thud nearby.

"Ah. Just waiting for him to arrive. Stay," he said to Dog.

Dog growled and followed him anyway.

The powered armor stood fifteen feet tall with blocky, powerful arms and heavy plating, more in line with a unit meant to take on tanks than a lone swordsman. Kikuchiyo spared a glance at Dog and jerked his head back at the power suit. Dog let out a *wuff* and padded to the clearing's edge.

The suit's helm slid back and Prime's head emerged between the monstrosity's metal shoulders. "You think it cheating, don't you, brother?" Prime said. "Unfortunately, emperors are not allowed to be sporting in their conquests."

Kikuchiyo hooked thumbs into his sash. "It is said the great Musashi faced opponents with a wooden sword against their steel, once winning a duel with a boat oar. You merely saved me the problem of finding a canoe paddle."

"Is that so? Then let us end this. I can't have an enemy at my back."

32

Death had more advantages. The bullet lodged in her shoulder wasn't ideal, but after the initial sting, the pain disappeared and she wasn't leaking blood all over the place. She slid farther back from the monolith's edge and pushed her awareness back into the machine. Astbury's tendrils had dismantled her earlier work and converged on the monolith's core. She wedged herself at a choke point and built a wall with the last uncorrupted light motes flowing through the machine. Green tendrils snapped at the wall, finding weaknesses and wriggling their way between the uncorrupted motes, then weakening the bonds between them.

One struck too close to her own awareness and Cora instinctively slapped it away, fear adding more strength to the strike. The tendril shriveled, turning pale and condensing into an uncorrupted mote. She struck at another, then another, cleansing each tendril and using it to reinforce the wall. With more instinct than thought, she struck as hard and as fast as she could, turning each corrupting tendril into another brick in her wall. The corruption slowed; her wall could hold if she were fast enough.

I've got you now, Ian.

Astbury's presence soon retreated altogether, and she cast about, searching for new attacks. A high-pitched wail tickled her ears. Astbury felt close, but where was he? Her concentration fell apart. The world within the monolith faded from her mind's eye as the screaming grew louder and the ground shook beneath her.

She opened her eyes and Astbury, minus his long black duster, dropped the final six inches to land on the monolith's top. The jetpack's scream faded, and he brought up his gun.

"It occurred to me I was fighting this battle altogether wrong," he said. "The wrong domain, if you will. The problem with engineers in general, and necros in particular, is they get tunnel vision. Our vocation's arrogance is believing one must solve all problems using its skills, charming a deader when a rope is quicker and more reliable. Quite stubborn, wouldn't you agree?"

"You talk too much," she said.

"You're right," he said, and fired. The bullets burned as they passed through her chest and almost sent her staggering over the monolith's edge. Panic gripped her as she scrabbled on hands and knees while Astbury ejected a magazine and brought another from a leg pocket. "Still alive? But of course, you're a deader now. You're so lifelike; talk about getting stuck in the wrong domain."

A sizzling plasma ball spattered against Astbury's gun. Skye's lanky form leaped the gap between monoliths, gun centered on Astbury's chest. "It's okay, you're just an amateur," he said.

"Nice shot, captain," Astbury said, shaking out his empty gun hand.

Skye shrugged, but kept his weapon centered on the necro. "Your buddies ran and your deaders are just stumbling over themselves with no one to direct them. Party's over."

"Is it?" Astbury turned his gaze and pointed. "The emperor and Blood Weeper are at the portal's very edge now."

"For all the good that will do him," Cora said. Her words came out jerky and wheezy as air leaked through the holes in her lungs. "Your army's finished, colonel. Scattered and on the run."

"That is a setback, but at this point I doubt my Prime really cares about his toys now that he's so close to his goal." Astbury readjusted his cavalry hat and scratched at an itch on his scalp. "Funny thing, this artifact. Opening the portal to the Creator's world is only a matter of finding the barrier's thinnest spot and giving it an impulse. My deaders primed the system, and I was about to open a stable gate when you two showed up. Pity. I think it will be interesting to see what happens with two of the Creator's avatars so close to an unstable gate and poking it."

"You're saying it's all going gooey-kablooey?" Skye said.

Astbury pulled a face. "Thank you for the eloquent summary, captain. I can't say for certain, but a 'gooey-kablooey' is certainly possible. Should we go and see?"

"I should shoot you now," Skye said.

"Oh, but I surrender!" He held out his wrists. "You could shoot me, but you'd lose all the knowledge locked in my head. Ask Miss Pierson. For all her strength, my more modestly powered but infinitely more complex approach nearly won the day."

"Cora?"

"It's true, but I don't know. Maybe with a few more months of study…"

"This relic's potential is limitless," Astbury said. "It could provide everything the Badlands needs and more if we unlock its potential. And it's not the only one," he added with a shit-eating grin.

Skye shook his head. "Nah, I'll just shoot you now."

Cora placed a hand on Skye's arm, and he lowered the gun.

"You're kidding, right? After what he did to us?"

She lifted her shoulders. "We can always kill him later."

Skye smiled. "True." He gestured with the gun. "All right, Astbury. Giddy-up."

Kikuchiyo danced from foot to foot as he charged in, changing elevations and cutting off angles as the armored suit's shoulder-mounted guns spat out their bullets. He rolled to the right, the twin guns converging on him as he closed. Prime's suit twisted and a fist as large as Kikuchiyo's head descended. Kikuchiyo waited until the last moment and sprang. His katana flashed in an *iaijutsu* draw and electricity crackled as the blade passed. He landed behind the suit, the spinning barrels of its shoulder guns whirring to a stop, their exposed power cables severed.

He dodged as the suit's leg drove a backwards kick into a nearby monolith and cracked it. Prime pivoted and faced Kikuchiyo with a speed and precision belying the suit's bulk. The suit's fists clenched and meter-long claws extended from each arm and locked in with a pneumatic hiss.

"I don't need guns to kill you, brother," Prime said.

Kikuchiyo raised his katana and charged in. He feinted a slash at the suit's knee joint and jumped away as a claw swiped. He planted a foot and pushed off the damaged and now-darkened monolith, landing on the suit's back. His hands and feet scrambled for holds as servos whined and the suit whipped back and forth trying to shake him off. A claw reached over the left side and stabbed blindly, nearly skewering him. Then Prime threw the suit backwards into the monolith.

Kikuchiyo drove his legs and swung free from an inert shoulder gun as the suit's plating screeched and ground against the monolith. Kikuchiyo completed his arc and drove the katana between the seams in the suit's helmet. He met resistance, then nothing. The suit froze, and for a moment he thought the fight had ended. Then the suit's arm swept him from his perch and sent him flying.

Pain. His body refused to tuck and roll as the ground came to meet him. He didn't remember the landing, only opening his eyes and finding himself twenty feet from Prime's suit, still slumped against the monolith. Hazy gas escaped from the cracked helmet and a hacking cough echoed from within. Prime's blotchy face emerged and hacked some more. One eye's sclera had turned blood red and Prime grimaced.

"You missed, brother," Prime said. "And you lost your favorite sword."

The katana had flown free and lay in the dust near Prime. The weapon looked like a toy in the suit's gauntlet as Prime picked it up.

"I should kill you with it. But what if I did this?" Prime turned the sword in his suit's right gauntlet and pinched its blade with the fingers of the left.

Kikuchiyo cried out as Prime bent the blade almost to a right angle before it shattered with a snap like a gunshot to Kikuchiyo's heart. The pieces dropped to the ground and Prime's boot rose and stomped it into the dust.

"You said it was dead metal, didn't you?" Prime said.

Kikuchiyo's hand went translucent as the rage boiled in his throat. He tried pushing it down but it would not yield. His eyes burned as the blood trickled free and onto his face.

So be it. One last pass before I am damned.

Kikuchiyo pushed himself to his feet and drew the wakizashi. Prime's eyes widened and he took a ground-shaking step back.

Thunder crackled overhead, and a light erupted from the emerald stones, reaching into the storm's center. Prime let out a sigh and backed away from Kikuchiyo towards the growing portal.

"Too late, Blood Weeper. Better luck next life."

The wakizashi, like the katana, was a slashing battlefield weapon, meant to engage enemies in close combat. If a samurai wanted to defeat an opponent at a distance, he would use a weapon designed for such, like the bow. That was proper. What went through Kikuchiyo's mind was not proper at all, something a traditional samurai would never contemplate. But as many pointed out, he was not a traditional samurai. He was Ryan's cheap copy, fueled by B-grade movies and bootleg anime. Kikuchiyo whipped his arm down and let the wakizashi fly. The blade spun end-over-end and Prime's eyes grew large even as his suit's arms came up to block it, too slow.

Prime dropped to a knee as the wakizashi clove the air where his exposed head had just vacated. Kikuchiyo's heart sank.

I have failed, but I will die with honor.

Kikuchiyo set his feet and readied himself.

"Of all the stupid tricks," Prime began.

A black-and-white blur leapt from the shadows and Dog's teeth sank into Prime's neck. Prime screamed and Kikuchiyo charged, ignoring the bone-on-bone grinding in his body. He closed the distance as Prime's gauntlet closed around Dog and threw him free. Kikuchiyo hit Prime with a ridge hand to the temple, stunning him and following up with a palm strike to the nose. Cartilage crunched and crumbled, driving into brain tissue as his head snapped back. Prime dropped, and the light faded from his eyes.

Duty discharged.

The rage drained from him, leaving behind aching hollowness where a soul should be. Duty, and his promise to Jasmine, had taken its place, but now there was nothing filling the void inside him, nothing keeping the fade from erasing him completely. Kikuchiyo's unburdened shoulders unknotted, and he stood taller. The air turned sweet and he savored it.

With the rage gone, the fade's pull on his flesh eased but his fate was sealed. Did he have minutes, seconds? How should he spend his last moments? He turned away and went to Dog. The animal lay on his side, blood bubbling from mouth and nostrils with each labored breath. The hollowness within him doubled. Blue and brown eyes focused as he approached, and a tail thumped twice in the dirt.

"You should not have done that," Kikuchiyo said, and stroked Dog's head. "Now we are both dying, yes?" The void within him grew. "Now who will remember me?" He wiped at Dog's bloodied muzzle with a corner of his kimono. "I am sorry I did not treat you better." His blood-stained fingertips went translucent and he fought against the fade. He would not leave before Dog, he told himself.

Dog's eyes shifted to Prime, and he growled in the back of his throat.

"He can't hurt us anymore," he whispered in Dog's ear. "He..."

Behind him, something hissed. He turned as Prime's armor whined deep within its shell, building. Kikuchiyo rose and took in Prime's ruined nose reforming. The whine crescendoed and Prime's body jerked with a muffled *whump*. Dog let out a strangled bark and Kikuchiyo shook himself loose, taking a step forward as Prime's eyes blinked and he inhaled sharply. Duty returned, filling him and rooting him once again in the present. His flesh solidified.

Kikuchiyo leapt, extending his heel—

Prime rolled and knocked him to the side with a servo-assisted block. Kikuchiyo rolled and pushed himself up, as did Prime.

"That hurt," Prime snarled.

"The first death always does," Kikuchiyo replied. "As does the second, and the third. When you have died your hundredth time, you realize it will never get better. After the first death, we lose the balm of ignorance forever."

A glass vial ejected from Prime's armor and shattered on a nearby monolith. The motes dancing through the stone flashed and scintillated in waves radiating from the impact point.

"Blood of the Redeemer," said Prime. He circled to his left and Kikuchiyo matched him. "Pity you're out."

228

33

———

Prime charged in and Kikuchiyo fell back. He aimed a kick at Prime's armored knee, which sent the suit swaying, but Prime recovered and backhanded Kikuchiyo in passing. The stones pulsed in an erratic rhythm. The clouds ripped apart and the blue light reached down to the emerald stones in a blinding chaotic twister. As it faded, sunlight filtered through a gash in the air, showing blue sky.

"At last," Prime said. His dazed grin turned into a scowl as he found Kikuchiyo standing in his way, settling the recovered wakizashi into its scabbard.

"You cannot defeat me, Blood Weeper. This is destiny. The old world calls to me as I do it. Humanity spins fractured dreams canceling each other out, or at best, staggering like a drunken sailor in a dark alley. They will flourish under my direction until they produce one who can replace me. It is not Ryan who cast off his dross; he *was* the dross. Step aside, Blood Weeper, or be destroyed."

Kikuchiyo hooked thumbs into his sash and took in a deep breath. He kept his eyes fixed on Prime's and let the silence stretch between them. Prime, the former majordomo, for all his talk of power and superiority, couldn't stand still. His eyes darted between Kikuchiyo and the rift's ragged edges within the stone circle. On the portal's other side, a stony beach ended in turquoise waters where several boats with brightly striped sails jockeyed around a buoy to the sounds of bells, cheers, and the buzz of a helicopter.

The wind pushed through, carrying the tang of salt air, and a sense of familiarity enveloped Kikuchiyo, a thousand tiny details reminding him how much was missing from the Badlands, how sad its aping of the dreamer's world, the Twins's reality. But it was not his reality. Distant memories called it home, but the more he opened himself, the more alien it became.

"Isn't it beautiful? Like seeing color for the first time," Prime said.

"It's not for us, not anymore."

"I am going."

"You will not."

Prime nodded. "If it must be so." He bent at the waist in a military-style bow. Kikuchiyo returned the bow and set his feet. Prime settled into a fighting stance, right leg forward, clawed arms up and protecting his head.

Kikuchiyo stood with arms loose at his sides. Prime took a shuffling step forward, then another. The third step brought Prime to the edge of his range, but beyond Kikuchiyo's. The samurai stayed relaxed.

Prime's right arm snapped out, claws extended to rend through the samurai's torso.

As the arm descended, Kikuchiyo swayed from the claws' path before drawing his wakizashi and shouting a *kiai*. Prime's left hand swept across to bat the sword away, but the wakizashi passed through an impossible arc that found its blade passing through the gaps between the twin claws and continue unimpeded.

Pain blossomed in his chest, and the world stopped. When it started again he was slumped forward, impaled on Prime's right claw.

Prime smiled for a moment, then his head slid from his shoulders.

Kikuchiyo lowered his head. It was done, and now he could die. Blood bubbled around metal claws with every shallow breath. He looked to Dog, who watched him from the corner.

"Now I know how you feel," he managed, and Dog thumped his tail in the dust. The sea breeze faded and the sunlight dimmed.

34

———————

The storm above winked out as Cora and Skye found Kikuchiyo slumped over Prime's body and Prime's head in the dust with eyes staring at the closed portal. Dog lay in the corner, eyes closed and dust caking the blood around his muzzle.

"We're too late," Cora said.

"At least the portal closed," Skye said. He gestured with his gun. If having hands bound before him and a gun poking his back bothered Astbury, he didn't show it. Astbury walked around the bodies like a man strolling through a park. He crouched by Prime's head and picked it up, turning it this way and that in his bound hands before chuckling and setting it back down. "Who would have thought the old man had so little blood in him?"

Cora approached Kikuchiyo's impaled corpse. He was finally at peace, all traces of anger gone. "Better luck next life," she said. She rested her hand on his head, which shifted under her touch, and he groaned. "He's not dead!"

"We can't do anything for him," Skye said. "You move him and he'll bleed out in a second if the shock doesn't kill him first."

Prime's armor hissed, and from within it an angry beep sounded.

"There might be a way to save him," Astbury said.

Skye brought his gun up. "Listening."

"Prime had vials of godsblood built into his suit. It's been dosing it ever since our fearless emperor lost his head. If you hurry, you might get to a vial before the system runs out. Maybe enough to save the Blood Weeper."

The armor hissed again and beeped.

"Another dose lost," Astbury commented.

Cora went to the armored suit and fumbled at the seams. "Where's the release?"

"The manual releases are a bit tricky. I could tell you, but I think it's time to renegotiate the terms of my situation."

"Skye, don't," Cora said. Astbury turned and blinked as he looked down the barrel of Skye's gun.

"A life for a life," Astbury said. "I get you a vial, you let me go."

"You turned people into deaders on an industrial scale. Nuh-uh." Skye took a step back and gestured with the gun. "You get the vial right now and you get to keep breathing. Refuse and I shoot you where you stand."

"That's not much of an offer," Astbury said.

The armor hissed and beeped.

Cora put her fingertips against the necro's temples and let power trickle through them. Astbury went rigid and made a choking sound. "Imagine yourself in a steel box under the desert sun, baking until you turn deader. Then imagine your journey through this maze after I've reprogrammed it, and you spend eternity with all your nerve endings raw and exposed. Your every step will be like standing on a hot griddle, every breeze like a razor storm."

She cut the power, and Astbury stumbled. "And the hero shows her true face," he said. "Fine." He went to the suit and reached inside the gore-splattered collar.

Skye put the gun to his head. "Careful now."

Astbury kept his gaze fixed on Cora, and a panel in the suit's torso hissed open. "I'm deactivating the auto-injector."

"Go on," Skye said.

He reached inside the compartment and flipped a switch. A telltale inside the panel changed from green to yellow.

"That's enough," Cora said. "I can take it from here."

Astbury stood with two glass vials filled with red liquid and smirked. "You want me to put these back? They're the last two."

Cora was about to give her retort when the light in the panel changed to red and started blinking. "That's not—" she began, then the panel sparked and exploded.

Astbury tossed a vial at Skye.

"Catch!"

Astbury's shoulder knocked her to the ground. She watched the vial's slow tumble as Skye lurched and dropped his gun. He stretched out and skeleton fingers closed around the vial as he hit the ground. Glass tinkled, and he rose, cupping his living hand under the dead one as it opened.

"Still intact," he said and let out a breath. He handed the vial over and grabbed his gun. "I'll get Astbury."

Flames emerged from the armor. "No, I need you here."

Skye fumed, but holstered the gun and nodded.

"When I say, pull him off the claws."

"Got it."

"*Kekkou desu.*" Kikuchiyo's eyes fluttered open and with a trembling hand, pointed to Dog. "Him."

"Sure," Skye said, while shaking his head at Cora.

"You can save him after we save you."

Kikuchiyo pushed the vial away. "No, Cora. See... to Dog."

"He's already dead, Kikuchiyo," Skye said.

"No, he is not. Please, Cora."

"Cora," Skye said, but she was already up and moving. It was a strange thing, the boogeyman asking you for a favor. Stranger that she should agree.

She went to Dog and placed a hand on his ribs. Dog's blue eye opened and his tail twitched. She supported Dog's head and poured the godsblood down his throat, then sat back as his black-and-white-furred body began spasming. Flesh bubbled and flowed; spine and limbs lengthened. His rib cage expanded and spread, paws morphed into fingers and toes. When the spasms stopped, motes flowed from the nearest monolith in a swirling mass, flowing over the black-and-white fur and bathing the body with light.

∼

WHEN THE LIGHT FADED, Dog inhaled a deep breath and pushed himself up on furry human-like legs. He stood and ran claw-fingered hands through a shock of long white fur atop his canine skull.

"Dog?" Cora said.

Dog took halting steps past her and came to crouch next to Kikuchiyo's still form. He slid closed Kikuchiyo's unseeing eyes.

"He knew," Dog said in a low voice, crackly and raw.

"Knew what?" Skye said. He rested a hand on the butt of his holstered gun. Cora removed it.

"His time was over." His paw came away stained from Kikuchiyo's wounds and he used a bloody claw to trace two short lines from the corner of his eye.

"What do you want done with his remains?" Cora asked.

Dog grasped Prime's head and placed it on the suit's armored torso. "Build a pyre for them both."

He spent a minute collecting Kikuchiyo's weapons, then tipped the discarded godsblood vial over the katana's broken edge. A drop fell onto the metal and he joined it to the other half of the blade. The steel rang with a sweet note.

He handed the wakizashi to Skye. "For you." Dog held the fused blade out to Cora. "For you."

"Don't you want them?" Cora asked.

"I don't even know how to use it," Skye said.

"Then learn." Dog waved a paw and cast his gaze around the stones. "There are more places where the barriers are thin and dreamers may cross over. I will find these places, seek out these new creators."

"To guide them?"

Dog growled. "No, to defend their creations."

"What if their creations don't want saving?" Skye asked.

Dog stared at the bodies. "They will all need saving, sooner or later."

∼

Kikuchiyo and Prime lay wrapped in shrouds, side-by-side on the pyre set outside Twisted Bluff's gates. Citizens took a break from clearing the battlefield and repairing their town, filing past to curse, pray, or just stare before moving on. When all had finished, Queen Beatrice addressed the crowd. Her words washed over Skye, who knew he should be paying attention, but couldn't give a damn right now.

Cora leaned in and lowered her voice. "Not one for speeches?"

"Seems like we're dishonoring him somehow," he said.

"Because he's being cremated with Prime?"

"There should be a third body there, but we let him go."

"Astbury can't hurt us here. His deaders will wander around the maze until they become citizens, and the queen will send more excursions through the Wall to dismantle the farms."

"If he makes it back to the Empire…"

"You mean if he doesn't get eaten by a sand fury or wild Eddie? There is no Empire, no one left strong enough to keep it all together."

"It'll be civil war."

"Perhaps. You could go back to Paradise City, help it throw off the Imperial yoke."

"Naw, that's a sucker's bet." Skye straightened his arm and inspected his skeleton hand. "I'm still a fugitive as far as they're concerned. Shit like this hand ain't going to help my case any. I might wander around a bit, see what else comes up. How about you? Sticking around here to learn more about the maze, neo-dead royalty…"

"The Labyrinth has everything a neo-necro could want, and the queen hints at my being part of something larger here."

Her face remained blank, but he knew better. He gave her a smile. "But?"

"They're polite enough to my face, but they don't trust me. And why would they? That incursion pulse didn't care who it killed, and they all know I'm responsible."

"Sometimes that's the thanks you get when you try to help."

She grinned back. "Speaking of, we never properly thanked Astbury for all his help."

"That we did not. Think Dog wants in?"

"I don't know. Let's ask." She glanced to the stage where Dog's seat was empty. "Where'd he go?"

The creature had slipped away during the speech and Skye nudged Cora as he spotted him at the crowd's edge, holding hands with a specter in a yellow party dress, their heads bowed together. She kissed his forehead and flew away. The queen's speech ended and the pyre lit. Dog's blue and brown eyes took in the pyre before walking away, head up, tail erect. Cora and Skye kept vigil as it burned, and in the desert, Dog's form shimmered and disappeared.

"Not a bad idea," Skye murmured. "Sneaking out before he's missed."

Cora bumped his shoulder with hers. "Not bad at all."

"Shall we?"

"Let's."

BONUS FEATURES

Get The Good Stuff!

Is this your first visit to the Badlands? Would you like to know more about deaders and necros? If you sign up for my mailing list I'll send you a free ebook you can't get anywhere else: Black Betty: A Badlands Story, featuring everyone's favorite necrosonic engineer, Helgo. (Hmm... I wonder if Black Betty is related to Queen Beatrice?)

Sign up at WadePeterson.com

If you just want to do the simplest thing

If all that is too much but you enjoyed my book, please consider leaving a review. Reviews are the lifeblood of indie books like this and I would consider it a personal favor — just a quick star rating with a sentence or two can make a huge difference in convincing others to give this book a try.

I am on a quest to get 100 reviews of this book and I can only do it with your help.

<u>Of course I'll leave a review!</u>

What Else can I read?

I'm always writing. Check out my complete list of available books here or at wadepeterson.com.

AUTHOR'S NOTES

Hello, Traveler!

Writing Enter the Samurai was a frightening delight. Frightening because I was stretching out into unknown territory with new characters and a delight because I love the hell out of exploring the Badlands universe and adding layers to its history. Kikuchiyo has always been my favorite villain, all bottled-up anger lashing out in all directions, an unstoppable force venting his creator's frustrations upon the world. He's that dark little kernel inside my teenage self that thankfully never blossomed. But after the events of Badlands Cursed, Kikuchiyo had to change his nature as the nature of the Badlands itself changed. What happens when your living gods leave and haven't picked up after themselves? What does a jobless avatar do with himself?

One question led to another and soon the story came tumbling out. In stutters, fits, and up blind alleys to be sure, but I eventually found my bearings and finished the story. (The scenes and ideas I had to cut out will find homes in the next Badlands novel) What did you think? I hope you enjoyed reading my story as much as I loved writing it!

Tag me on social media or send me an email letting me know what interests you or what you want to know more about— I'm writing more Badlands stories and you can help shape the next one.

Wade Peterson
February 2021

<<<<>>>>

ABOUT THE AUTHOR

Wade Peterson is a man. He's pretty sure he is, anyway. When he's not writing, he's busy unlocking the secrets of Texas barbecue, wrangling two demonic cats, tormenting his kids with dad jokes, and agreeing whole-heartedly with his wife's wine selection for the evening.

Click on the icons below to follow Wade on social media for updates, fun pictures, and the occasional cat video. Of course the best stuff is at wadepeterson.com (just saying).